SPIRITS OF PEPIN

SPIRITS OF PEPIN

A No Ordinary Women Mystery

by
Barbara Deese

NORTH STAR PRESS OF ST. CLOUD, INC.
St. Cloud, Minnesota

ISBN: 978-1-68201-032-7

Cover art by Jake Karwoski, Monster of the Midwest, LLC

First Edition: September 2016

Printed in the United States of America

Published by
North Star Press of St. Cloud, Inc.
P.O. Box 451
St. Cloud, Minnesota 56302

www.northstarpress.com

"I believe that these circles of women around us weave invisible nets of love that carry us when we're weak and sing with us when we're strong."

~ SARK, *Succulent Wild Woman*
(Susan Ariel Rainbow Kennedy)

Cruising down the highway, windows open, platinum hair blowing every which way, Louise Trenton pretended she was twenty-five again. The radio was tuned to an oldies station, and when the Eagles came on, she cranked up the volume. "Take it easy, take it easy," they sang as if they knew the messy turn her life was about to take.

By the time she got to the marina her heart was lighter. It was a hot June morning in the old Minnesota town of Red Wing. The sky was unremittingly blue and a mere whisper of a breeze blew across her sun-warmed face. Nestled between a shiny new sailboat and another cabin cruiser, the *Time Out* beckoned. The vintage boat, with its newly refinished wood trim, had a classic look, much nicer, she thought, than its modern counterparts.

She removed the blue mooring cover and began her routine, checking lines, oil and fuel levels and making sure electronics and engine were in working order. She heard the racket and lifted her head. The rest of the No Ordinary Women book club had arrived in two cars, Robin and Grace from Minneapolis, Cate and Foxy from Saint Paul. Meeting them on the weathered dock, she helped them haul a ridiculous amount of gear to the boat.

Once the coolers, grocery bags, canvas totes, and small luggage were on board, Louise removed her oversized sunglasses, positioned them on top of her head and drawled, "Okay, let's go through a few safety warnings. Don't take it personally. I swear it has nothing to do with our history of rushing into things headlong."

Grinning as if she'd been dealt a compliment, Grace turned and tripped over Robin's foot. "Headlong? Us?" she said when she'd recovered her balance.

Louise didn't crack a smile. As reluctant as she was to dampen their enthusiasm, she didn't want some preventable injury spoiling the trip for everyone. "Thank you, Grace, for demonstrating what not to do."

Grace stood tall. "Hey, if I have nothing else to offer, at least let me serve as a bad example."

Louise chuckled along with the others. "What I was about to say is, with all the cleats and uneven wood, you have to watch where you're going. Just think of marinas and boats as accidents waiting to happen." She resumed her boating orientation by opening a locker under the bench. "Listen up. If anything goes wrong, the first thing you do is put on one of these." She reached into the locker, pulled out an orange Mae West vest and demonstrated how to buckle it before stowing it again.

They traipsed below deck, where Louise introduced them to the salon, the berths, and the head, making sure they knew the proper boat terms. In the galley they loaded items into the small refrigerator and Louise showed them where to find such essentials as the fire extinguisher, wine glasses, and corkscrew.

Returning topside, they got a detailed tutorial on leaving the dock. "The idea is to get the boat out without damaging anything, animate or inanimate," Louise told them. When they were finally ready to take off, Cate and Robin detached lines and coiled them on the deck, as instructed, and Foxy and Grace pulled up and stowed the fenders. Louise took the helm seat. Her friends settled on cushions behind her. Backing into the channel, she finessed the cabin cruiser past fingers of docks in the Ole Miss Marina and out into the Mississippi River, heading toward Wabasha.

Despite their almost giddy mood, Louise's mind kept flashing on the situation awaiting her at the end of this getaway. Her father had been slowly but inexorably losing his ability to function. Now that things had reached a crisis point, she and Dean needed to figure out new arrangements for him. Her father, a man used to giving orders, was not about to take direction from his daughter, making it a tough couple of weeks. Dean had insisted she keep her weekend plans with friends. The inevitable and unpleasant battle over her father's welfare could wait for a few more days.

They cruised at a leisurely rate for a while, then, one by one, Louise invited them to try their hand at the helm. Alone among them, Foxy, with her reddish mane knotted on the top of her head, demonstrated a real instinct for operating the throttle and wheel and correcting for wind and current.

By late morning they were passing the quaint little shops of Stockholm on the Wisconsin side of Lake Pepin, the name given to this wide, thirty-mile-long stretch of the Mississippi. Founded by Swedish immigrants in the mid-1800s, the village now had a thriving artists' community. Unfortunately, because there was no public dock, they couldn't stop. Snacking on fruit and cheese, they drifted lazily toward the town of Pepin, which they planned to explore on foot. On the hills to their left, trees were swaying. Louise noticed the increasing wind too late, and made a grab for her straw boater hat. It lifted off her head, went airborne and skittered across the water's surface. "Dang it all! I loved that hat!" Louise's southern accent was more pronounced than usual.

"Me too. You looked very *Great Gatsby* in it," Grace said.

"You've got the right era." Louise watched her hat sink out of sight.

"I suppose it was from your shop."

"Naturally. Antiques for an antique." Louise and Dean owned an antique shop in Minneapolis named Past Tense. With her flair for vintage fashion, Louise often sported a hat or brooch or ring from their inventory. For years, Past Tense had defined their lives, then one day when Dean was gathering up paperwork for their accountant, he turned to Louise and said, "Tense is the only part of this business I'm feeling right now." That's when they decided to buy the boat and started spending less time in the shop. They began grooming their assistant to take over permanently when they were ready to sell the business.

Robin refilled their plastic cups with lemonade. With her pale complexion and hair, she tried to stay in the shady corner of the bench. For the third time that day she commented on how peaceful it was on the water.

Louise said, "If we'd had to call off another weekend, I was fixing to put the boat up for sale." She laughed to let them know she wasn't serious. However, between bad weather and engine problems, scheduling time on the boat had been problematic.

Swiping a long strand of hair off her face, Cate lifted her cup. "To our fearless and peerless captain." There was a muffled plastic thunk when they touched glasses.

With a broad smile, Robin proposed a second toast. "May this be the first of many adventures aboard the good ship *Time Out*."

"Adventures?" Grace paused with her drink in the air. "Robin, did you just wish for more adventures? Is that really wise?"

Robin lowered her sunglasses on her nose. "Oh, come on, Gracie! We all saw how you channeled your inner Nancy Drew when—"

Grace objected. "Hey! It wasn't just me. I had plenty of company snooping around, if you remember."

Robin looked pointedly at Foxy, whose leg had been badly broken in their most recent escapade. It still ached at times when the weather was damp or cold, Foxy had told them, or if she stood too long, which had kept her from taking on new massage clients.

Sipping lemonade and nibbling the last slivers of Wisconsin cheddar and apples, they talked and laughed and watched the boats go by—powerboats, fishing boats, sailboats, tugboats. They were near Pepin, the village that shared a name with the lake, when a flock of raucous seagulls appeared from nowhere and circled the *Time Out*, demanding a handout. Seeing Foxy about to offer them food, Louise gave a stern shake of her head. "They'll never leave us alone if you do." Foxy pulled her hand back. The birds circled her for a while before moving on.

High overhead, a bald eagle soared. Robin caught its movement and raised the camera hanging around her neck, adjusting settings by feel as she rotated from the waist to pan the bird in flight, clicking as she and the bird moved in sync.

Leaving Foxy at the wheel, Louise moved to the rail to read the water, which had taken on a slightly darker hue, and though the change was subtle, its surface was more fractured—more indications the wind was picking up. Louise reclaimed her chair so she could turn the radio dial to the weather station. Winds gusting to thirty-five miles an hour were predicted by mid-afternoon, a significant increase from the morning forecast. "If we stop in Pepin, we won't be on our way again for two or three hours," she said. "I'm worried we'll be bucking the wind if we wait too long. Do y'all mind if we just mosey back? That way we can cruise around a bit and duck into the marina if it starts to get dicey."

"Our fate is in your hands, Captain," said Cate.

And so they made a slow turn, passing on their port side the marina at Lake City where they planned to dock for the night. A little while later Louise pointed to a park and adjacent campground. She was about to give them a history of the area when Robin's sharp words stopped her.

"What is that boat doing?" She lowered her camera and pointed to a sailboat ahead of them, its sails flapping in the stiff breeze.

Louise eased up on the throttle and together they watched the boat's erratic course, traversing the water in a drunken path, first toward the Wisconsin side, then to the Minnesota side, then downriver until a gust blew it in a different direction.

"That's not good," Louise mumbled to herself. To the others, she said, "See, the reason those sails are flailing around like that is they aren't filling with wind. It's called luffing." She took off her sunglasses and squinted. Unable to see what she wanted, she shoved a pair of binoculars into Grace's hand. "Can you catch the boat's name?"

"Maybe the crew is practicing maneuvers," Grace suggested, peering through the binoculars. The boat twirled several degrees clockwise. Grace shook her head, unable to catch the name.

Foxy said, "I've heard about boats being overrun by drug runners. They incapacitate or kill the crew and take over—" She stopped when Cate and Robin started giggling.

Grace snorted. "I don't think we need to worry about pirates on Lake Pepin, but if I see anyone with an eye patch—"

"Look." Louise pointed. "The boom is swinging free. That's the big bar at the foot of the mainsail, and it should definitely not be doing that. I don't think anyone's in control of that sail. It's been going on way too long for it to be an accidental jibe.

"Jibe?"

"Right. When you're sailing downwind and the wind starts filling the wrong side of the sail, you have to get the sail to the other side of the boat to catch the wind so it can drive your boat." Louise paused until she saw comprehension on their faces. They were listening intently. "Jibes are regular maneuvers, but it's those unplanned jibes you have to watch out for." She wiped sweat from her

6

upper lip. "That's when you're not paying attention and the sail suddenly catches a pocket of wind on the wrong side. If that happens, the whole thing can swing by itself. It can happen at lightning speed and you might not have a chance to get out of the way of the boom." She cast another look at the sailboat. "A good sailor knows never to be in the way when it crosses the center line. A full sail packs a huge wallop."

They were exchanging glances as if trying to determine how seriously to take it.

Louise didn't like the way the seagulls were flocking around the errant sailboat. "What I'm trying to say is a swinging boom can bash your head in, or even throw you clean out of the boat."

Standing with one hand on the rail and peering at the sailboat through her camera's telephoto lens, Robin said, "Rats, I almost had it. I think it's—agh! It spun before I caught the name, but I think it starts with a W. Could it be Way-something?"

Louise bit her lower lip. "*Wayward Wind?*"

"Very well named," said Robin.

"I know that boat. There aren't a lot of sailboats out of Red Wing, but that's one of them. I'm surprised. The owner is a decent sailor." Louise snatched up the radio and spoke into it. "*Wayward Wind, Wayward Wind,* this is *Time Out.* Over." She waited and repeated the words, adding, "Do you read me?" She told her friends to sit down and hold on, then pushed the throttle forward and turned in the direction of the sailboat.

The radio crackled and then a male voice, high pitched and nasal, said, "*Wayward Wind, Wayward Wind. River Rat* here. You need help?"

The five women held their breath, waiting to hear whether or not this new caller was able to make contact with the incapacitated boat.

Cate stood and with a jerk of her thumb indicated a houseboat approaching the troubled sailboat from a different angle. "Think that's the *River Rat?*"

Louise watched it before nodding. Into the radio she said, "*River Rat*, this is *Time Out*. Can you see anyone at the wheel?"

"Negative," he replied.

"Switching to six-eight." Louise twisted a dial.

"Is that a police code or something?" Grace asked.

Louise was all business. "We were on the distress channel. As soon as you make contact, you're supposed to switch to a different channel to free it up for emergencies." She took a look at her inexperienced mates and sighed. On the new working channel she said, "Not sure how close we can get. She keeps changing course. I think someone'll have to board her."

"I'm alone here, so it's a no go for me," said the nasal voice. "I dunno, with that boom swingin' . . ." He cleared his throat. "Keep an eye on her. I'll put out a call for help."

Louise watched as the bow of the *Wayward Wind* swung again so it now pointed directly at the *Time Out*. It wasn't exactly a runaway train hurtling toward them, but even moving slowly, it was several tons of unruly wood and fiberglass and metal that would bounce around until it crashed into something—another boat or the shore. Boaters who weren't on the radio might not be aware this bumper car with sails was without a captain.

"Now would be an excellent time to put on your life vests!" Louise said. The others complied hastily and without question. As soon as she'd donned her own, she adjusted the throttle and turned to the long-legged redhead. "Think you can steer this for a bit, Foxy?"

Foxy puffed out her cheeks. "I guess we'll find out." She looked less than confident as she wedged herself into the helm seat.

"Try to get us a little closer." Louise observed how she maneuvered the vessel and nodded approval. "Okay now, try to keep enough distance so that the other boat won't veer into us." Turning to address them all, Louise explained she was going out in the dinghy—the smaller boat used as a tender by larger vessels—to try attaching a line to the *Wayward Wind*. "I need one of you to come with me."

"I'll go." Robin was on her feet. She helped Louise untether the dinghy and held onto the line.

Thinking through the next steps, Louise grimaced. "This won't be easy with the wind, and I will never hear the end of it if I damage our boat." The tip of her tongue poked from between her lips as she thought. After a short moment, she hauled a thick nylon towrope out of its locker, surprised at its weight as she slung the loops over her shoulder and stepped down into the waiting dinghy. When Robin had settled in the bow of the little boat, Louise started the engine and they hooked around, heading for the sailboat.

Foxy's job was to hold the *Time Out* in close but not too close proximity. Grace and Cate, the remaining crew, could do nothing but watch.

As soon as they were almost directly under the front end of the *Wayward Wind*, Louise adjusted the dinghy's angle and gave the engine a little shot in reverse. Both boats dipped, unfortunately not in sync. "Okay, give it a try," she called over the idling motor.

The first time Robin tried to stand, the wake from a passing speedboat rocked their little vessel, throwing her off balance and pitching her back hard against the molded plastic seat. When she stood again, she took Louise's advice and flexed her knees to better adjust to the rocking motion.

Finally Robin stretched to her full height and made a grab for the large metal loop at the tip of the jutting prow. On the sixth try, she caught hold and hung on, even when the larger boat nearly lifted her off her feet. With a length of the towrope draped over her shoulder, she rode the wake caused by yet another passing speedboat and waited for an upswing. When it came, she timed it just right and threaded the line through. Raising her fist in triumph, she wobbled and fell back again, wincing as her tailbone smacked against the thwart.

Louise pulled, testing the knot. It held. Then, instead of returning to the mother ship as planned, she left the towrope secured to both vessels and turned the dinghy toward the other end of the sailboat, hugging the side until they were behind the *Wayward Wind*.

"What are we doing?" Robin called to her.

"I have to find out what happened to him." She called out, "Ahoy!" There was no response. "I'll hold us steady. See if you can look over the side."

Robin grabbed an aluminum rail on the sailboat to steady herself as she stood. "Can't see," she said with a shake of her head.

Louise bit her lip. "See that step there?" She pointed to a narrow ledge jutting out from the stern, near the water level.

Robin hoisted herself up and stood on tiptoes to peer over the hull. She gasped. "He's not moving!" Before Louise could stop her, Robin had scrambled up the short ladder.

"Whatever you do, don't move him," she called as Robin disappeared over the edge. Seated alone in the dinghy, Louise swallowed hard, remembering that awful day. It had happened five decades ago, yet the images were still vivid:

Her brother, barely six years old, sprawled on the rocky path where the horse had flung him. Her mother dismounting, her boots slipping in the mud as she ran to him, snatching him into her arms even as the trainer yelled at her not to move him. And then later. Her father taking his daughter's small hands in his. Telling her Bobby could have survived the injury if her mother hadn't picked him up. The little coffin a month later. Her mother, dressed all in black, leaning down and begging forgiveness from her only son just before the lid lowered forever.

Louise had been only three and a half, but she'd understood two things—her Mama was the reason little Bobby died, and Daddy could not forgive her. Ever. Much later she came to understand how that impulsive act of motherly love had severed the little boy's spinal cord.

Suddenly Robin's head popped over the edge. Her eyes were big and her voice was small. "I think he's dead." In a rush, she did her best to describe the scene to Louise.

Louise took her hand away from her mouth long enough to say, "Did you touch him?"

Robin shook her head.

Craning her neck to check on her own crew, Louise was alarmed to see Cate and Grace standing on the high point of the deck, totally ignoring her safety instructions about always having a handhold on the boat. As she watched, Cate lost her balance.

That decided it. "We're going to let the professionals handle it."

* * *

WHEN THEY CLOSED IN on the *Time Out*, Robin tossed the rope attached to the front of the dinghy. Grace caught the painter deftly and tethered it to the starboard cleat, with Louise coaching her.

Turning to see the *River Rat* motoring toward them, Grace said she'd heard on the radio that help was on the way. Robin scrambled out of the dinghy. Gripping the thick towrope several feet from the end, Louise leveraged it against her shoulder to gain some slack before wrapping it in a figure eight around the large cleat.

The houseboat pulled up alongside. From the houseboat, a young man in a fishing hat watched them securing the lines and gave a nod of approval. "I been on the horn with the harbormaster," he called out, "and he wants you to keep her neutral or super low throttle, okay? They're sending out a twenty-four-foot fireboat with a crew to board her and take her in."

Louise nodded, hoping she gave the impression of confidence.

"You get a good look?"

"Not really," Louise hedged. "Enough to think the captain might be unconscious." She didn't repeat Robin's description of the bloody wound.

"Christ! I'll let 'em know." He spat overboard. "I'm gonna hang out 'til they get here. Make sure nothing comes loose, ya know."

"Thanks, we're good," said Louise.

He scratched his neck and squinted like he wasn't sure she could manage without him. "Hate to see that cleat pull out."

"I think we've got it. Thanks for your help."

With a shrug, he motored off.

Louise wondered if she'd been too hasty sending him away. She squatted and checked the lines again before returning to the cockpit and relieving a grateful Foxy of her duty. On the radio once more, she talked to the Lake City Marina, confirming what *River Rat* had said about a casualty on board. The harbormaster assured her a rescue boat was on its way. "Just keep her slow and steady 'til we get there. Soon as our guys board the *Wayward Wind* they'll bring her right in. We got medical people standing by."

"Hurry!" Louise said under her breath.

Seeing her expression, Cate asked, "What aren't you telling us?"

Once more the image of her brother's nearly lifeless body came to mind and she shook her head to clear it. "I'm just . . . I never rescued or towed a boat before."

Grace groaned. "Now you tell us!"

Louise tried to smile along with the others, but based on what Robin had told her, she did not expect a good end to this.

Perhaps a quarter of an hour had passed when they saw the flat, silver rescue boat. Its captain held up a hand in greeting as he passed on his way to the sailboat, and Louise waved back. Soon a bandy-legged man clambered from the rescue boat onto the larger vessel. In the cockpit he stooped down, out of sight. Moments later he stood again, opened his arms, crossed and opened them again, signaling his partner on the rescue boat. Then he hauled on the halyard, and the mainsail began to collapse. He did the same with the jib.

"What's happening?" Robin and Cate asked.

Louise didn't have much experience with sailboats, but she knew enough to recognize the emergency maneuver. "They dropped the sails and tightened the boom lines so they can motor into the harbor." She pointed to the man at the helm and then at the discharge of water behind the boat, an indication the engine had kicked in.

In a minute the radio crackled to life. There was static, and then a single word came through clearly: "unresponsive."

More words broke through the white noise as the man who'd taken charge of the *Wayward Wind* talked to his partner on the rescue boat. He referred to a nasty head wound, followed by a comment about there not being a lot of blood.

More crackling, then, ". . . revive him?"

The answer came after a long pause. "Negative. No pulse."

The stunned women looked to Louise, but her eyes were closed and her lips pressed shut.

Cate picked at a tear in the knee of her jeans. "How do we get ourselves into these things? It's like we're some kind of murder magnet."

Louise's eyes snapped open. "Who said anything about murder?"

Cate arched an eyebrow. "Trouble magnet, then."

Louise rubbed her forehead with the heel of her hand.

Grace looked like she was about to cry. "It started out such a beautiful day."

Foxy looked off in the distance. "You'd think we'd know by now. Good beginnings don't always make for smooth sailing," she said.

The rescue team detached Louise's towline. It took three of them to haul it in. By the time the tandem boats passed them, Louise allowed herself a moment of relief. She idled the engine, stalling so they wouldn't arrive in Lake City at the same time as the *Wayward Wind*. There was bound to be commotion, and she'd just as soon slip into the marina unnoticed.

Silence fell over them as they slowly made their way through the choppy water. Louise's mind kept going over the scene as Robin had described it. When she recognized the distinctive aroma of barbequed meat wafting from shore, she was jerked back to the present moment, startled to see how close they'd drifted to Hok-Si-La Park on the Minnesota side of Lake Pepin. A few colorful kayaks clustered at the water's edge. Swimsuit-clad bodies dotted the beach and a couple of swimmers ventured farther from shore. She quickly corrected her course, and then radioed the marina to find out where they would dock for the night.

Proceeding past the breakwater, built to protect boats from the river current and wakes caused by larger boats, she steered past the pier where the *Wayward Wind* and rescue boat were tethered. Foxy and Grace went fore and aft, slipping the cylindrical fenders from their cages and dropping them over the sides.

"Let the wind take us in," Louise instructed her friends, "and stay on the boat 'til I tell you." Approaching the dock, she threw the engine in reverse to slow their forward speed, then gave a thumbs up to Grace and Robin, who easily stepped off the boat to secure the docking lines.

Nearby, a boat horn sounded, and then another. Over the radio came a new voice. "Nice work, *Time Out*." More horns sounded, apparently the boating community's version of a standing ovation.

Grace waved at the people popping their heads up from docked boats like a colony of aquatic prairie dogs. Louise kept her head down as she made sure all the lines were secure, coiling the excess on the dock.

"We're celebrities," Grace said, coming up beside her.

Louise's smile was tight. "It's not like we saved anyone's life!" But at least they hadn't killed him by moving him, she thought.

The others' eyes followed where hers had landed. Two men aboard the *Wayward Wind* hoisted a stretcher up and over the rail, where four hands waited on the dock to receive the pallet and the still figure that lay on it. The man was not covered by a sheet. He had a shock of dark brown hair. His shirt and shorts were white, his shoes green. The emergency crew moved almost casually as they fed their cargo through the open maw of a waiting ambulance and shut the doors.

"Doesn't someone usually get in back with the patient?" Robin said. Immediately realizing the answer, she clamped a hand over her mouth.

No lights flashed as the ambulance drove off.

Louise said she wanted to stay on the boat until the fuss died down. "By the way, girls, I think it's safe to take off your life vests now," she said, and they had a moment of levity as they returned the vests to the locker. They huddled in the cockpit, from where they could see both men from the fireboat had remained on the *Wayward Wind*. One ran his hands the length of the boom, pausing on what

Louise guessed to be the point of impact. They crouched to examine the deck. They stood and walked the length of the boat. Finally they hopped onto the dock, reattached the vinyl-coated lifeline to the stanchion of the sailboat and hung a KEEP OFF sign from it with duct tape.

Louise frowned. Something wasn't right.

"What time is our dinner reservation? I can't believe I'm hungry again," Foxy said, interrupting her train of thought.

Louise was taken aback by the question, but Foxy had been right to pull them back to normalcy. She said they still had plenty of time, so the five of them spread out on the U-shaped settee around the table. Cate offered to open a bottle of wine, but no one was interested.

Grace broke the silence. "How well did you know the boat's captain?"

Scratching her head, Louise ran into a spot of sunburned scalp and winced. "I guess I knew him, in the sense that everyone's aware of the other boats and their owners. We don't exactly know each other, so much as we know about each other. I remember he's an attorney, maybe mid or late forties. Not flashy. Not like the owner of that brand new Carver motor yacht I pointed out earlier. Dean says that guy's so rich he has to buy a new boat every time he gets one wet."

That got a laugh. Louise started to lighten up.

"So what's this attorney's name?" Cate asked.

Louise shook her head. "You know, I'm completely blanking. I remember his wife is quite pretty, several years younger than him, and they have two little boys. He's kind of an odd duck, not real sociable. The *Wayward Wind* is a big boat for one person to handle. People talk about how dumb it is for him to sail solo all the time."

"I guess they were right," Robin mumbled.

"I wonder why he wanted to be alone," Grace said. "How about his wife? And kids? You'd think they'd love sailing with their dad."

"I'm sure they would, but they're at that age when they're a handful. Dean and I saw the family last summer. They hadn't even left the dock and he—Why can't I remember his name?" She pulled at her bottom lip before continuing. "Anyway, he was carrying on about those boys, telling his wife it was a stupid idea to bring them. It's not like they were monsters, just being kids, you know. Anyway, after putting up with his grousing for a while, the mom grabbed them up, one on each hand, and took them down below. She came topside again by herself and pitched a hissy fit with a tail on it. As I recall, they went at it for a while."

Foxy said, "You mean it got physical?"

Louise truly grinned for the first time since spying the unmanned sailboat. "No, just boat sex."

She waited for someone to ask, and Grace did. "What do you mean, boat sex?"

"It's when you argue until someone says 'screw you' or other words to that effect, depending on your vocabulary, and the other one says it back. I'd guess every couple in this marina has had boat sex at some time or another."

In mock horror, Foxy said, "Surely not you and Dean!"

Louise laughed a throaty laugh. "Oh, I'm not saying I use those exact words. When he really gets under my hide, I just bat my eyes and say, 'Well, bless your heart!' It gets the point across."

They heard clomping along the dock and looked up to see a cute, round-faced woman in denim shorts and tank top approaching. "Knock, knock," she called out in a singsong voice.

Louise invited Betty Jo to join them. At least she remembered *that* name. She and Dean had had some interactions with Betty Jo and her husband, but, like their other marina friends, they didn't know each other well.

"Oh thanks, hon, but I just came to let you know we've got a pitcher of margaritas and chips with salsa. The *Siren*'s just over there on the next dock. " She pointed to a sailboat with green sail covers.

Several minutes later, they were aboard the *Siren* with Betty Jo and her husband, Jack. She'd barely shoved drinks into their hands before their hostess revealed the real reason for the invitation. "We heard that whole thing on the radio and wanted to get the story first-hand, before anyone else," she said. "Did you really try to tow the sailboat?"

"We just used the towrope 'til the fireboat got there."

"You think he's dead?"

Suddenly weary, Louise leaned her elbow on the table. Knowing Betty Jo, she'd keep poking around until she got the answer. Might as well get it over with. "Might be. They didn't look like they were in a hurry to get him to the hospital, did they? I'm assuming it was the owner. I recognized his shoes, anyway."

"Those neon green Topsiders?"

Louise nodded. "He always struck me as the buttoned down type. Those shoes were so out of character." To preempt further inquiry, she said, "But listen, we don't know any more than you do."

Undeterred, Betty leaned forward, her eyes wide, "But you were there. Did you see him? The way people were talking, it sounded like his head was split open like a melon."

Her husband slammed his drink against his thigh and, swiping at the sloshed liquid, said, "For the love of God, Betty Jo! Why d'ya have to be such a ghoul?"

"Well, you were just as curious as I was." After shooting him a withering look, she changed the course of her questioning. "Do you remember that time Bryce's wife spent the night with him on the boat?"

Only then did Louise recall his full name. Bryce Morgan. And with the name came the memory of that night. Betty Jo and Jack, along with Louise and Dean, had witnessed that uncomfortable little spectacle from where they sat having cocktails on the dock. Chagrined, she also remembered how all four of them had shaken their heads and cracked jokes as if the show were being put on purely for their amusement.

"That was ugly," Louise said, tightening the corners of her mouth. "I felt bad for his wife—all that youthful exuberance getting stomped on."

"Yeah, he was pretty tough on her," Betty Jo admitted. Then she started telling about the incident, with Louise filling in some missing details. Jack stared into his drink, clearly uncomfortable.

From all appearances, Bryce and his young wife Lexi had been anticipating a romantic evening on the boat. There was a particularly lovely sunset that night, and the two couples, Betty Jo and Jack, Louise and Dean, had set up deck chairs at the end of the dock to drink a cocktail and watch the sun go down. Gathered in a semicircle, they'd had a good view of the next dock over, and of the *Wayward Wind* and its occupants.

They lingered after the sun set. The evening was still on the sultry side. They hadn't intended to invade anyone's privacy, yet they'd found themselves looking on as Lexi carefully lit little tea lights and placed them along the edge of the fiberglass deck. Soon Bryce came up from below, took one look at her attempt at ambience and blew the candles out, and he launched into a lecture about fire hazards. Louise admitted he had a legitimate safety concern, but thought he came across as unnecessarily harsh. Although neither of them yelled, the couple's voices bounced off the water. The more he'd berated her, the more Lexi's shoulders had sagged. For a while she'd sat cross-legged on the forward deck and sulked. After a while Bryce had crouched next to her, talking too quietly to catch his words, and began rubbing her shoulders. Soon she'd ducked below. When she came up in a few minutes, she was wearing a flimsy nightie.

Interrupting her story, Louise turned to Jack. "Oh, yes, I remember the way you and Dean gawked at her, hoping the wind would blow her nightie up."

"Aw, c'mon, we just did that to give you gals a little grief," he said.

Cate's eyebrow went up and Grace snorted.

"Uh-huh." Louise let those two syllables carry her skepticism.

"Bryce took one look at his wife's kitten-heel sandals and said if she wanted to be invited on the boat again, she needed to wear proper boat shoes, and she yelled something about wearing tennis shoes with a negligee," Betty Jo continued. "She scurried down the ladder and pretty soon this shoe flies up from below and clangs against a stanchion before it hits him on the shoulder and ricochets off into the water."

Foxy clapped her hands together and said, "Oh, I would love to have seen that."

"I would've bought a ticket to that show," Robin said. "Then what happened?"

Jack said, "As I recall, Bryce ducked just in time or the second shoe would've clobbered him."

Robin and Louise exchanged a look and the mood shifted.

Betty Jo offered a second round of margaritas. The book club women declined, explaining they had dinner reservations at Nosh.

Holding up his drink, Jack said, "Well, we're noshing on the boat tonight. Maybe you want to join us after dinner for that presentation over at the campground."

Louise shook her head. "Sorry, I don't—"

"You know the place, it's just past the Skyline Restaurant," Betty Jo explained. "Some ghost hunter is doing a program. It sounds interesting."

"Ghost hunter?" Robin and Cate said at the same time.

She seemed pleased to have information they did not possess. "Some guy from the Cities is writing a book about the weird goings-on here on Lake Pepin. He's got a lot to work with, what with the

Indian maiden and the ferry disaster and all. I guess there are even haunted houses right here in Lake City."

Louise rolled her eyes. "Not to mention Pepie."

Betty Jo shook her head. "No, it's not about Pepie. The guy's only researching real things."

"I see," said Louise. "Ghosts and haunted houses but not lake monsters."

"Exactly!"

Mom?" Lexi Morgan heard the childlike quaver in her own voice.

"For crying out loud, Lexi, I've been trying to reach you for hours." Her mother's tone was sharper than usual. "Are you okay?"

Slouched on the kitchen stool with a growing pile of sodden tissues in her lap, Lexi dabbed at her eyes as she spoke into the phone. "I just picked up the boys from Zan's." She and her sister often took turns watching all four kids for a day, sometimes for a whole weekend, just to give the other a break.

Her mother's voice shifted from concern to annoyance. "I know. I called Zan this morning when I couldn't get you either at home or on your cell phone. Where were you, anyway?"

"Listen, Mom. Something happened. It's bad."

There was a tiny gasp at the other end. "Is it Zan? Is she okay?"

Why did everyone worry about her younger sister? She might be a size two, but she was stronger than she looked. "It's Bryce. He was in an accident. The police called right after I got home."

"Is he okay? What happened?"

"No, Mom!" she yelled. "He's not okay. I'm not okay." Lexi's heart pounded, afraid she couldn't get the words out. She paced from kitchen to sunroom, circling the room and wondering how its white wicker chairs, pale gold walls, and a jungle of potted plants could be so cheery on this, of all days. She took a deep breath. "Bryce was on the sailboat, and he—"

"Alone?"

"Yes, Mom, he was alone. As usual." Lexi felt sweat beading on her forehead and upper lip. "He was all by himself when the boom caught him on the corner of his head. It was a bad accident."

There was a long pause before Alice said, "The corner of his head?"

Her inane questions made Lexi want to scream. "Wrong word. It was, you know, on his temple. It hit him hard, and . . ." She paused and took a deep breath. "They said there was brain damage."

"But is he okay now?"

She wanted to hurl the phone against the wall. "I told you already. He's not okay."

"Mommeee!" Her younger son Brian careened around the corner, naked except for a red Superman cape. He stopped, his large eyes growing larger. "Why are you crying?" he asked her.

Lexi tried to scoop him up with one arm, something she could have done just a few weeks ago, but he'd gotten too big for that. "Mommy's having a really bad day," she told him.

Superman nodded and jammed his thumb in his mouth. She really did have to wean him from that habit. "Go get some pants on," she told him.

He stuck his arms out in flight. When he soared off, she returned the phone to her ear.

Her mother was mid-sentence. ". . . what to tell your father. Are you saying Bryce is dead?"

Lexi shuddered. "Yes, Mother, he's dead." She explained she was calling because she needed her mother to stay with the boys so she could drive down to Lake City, where Bryce's body lay at the funeral home.

She heard her father in the background saying, "What's wrong, Alice? Let me talk to her."

"We'll be right there, honey. Dad will watch the boys. I'm going with you. You're not going to drive alone." Her mother was always so decisive. She hung up before her daughter could object.

Lexi made a beeline to the liquor cabinet and poured herself a small glass of sherry, drinking it down in two gulps. She hoped it would give her just enough courage to gather her sons to her and tell them their father wouldn't be home tonight. Or any other night. At five and not-quite-four, BJ and Brian had no real understanding of death.

She mustered her courage and went upstairs to their room. The boys barely looked up when she walked in, sat on a bed and did her best to tell them their daddy bumped his head and was hurt badly. When BJ asked if he could see him, Lexi shook her head. "Not today, sweetie." Brian, now wearing pull-on shorts with his cape, asked if Daddy was in the hos-tipple. "No," she answered truthfully. "Grandma and I need to see Daddy right now, so Granddad's going to take you two hooligans out for pizza."

"Hool-gan, hool-gan," Superman chanted, flapping his cape. His brother joined in, and she slipped out of the room while they were still giggling. Maybe one day the boys would think back on this moment and be embarrassed by how easily silly words and pizza with their grandfather had turned their attention away from their father's untimely death. For now, the distraction was simply a reprieve for all of them.

She could only imagine what her parents were saying right now. Her mother had never warmed up to Lexi's husband, although she never came right out and said so. It was more complicated with her father, who could be disparaging Bryce one moment and slapping him on the back the next, sharing a joke, just one good old boy to another. Her sister Zan was the bluntest of them all. She flat out hadn't liked Bryce.

When they arrived, her father, his eyes shining with unshed tears, gave her a gruff hug. Following close behind, her mother opened her arms and pulled her daughter into a tight embrace, stroking her hair. Lexi knew her mother wanted to comfort, but today she was impervious, as though encased in a hard shell. No hug or cooed words would console her troubled spirit today.

Brian and BJ clutched their granddad's hands and dragged him into the living room. "It's like being taken down by kudzu vines," he said with a smile. The boys brought him to the floor and spilled the contents of a big plastic bin in front of him. "Oh, boy, Legos!" he said, as if he'd hoped for nothing more.

"Honey, I know you don't like us butting into your life, but maybe now you'll accept our help," her mother said.

"Maybe now?" There was no mistaking her mother's intent. Maybe now that Bryce was out of the picture, Lexi would realize she couldn't handle things like an adult. "I can handle it."

"Yes, I suppose you can. You've been raising the kids pretty much by yourself, anyway. Now you can do it without so much, uh . . . direction."

When Alice walked out of the room, her father rose to his feet, and placed a hand on Lexi's back. "I'm sorry, sweetheart. Your mother didn't mean it to come across that way. She can't imagine what you're going through." He spoke close to her ear, as if they were co-conspirators. "You know she's just worried about you. She doesn't mean to be unkind."

She hated it when her father interceded like this, making excuses for her inappropriate comments. "So you're saying she has Tourette's?" It was the kind of snotty retort she might have given as a teenager.

His mouth tightened. "You don't need to take that tone. We have eyes and ears, you know. We've both been concerned about your husband's temper."

Lexi fled to the bathroom, where she shoved her face in a bath towel to stifle her scream.

5

Louise had her favorite restaurants on Lake Pepin and this one was on her short list. She was sure her book club friends would appreciate the inventive menu and artistic presentation, unlike Dean who, truth be told, would be happy to eat bologna sandwiches on the boat every day. Positioned on the other side of the marina parking lot, Nosh was usually busy. The weathered building might have been mistaken for a boathouse or a dive, although the interior had an air of casual elegance. They were led to a table on the patio with a spectacular view of the marina and lake.

Perusing the menu, they ordered tapas, salad, roasted morel mushrooms and two entrees to share. Before the food arrived, a middle-aged man in cargo shorts and polo shirt got up from his table and came to ask about "the guy from the sailboat." Louise said they didn't know much and suggested talking to the fireboat crew to get whatever information he was looking for. When he returned to his table, they saw him shrugging at his dinner companions.

After they'd eaten every morsel, Louise excused herself. Robin jumped up, following her into the bathroom. "You don't seem yourself," she said to Louise. "Your mind is still back on that sailboat, isn't it?"

"I'm uncomfortable with all this interest in Bryce Morgan's death, like it's just another titillating story." She stepped into the stall and kept talking. "I'm not interested in giving lurid details. The more we talk about it, the more I worry we're being just as ghoulish as Betty Jo."

In the stall next to her, Robin sucked in her breath, and Louise prepared for a rebuttal, but what came out was, "Do you really think we're like that?"

"No . . . maybe. I mean, back when we discovered our first body, we just jumped in, and now we keep finding ourselves in these awful situations."

"Oh, Lord, our first body! When you put it that way . . ."

"It was all very scary and sad, but it was also . . . exciting . . . invigorating to be putting our brain cells together to solve a real mystery."

"But if it weren't for us, that death would still be listed as accidental. We helped to solve it," Robin protested.

At the sink, Louise pumped the soap dispenser and talked over the running water. "And here we are again. Another death that looks like an accident, but is it? Are we sure it was an accident?"

Robin came to stand next to her. They looked at each other's reflections as they talked. "You don't really think he was murdered, do you?"

Louise shrugged. As much as she wanted to let it go, she had to ask. "When I watched those guys going over the sailboat, I thought something was a little off."

"About the rescue team?"

She checked herself in the mirror. "No, something about the boat, but I can't put my finger on it." Louise continued to wring her soapy hands together under the faucet.

Robin said, "Think your hands are clean enough, Lady Macbeth?"

Looking at her compulsive behavior, Louise almost laughed. "You know I always wanted to play Lady Macbeth? Only on stage, though." She'd gotten the acting bug in high school and had considered majoring in theater, but her parents wouldn't hear of it.

"Real-life drama isn't as fun as it looks."

Louise leaned into the mirror and smoothed her hair. "Today I remembered something Daddy used to say. He'd say, 'It's all fun and games until someone pokes their eye out and sends the other one looking for it.'"

Robin started to laugh, but Louise cut her off. "No, really. Think about it. It's like the way we keep dragging each other into dumb situations, and one of these days, that one eye's gonna take off for good and the second one's gonna get lost looking for it."

"That's quite the mental image," Robin said, and crossed her eyes.

Louise guffawed. "Yeah, I may have wrung too much out of that metaphor."

Stepping into the hall, their way was blocked by two figures. A man wearing a white smock and a florid face was chiding another man for being late to work. "I don't care if she's Ange-frickin'-lina Jolie. It's a full house tonight and we've got people griping about the service."

The one being called out for tardiness scratched his curly mop of dark hair and said, "What'd you expect me to do? Her boyfriend stranded her at the restaurant. She can't exactly walk back to Red Wing."

The other guy gave a derisive snort. "Yeah, you're a real knight in shining armor."

The curly headed guy shrugged.

"You know what, Chad? You're full of crap and you know it. You really expect me to believe you picked up a strange girl just cause you're such a nice guy?"

Suddenly aware of the women only a few feet behind them, they spun their heads around. The men stepped aside, and as Louise and

Robin hurried past, the one in the white smock said, "And what were you doing at the Skyline, anyway? Looking for another job?"

Chad's answer was unintelligible.

"Well, that was unpleasant," Louise muttered when they were out of earshot.

They sat down at their table ready to tell the others of this strange conversation, but were interrupted by a voice calling Louise's name. Turning toward the voice, they saw Betty Jo weaving through the tables toward them. She planted her hands flat on their table, leaning forward to show plenty of cleavage. "We've rounded up a couple vans for the ghost lecture. There's room for five more and we leave in twenty minutes. C'mon, it'll be fun."

Louise looked to her friends and sighed. "Well?

Cate nodded her head vigorously.

"It sounds like a perfect diversion," Robin said, and the others agreed.

She threw cold water on her face and emerged from the bath-room as ready to face what lay ahead of her as she would ever be. Opening the door to the garage, Lexi found her mother already behind the wheel, adjusting the rearview mirror and fussing to reposition the seat. Alice motioned for her to get into the passenger seat of her own car.

As soon as the car was in motion, Lexi confronted her. "I always knew you and Dad weren't wild about Bryce, but I didn't realize you actually thought he was a threat to us."

Her mother concentrated overly much on the road. "Only when he flew off the handle."

Lexi felt cold inside. "Bryce never laid a hand on me. Or the boys."

"You can hurt someone without physical violence, you know."

That struck close to the bone. Lexi was all too familiar with the kind of hurt that didn't leave bruises. Her eyes welled up. Tears rolled down her cheeks and onto the front of her sundress. "Well, you won't have to worry about that now, will you?"

Sighing heavily, Alice stared straight ahead.

In the ensuing silence, Lexi had ample time to reflect on the concerns her parents—and frankly, a few other people—had about Bryce. He'd been such a dichotomy. The first year of their marriage, she'd made and revised lists of his qualities, both good and not so good. Now she just kept the ledger sheet it in her mind. Either way the pattern held, and most days the plus side was longer than the minus side. There was smart, handsome, take-charge Bryce with a charismatic smile. The one who wept openly when his sons were born, and in the privacy of their bedroom demonstrated surprising tenderness. This Bryce could melt hearts with a smile. And then there was vain, ambitious Bryce who could use his words like rapiers, yet was too thin-skinned to handle criticism himself. That Bryce was so exacting, so disparaging, no one could hope to live up to his expectations, although she'd certainly tried.

Recently the two aspects of him had become more equal, the crack between them widening, like the shifting of tectonic plates. Lexi felt as if she stood on his fault line.

Unbidden, the memory came to her of the day he'd come home sizzling with excitement about the sailboat he'd bought. He hadn't consulted her, naturally, but poring over the brochure and seeing the joy in his face, she'd gotten drawn in by his enthusiasm. For days they'd painted word pictures of romantic sunset cruises for the two of them, and leisurely day trips with the boys. She could pinpoint the sickening moment she'd realized the boat wasn't about strengthening their marriage or their family life after all. On that single, failed trip with the boys, she'd seen in a flash it had been all about Bryce all along. The *Wayward Wind* was nothing more than a very expensive man cave.

"I can't believe you're jealous of a boat!" he'd exploded when she questioned the number of hours he spent alone on the *Wayward Wind*. "Anyway, aren't you always badgering me to take time off?"

He had her there. There were people who still saw her as sweet, but she knew she'd hardened in some ways, and for that more than anything else, she resented him. When it came right down to it, what she hated about Bryce was who she'd become.

With her mom driving in their self-imposed silence, freewheeling thoughts and memories tumbled in Lexi's head like so much laundry. From the first "I love you," she'd made Bryce the hub around which her world turned. From the moment she'd found the engagement ring in her wine glass, she'd been unable to imagine her life without him in it.

When had that changed? She couldn't remember the incident that had been the impetus, but one day she found herself finding perverse consolation in imagining what life would be like without him. It happened with some regularity after that. One particular incident floated to the top. It was the time she'd forgotten to pay a bill. He'd looked at her with that cold, hard stare of his and told her, "You should be damn grateful. If it weren't for me, you'd be utterly helpless."

Helpless! He hadn't known her very well, as it turned out. Even in this maelstrom of longing and remorse, she detected a glimmer of hope—even empowerment. If God was truly a just god, once this trial passed, she would look back on this someday and see how strong and resourceful she'd been in seizing the opportunity to fashion a different kind of life for herself and her children.

The closer they got to Lake City, the less Lexi wanted to dwell on marital discord. Instead, she wanted to remember all the reasons she'd been attracted to him in the first place. Whatever and whoever Bryce Morgan had been, she was traveling to this town of three thousand people to identify his remains. Maybe it would be less horrifying if she could think of him as "the deceased," rather than picturing that brilliant, stubborn, mercurial brain of his shattered.

Arriving at the funeral home, she felt numb, as if someone else inhabited her body and was going through the motions for her. Walking into the dimmer light with its soothing decor, she couldn't reconcile it with the brutality of Bryce's death. The incongruity of it struck her, and she felt like she'd been dropped into a theater set.

34

Barbara Deese

She'd played the lead in her senior class play, *Mary Poppins*, and that felt more real to her than this. If only she had an umbrella, maybe it would lift her on a breeze and take her away.

A man in a black suit jacket too heavy for this hot day met them in the lobby and guided Lexi and her mother into an office, where he introduced them to a doctor, a young woman with round glasses and closely cropped hair, who said she wanted to talk to Lexi for a bit before letting her see her husband. As the doctor explained, she had already examined Bryce's body and determined approximate time of death, but before making the official pronouncement, she hoped to have a family member corroborate his identity.

"There's no need to put her through any more pain," her mother said, standing and putting a hand on her daughter's shoulder. "I'll do it."

Lexi's eyes lifted and she felt a flood of love for her mother, whose offer was nothing less than a stay of execution. Slowly, like a marionette's, her head moved up and down.

While they were gone, Lexi examined the samples of memorial folders and note cards, all with peaceful images of flowers and soaring eagles and sunrises over shimmering water. How, she wondered, did those pastel, innocuous pictures have anything to do with blood and brain matter defiling the *Wayward Wind*'s pristine deck?

An open cabinet to her right displayed rows of urns—wood, marble, bronze—in various colors, shapes and sizes. She was disturbed to think a human being, especially one with a personality as big as Bryce's, could be reduced to no more ash than would fit into a child's shoebox.

Her mother appeared in the doorway. How long she'd been standing there, Lexi didn't know. Her red-rimmed eyes fixed on Lexi's. She nodded her head and her lips quivered as she tried in vain to be strong for her daughter.

The finality of her unspoken answer left Lexi bereft. "Why did it have to come to this?" she muttered under her breath. Even as she spoke the words, she knew there would be no answer.

"Honey, we need to make decisions here," Alice said, and repeated the funeral director's question. "Do you want to go with burial or cremation?"

In her current floaty state and overwhelmed by all the decisions to be made, she went blank, unable to process the actions that went with those words, and so she shrugged and deferred to her mother's natural inclination to manage. "What do you think?"

Clearly uncomfortable, Alice said, "Sweetheart, it's not my call. Did you and Bryce ever talk about arrangements?"

Lexi shook her head.

Alice asked where he kept important papers, like his will or health care directive.

Lexi picked at a ragged cuticle. "I don't know. At the office, most likely. That's where he kept everything important."

"And what about the boat? You'll be wanting to sell it, won't you?"

With each question, Lexi felt as though she regressed a year or two until she was reduced to a child. It was not a particularly good feeling and with it came a familiar resistance to taking direction. She reminded herself she was quite capable, something that would probably shock her mother. Bryce had treated her the same way, even said she was helpless, but he was wrong. "We don't need to discuss what I do with the boat," she said, emphasizing the word "I." To the funeral director, she said, "I'll let you know tomorrow about arrangements." There, she'd said it. "I'd like to find someone to return the *Wayward Wind* to Red Wing. May we stay here and use your phone?"

The director nodded and flipped his Rolodex, scribbled on a slip of paper and handed it to Lexi. "Here are a couple names. He poked a finger at the paper. "I'd try him first. His price is reasonable and he may even be able to get your boat there tonight." He left them in the office to make calls.

The day had been emotionally exhausting for both of them. All she wanted was just one more hour, one more day before having to look into the sad and bewildered eyes of her sons. Before bracing for her father's comments. Before having to explain to friends and neighbors how she came to be a widow at the age of twenty-eight.

7

I'm pretty sure some of you came here with the idea that we're a bunch of crackpots," said the speaker, a man with thin ginger hair and deep furrows in his forehead. He had a little paunch and Robin guessed he was in his forties. Dressed in nice jeans, a golf shirt, and tennis shoes, he looked like the antithesis of a crackpot. "Sure, there are a few screwballs, like in any profession, but ghost hunting is real science. Talk to any of us and you'll see when it comes to ghosts, we're dead serious." There was a ripple of laughter in the audience.

About three dozen people were crowded into a screened shelter at the community park, all of them having paid a modest fee to hear about the supernatural. There was a slight echo in the room when the speaker introduced himself as Simon and explained that although he answered to the title ghost hunter, he preferred to be called a paranormal investigator. "I do my best to stay current with the scientific research, but most of the time I'm just listening to stories, taking lots of notes and looking for consistencies and inconsistencies." He scanned the room and his eyes seemed to fall on Cate, Robin and Grace sitting in a clump by the window. "Sometimes I find evidence of paranormal activity, but much more often I debunk it. I approach each situation with a healthy dose of skepticism. But here's the thing: I also believe it's folly to deny the spirit world exists."

Cate leaned forward, forearms resting on her thighs. Robin wiggled her eyebrows at her and Cate smiled back. Robin knew this was right up her alley.

Simon threw a glance around the room and rubbed the back of his head. "You know there's more to this universe than those things you can pick up with your five senses. I suspect you all believe that, or you wouldn't be here."

Grace elbowed Robin. "Should I tell him his fly is open?" she whispered.

Robin glowered and gave little shake of her head. She and Grace had a long and undignified history of giggling at the most inappropriate times and she didn't want to disgrace herself once again. Almost against her will, her eyes dipped to his crotch. Grace was right. By refusing to make eye contact, Robin hoped to avoid embarrassing both of them.

He hitched up his pants and continued. "Just because you can't see something, can't feel its mass in your hands, doesn't mean it doesn't exist."

Robin bit the insides of her cheeks.

His pale blue eyes searched the room and fell on them. "You know, until the microscope, nobody understood how disease spread, and they scoffed at the germ theory. It took a long time for people to accept that some things are too small to see with the naked eye." He gestured to the array of gadgets that lay on the table next to him. "But once you get your hands on the proper tools . . . "

The noise Grace emitted was like air slowly escaping from a balloon. Robin covered her mouth and coughed.

Cate smacked Robin's thigh with the back of her hand. "Shhh," she hissed. "When you make fun of him, you make fun of me." Cate could be very prickly about her own psychic abilities.

"His zipper's open," Robin whispered between her fingers.

Cate gave a disgusted shake of her head that clearly said, *Oh, grow up.*

Simon held up various pieces of the equipment, which he identified as full spectrum cameras, electromagnetic field meters to detect nearby spirits, and electronic voice phenomenon devices to record spirit voices. After describing their functions and giving very brief demonstrations, he turned to the reason he'd come to Lake City. He, along with three volunteers, had been documenting local unexplained sightings and odd phenomena. "There's a house not too far from here where people report doors shaking," he told the crowd. "They hear footsteps both inside and out." He picked up one of the metal boxes. "We managed to catch this on our EVP recorder. If you listen closely, you can hear someone say, 'Get lost.'" He pushed a button and they all strained to make sense of the whooshing and crackling.

"It just sounds like someone messing with the radio dial," Robin whispered. Grace nodded in agreement, but Cate wore an exasperated frown. "Well, what did it sound like to you?" Robin asked her.

Cate's mouth twisted and she let out a long sigh. "I hate to say it, but it sounded like someone messing with the radio dial."

Simon went on. "One shop owner claims he's seen the watery footprints of a little girl who drowned in Lake Pepin. Many times, in fact."

"How do they know who it was that made the footprints?" someone shouted out. "And how do they know she drowned?"

He hung his head for a moment. He looked peeved. Facing his questioner, he said, "First of all, just so there's full disclosure here, our electronics haven't picked up on any activity there, not yet, anyway. But here's the deal. Several years ago people reported seeing the ghost of a young girl and later said they recognized her from a photograph. The girl's ghost was seen several times, and each time she was in the vicinity of where the wet footprints were later seen."

The guy with the questions sat back, seemingly satisfied.

"All we can do is record what people tell us," Simon continued. "For years there have been reports of several ghosts who've taken up residence at the St. James Hotel in Red Wing." He picked up a sheaf of papers and went around the room dispensing a stapled report to each attendee. "I won't say much about the St. James spirits, since there's been plenty of documentation by other investigators, which you can read on your own."

"What about Maiden Rock?"asked a man with a nasty sunburn who sat in the front row. "You know, that place where the Indian princess Winona jumped off a cliff? Does she show up on your gadgets?"

Simon skewed his mouth to one side and sniffed. "The gadgets don't tell the whole story about any of these spirits. Besides that, not everyone agrees that the story about Winona really happened. More likely, it's a legend. See, 'Winona' isn't a proper name. It's the Dakota word for first-born girl." He addressed the rest of the crowd. "If you haven't heard the legend, a young girl, some say the daughter of Chief Red Wing of the Sioux tribe, leapt to her death rather than marry the man chosen for her."

The sunburned man pointed across the lake. "Yep, right over there at Maiden Rock." The woman to his right nodded vigorously.

Simon invited the couple to talk to him after the program. "Okay, look, we can go in all sorts of different directions here, but tonight I want to focus on the *Sea Wing* ferry. A lot's been written about that disaster. My assistants and I came here to find out what we can about paranormal activity on the lake itself relating to that accident."

The room was hushed.

Simon took a deep breath. His low, almost reverential tone re-minded Robin of telling ghost stories around the campfire.

"It was Sunday, July thirteenth. The year was 1890. The weather was hot and humid, a lot like today, actually. Hoping to cool off, some residents of Red Wing decided to take the *Sea Wing* ferry downriver to the National Guard camp right here on the shores of Lake City. Unfortunately they'd oversold tickets, and the riverboat ferry was overcrowded—over two hundred passengers, all told, and more than half of them women. Well, the captain took one look at the overcrowded boat and decided to put some of the overflow onto a barge and lash it to the big boat, so that's the way they set out." His eyes took on an intensity as he spoke. "The day was uneventful, that is, until the ferry left Lake City to return her passengers to Red Wing. Without warning, a storm blew in. The boat began to rock. It rocked so hard the barge cut loose of the riverboat, which saved the lives of all those on the barge, but ultimately doomed the other boat. If it weren't for those survivors, we may never have gotten such a detailed account."

He went on to tell the dramatic story of the capsized ferry that took the lives of ninety-eight people. Only seven of the women survived. Whether or not it had come in the form of a tornado—some of the survivors reported seeing a funnel cloud illuminated by a flash of lightning—the sudden and violent storm had struck with disastrous results. In the aftermath of this unprecedented tragedy, some claimed the ship's captain had been inebriated, although that was never proven.

"The *Sea Wing* was big news back then. In fact, for a while after that, Red Wing was known as 'City of the Dead.'" Simon directed them to a page in their pamphlets that showed a photo of the St. Paul newspaper touting the headline, "A Voyage of Pleasure That Ended on the Shores of Another World."

Betty Jo waved her hand over her head. "What about ghosts? Has anyone seen ghosts from the ship?"

A faint smile crossed his lips and he bobbed his head. "That headline suggests to me there might be ghosts from the *Sea Wing*, and that's exactly what we want to find out. We do know there haven't been a lot of sightings, but some people say they can sometimes hear the screams of terrified passengers. Unfortunately, nobody's gotten anything on an EVP meter, for instance." Then he resumed his story. "Whatever the cause, that top-heavy ferry flipped over end to end and got broken up pretty good. Just imagine the terror of the doomed passengers. Those who managed to survive were forever traumatized by it."

Looking at the rest of the audience, Robin had to admit Simon's telling of the *Sea Wing*'s fated voyage was captivating. She was just about to raise her hand to ask if the ferry had ever been recovered, when a bone-chilling cry caused the words to dry up in her mouth. The high-pitched screams were followed by more, jolting everyone in the room, including the paranormal investigator. Heads swiveled and eyes widened as a shape flew past the window of the log cabin, and then another, accompanied by more unholy shrieks.

One of the screams came from inside the room, in the vicinity of Louise and Foxy. Betty Jo was frozen in her seat, her mouth open, her eyes showing abject terror. Even Simon seemed unhinged for a moment.

Afterwards, most of them would admit they were shocked and immobilized until they realized the screams had come from a bunch of teenagers having a water balloon fight outside the building. A couple of the men claimed they'd figured it out right away.

Simon cleared his throat. "Well now, I've never had special effects like that before." He gave an embarrassed laugh and then tried to reel them back in. "You asked about ghosts of the capsized ferry. Over the years, there have been scattered reports, but—"

"I got a report for you," said a man wearing a battered fishing hat encrusted with lures. "Today our grandkids were down by the water and they came running back to the camper yelling about some-body drowning out there in the river. We hightailed it over and couldn't see a blasted thing. Now I'm wondering if maybe it coulda been one a' them drowning ghosts."

"If you want to talk afterwards—"

The sunburned man slapped his thigh and laughed. "Hey, I bet anything it was Pepie!"

"Listen to this," a woman in a purple caftan chimed in. "Just before we walked over here, our neighbor asks us where we're going and when we tell her we're gonna hear a ghost hunter, she says—get this—she says earlier today she saw the shadowy figure of a girl slipping between the trees. When she looked again she was gone, but she left wet footprints on the ground, just like you said."

"Maybe it was the creature from the black lagoon," another man suggested.

"Pepie," the sunburned guy repeated.

"Walking between the trees?"

"Coulda been."

"With long black hair? I don't think so."

A bald-headed man stood, as if to leave. "Wet footprints on a beach! Imagine that!" he jeered. They heard sniggers.

"Not on the beach!' the woman said, indignant. "It was down past those condos."

Simon shook his head. "We're veering off course here."

8

"A re you going to sell the boat, then?" her mother asked as soon as they stepped out of the somber funeral home into the light. Lexi ran a hand across her throat, feeling slightly nauseated. "Can you just drop it for now?"

"They have boat brokers, just like for real estate," she persisted. "We'll be driving through Red Wing on our way home. Maybe we could just make a quick stop at the marina and ask how we go about selling it."

Her stomach roiled at the thought of seeing the *Wayward Wind* again. A shuddering sigh escaped her. "Why do you feel the need to keep up that drumbeat?" she asked with rising panic.

Her mother apologized and slid in behind the wheel, leaving Lexi to sit once more as a passenger in her own car.

She would never again see a sailboat or think of the *Wayward Wind* without picturing it as the instrument of her husband's death. "I just want to go home," she pleaded as she unknotted the bun at the nape of her neck, letting her dark tresses tumble over one shoulder. When her mother assented, she tilted the seat back and closed her eyes, her mind a muddle.

There was so much to do. Someone would have to write the obituary. She supposed that someone was her, and she began writing it in her mind. Bryce would want her to mention his rising career as a civil rights attorney, and that he'd been considering a run for the Minnesota legislature. Or maybe not, since that wasn't actually public knowledge yet. A list of schools, degrees, and honors would be appropriate, perhaps a couple of paragraphs about the causes he championed. He'd been all over the news for two days last year, representing concerned citizens who became alarmed by a cluster of hate crimes in the more affluent suburbs of the Twin Cities. Lexi decided to talk to Delroy, the firm's senior partner. He'd have some thoughts on what to write.

But it wasn't just a matter of penning some words for an obit and planning a memorial service. From now on, Lexi would be the one to pay the bills and mow the lawn and change the furnace filters. Parenting decisions would be hers alone. When her family gathered at her house for Easter dinner, she would be sitting at the head of the table. She alone would attend parent-teacher conferences. There were only so many hours in a day, and now they would be stretched thinner than ever. It would be a lie to say she hadn't considered the possibility of being a single parent, but since Bryce had never been all that involved in the hands-on stuff, that hurdle had never felt insurmountable.

There were so many unknowns, but this much she knew: she would need to reinvent her life, and that meant choosing, for the first time, what she wanted that life to look like. Bryce would not be the hub of this one.

"I don't know about you, but I'm starving," her mother said as they entered Red Wing.

Eating was the last thing Lexi wanted to do, and said so, but in a few minutes, the car was parked outside a bar and grill and a server was plunking a plate in front of her. What she really wanted was a drink. After two bites of her burger, Lexi set it back on her plate and smashed it flat with the heel of her hand. Bright red ketchup spurted onto the table like a wound. She almost threw up.

Her mother kept up a patter of innocuous observations—a commentary on the weather, the food and casual décor, and the fact that Lexi needed to eat. But Lexi let the words slide over her. At least they were no longer talking about Bryce and burial arrangements and that damned boat.

Back in the car, the nausea Lexi had experienced immediately after choking down a couple bites of hamburger returned. She began to cough and gag, but nothing came up.

"Should I pull over, honey? Are you okay?" her mother asked.

What an asinine question. Of course she wasn't okay! "I'm fine, Mom. Never felt better." With a sigh, she reclined her seat and pretended to sleep.

Her mother wasn't fooled. It didn't take her long to get back to planning Lexi's next steps. "I think you should arrange for a reading of the will," she said in the same tone she used when suggesting that Lexi tuck her hair behind her ears "so everyone can see your pretty face."

"Reading of the will? Don't you think that's a little melodramatic, Mom?"

"It doesn't have to be a formal thing, but, honey, do you really know what's in there? I mean, all things considered."

"I know exactly what's in there. He's leaving everything to me."

"Are you sure that's what he actually did?"

Doubt hit her like an electric current. Of course Bryce had shown her the document, but as always, the legalese had made her eyes glaze over and she'd barely skimmed it.

Her mother patted her knee. "I'm not trying to borrow trouble, but you have to wonder. He didn't exactly provide for his first family, did he?"

Oh, God, not this again. "You know he and Mallory were never married, right?"

"I'm well aware he did not step up to marry the mother of his first child."

She sighed loudly. "It was Mallory's choice not to get married, you know. They were both still in college and neither of them had anything worth fighting over. I told you all of this. He offered to help, but Mallory didn't need or want anything from him."

"Is that in the Gospel according to Bryce?"

She didn't have the energy to argue.

"Does that seem plausible?" Alice asked with feigned nonchalance.

"The way he explained it, yes. Actually, he felt horrible about the whole arrangement." Her mother raised an eyebrow, but Lexi pressed on. "Like I've told you before, Mallory was really into the whole feminist thing. They both were, but she took it to a whole new level. Bryce said he felt like a sperm donor, and as soon as she got pregnant, she didn't want to be saddled with him."

"And you believed him." Alice sniffed, keeping her eyes straight ahead as she drove. "I can't understand a loving mother turning down help, and I think a decent man would've insisted on taking care of his little girl."

Lexi sat up. "Little girl! Mom, Courtney's almost twenty-three!"

"Maybe so, but she was an infant when she was born."

She groaned. "Yes, Mom, I do believe most newborns are infants."

Alice opened her mouth for a retort and then burst out laughing. "Well, you have me there."

For some reason, her mother's melodic laugh made Lexi burst into tears.

"Oh, honey!" Alice reached over to stroke her daughter's cheek. "Sometimes I get so focused I can't see I'm tromping all over your feelings. My God, you've been through something horrible and I'm chewing on you like a dog with a bone."

The last twenty minutes of the drive were pleasant. Just blocks away from the Morgans' home, Alice looked at her sideways. "By the way, you never did tell me where you were all day."

"Please, let's not go there. None of it matters now, anyway."

Try as she might, Louise could not sleep. It had nothing to do with the accommodations at the bed and breakfast, which were great. She was exhausted, and yet each time she closed her eyes, the day kept running through in her mind. Thinking about some of her decisions made her cringe. She had to admit one of her motivations to save the errant sailboat was pride. She'd been showing off her prowess as a boater, which wouldn't have been so bad if she hadn't put her whole inexperienced crew at risk. Her only real obligation in that circumstance was to radio for help, and she hadn't even been the one to do it.

Next to her in the comfy bed, Grace slept undisturbed in her Darth Vader mask, which was how she referred to her contraption for sleep apnea. Light snoring came from the room across the hall, where Robin and Foxy shared a queen-sized bed. Cate, whose husband accused her of chasing cars in her sleep, had claimed the twin bed all to herself.

Padding into the hallway, Louise stopped in front of the Victorian bookcase she'd admired earlier, randomly grabbed a paperback from it and crept downstairs to the living room. Covering herself with a crocheted afghan, she tried to get into the book, a moody and mystical novel about a man who killed people by the sheer power of his thoughts. "Great bedtime story," she said to herself after skimming the first three chapters. Closing the book and turning off the light, she closed her eyes. It had been a bizarre day, beginning with the wandering sailboat that held a very recently dead man, and ending with that peculiar presentation by Simon, the paranormal investigator.

She must have fallen asleep in the chair, because suddenly she jolted to alertness. She realized not only that she was shivering but that there was another presence in the room. She could sense it. Her eyes sprang open. Staring into the darkness, she focused on the stairway. At first, she wasn't sure what she was seeing. And then it took shape. The wraith, outlined by a faint light, began to glide down the stairs.

Immobilized by fear, Louise's breaths were rapid and shallow.

The specter floated across the floor and settled into the rocker next to her. "Can't sleep either, huh?" Cate asked from the shadows.

Louise yipped. "You scared me half to death!"

Cate gave a fiendish laugh. "Well, that makes two of us. I woke up from a bad dream and started down the stairs when I saw you. You scared me to death. The way the moonlight was shining on you, you looked like a ghost."

"I thought *you* were a ghost!" Louise shuddered.

Cate reached over to pick up the book Louise had been reading before she fell asleep. "Good book?"

"It's dark. I wouldn't recommend it as bedtime reading."

"Want a glass of wine?"

Louise sat up. "There's wine?"

Cate went to the sideboard where their hosts had set out a bottle of pinot noir, crystal goblets, and a corkscrew. She poured two glasses and they sat in the dim light of the moon, sipping their wine.

Knowing that Cate's dreams were sometimes prescient, Louise asked if she wanted to talk about it. "Was it one of those, uh—I mean, should we be worried?"

Cate's semblance of a laugh was not comforting. "I don't even know how to answer that. It was probably just me processing what happened yesterday. I was in the lake. I must've gone overboard. The water was so murky I couldn't see a thing. Then my feet touched bottom and suddenly I was on land, surrounded by gnarly trees. They started swaying and then I saw they were actually people. I couldn't see their faces. I started running and I looked down and saw wet footprints and wondered if they were from the ghost with long black hair."

Louise sat up straighter. "Wait! Who was the ghost? Did someone die?"

For some reason that cracked her up. "Do you know another way to make a ghost?"

Louise rubbed her forehead with the palm of her hand. "You dreamt you fell overboard and then there's a ghost with long black hair. Cate, listen to yourself. Are you telling me you dreamed your own death?"

"No, I don't think so. That's not the way it felt."

Louise stared at her, speechless. Then she put the wine glass to her lips and tipped her head back. "Okay then. After that lovely dream, I'm sure I'll have no trouble at all falling asleep."

When Cate apologized, Louise held up her hand. "Don't. I'm just thinking we shouldn't take the boat back to Red Wing."

"Our cars are there. What do you expect us to do, walk back? Louise shook her head.

"Swim back?"

"Good grief, no! Not if there's a chance you're going to wind up a ghost!"

Cate groaned. "My dreams aren't like that, with something happening exactly the way it does in the real life. That would be way too simple. No, the clues in my dreams are like puzzle pieces I have to put together. Sorry, you'd think I'd have a better explanation after all these years. Sometimes the pieces fit and sometimes it turns out it was just a silly dream."

Louise wrapped the afghan tighter. "How do you know if it's a real warning?"

"I don't, not always," Cate said. The furrow between her brows deepened.

Louise's hand went to her chest, where a ball of worry had taken up residence. "Can you just give me an honest answer? Do you think we should take the boat back to Red Wing?"

"Why on earth shouldn't we?"

"Catherine Running Wolf!" Louise said, invoking her full name. "Are you trying to drive me crazy?"

Cate smiled in the moonlit room.

Louise felt a chill running the length of her spine. "Don't you grin at me. All I can see are your teeth glowing in the dark."

Cate's smile got even bigger. "That's because I'm the Cheshire cat," she said, and the tension flowed out of them as they giggled.

"Now go to bed," Cate said after draining her wine glass. "And dream about Cheshire cats."

"No, that's creepy."

"Okay, polliwogs then."

Louise laughed. "Why polliwogs?"

Cate shrugged her shoulders. Standing, she reached for her friend's hand and hauled her to her feet. "I don't know. Because polliwog is a funny word and it makes you laugh."

"You know what worries me?" Louise said as they headed for the stairs. "That actually made sense."

There must be a word for this weird state of being, she thought,
a hybrid of weary and wary, focused and fatigued. Her thoughts
had gone all muzzy, like her body wasn't connected to her
brain, yet her nerves were amazingly calm considering all that had
happened. As if from a vantage point slightly above and behind her,
she watched herself move from one room to another, zombielike,
numb, but also alert.

Gliding into the bathroom, she was almost surprised to see she
cast a reflection in the mirror. Not undead, then, and hopefully still
in possession of a soul. She hadn't lost everything about herself, but
her eyes looked different, a change that was both subtle and pro-
found. They were the cold, flat eyes of a stranger. Her fatigue would
surely leave her in time, but she knew she had crossed an invisible
line and would never again be the person she'd been only two days
ago.

She gripped the counter with both hands. "I'm not a monster,"
she said to her reflection. "You know I've always tried to be fair." If
only he'd been reasonable, none of this would have happened.

She pulled her thick hair into an alligator clip and threw water
on her face. For the briefest moment a thought crossed her mind. The
thought escaped, but the alarm it had set up remained. She watched
the water running through her fingers and tried to remember. Blotting

herself dry, she looked again to see if the cold water had restored something of her old self.

When the thought came again, her eyes grew wide. Wasn't there just something on the news about surveillance cameras everywhere? Everywhere! They said the average person is caught on camera dozens of times a day. What if they were at the marina at this moment, reviewing the film, watching her get out of the car, walk across the lot and down to the boat to surprise him as he drank his morning coffee?

Chirping birds woke Robin at dawn. That, and a guilty conscience. She hadn't finished the book chosen for discussion this month. Although it was well written, the subject matter, a thorny father-daughter relationship, put her in avoidance mode. The storyline cut too close to the bone.

In her cotton pajamas, she stepped with bare feet onto the grass still wet with dew to do her morning yoga sequence. She skipped the "down dog" position because it put too much pressure on her arthritic wrists. Her tailbone ached where she'd slammed against the dinghy's seat, and her shoulders weren't too thrilled with her, either, each twinge reminding her of yesterday's antics. Over the years she'd tried other forms of meditation, but found when her body wasn't in motion, her thoughts ran amok. The Buddhists referred to those whimsical and uncontrollable thoughts as the "monkey mind." Some days they made concentration or tranquility almost impossible.

This morning, not even yoga kept those drunken monkeys from chattering. Thinking about two little boys, fatherless because of a random boat accident, she found herself sucked back to her own childhood, when she'd lost her father—twice. The first time was when he turned himself in for kidnapping her during a custody battle, and the second when he'd died shortly after his early release.

She powered through the rest of her routine. Before going back inside, she took time to run her toes through the grass while she admired the garden's palette of lavender-blue bellflowers, speckled toad lilies, pink bleeding hearts, and yellow coneflowers.

In the living room, she picked up the book club book and opened it to the page marked with a Hennepin County Library receipt. In no time she was engrossed in the story. Just as in real life, the family's controversy never truly ended. Instead, like in "The Sorcerer's Apprentice," the end of one problem splintered to create ever more problems. She turned the final page and set the book aside. She smelled coffee and wondered when the coffee urn had appeared on the sideboard. She heard a commotion on the stairs and realized the aroma must have lured Louise and Foxy down.

Louise came downstairs, scratching her tousled head. "I know, I look like hell. Whenever I've had trouble falling asleep, I go to my happy place. Unfortunately, that's always been a rocking boat."

"I can see where that might pose a problem." Robin rose and poured coffee into three china cups. She and Foxy and Louise waited for the others to wake up, sipping the rich brew and enjoying the warm, homey smells coming from the oven.

Soon their hostess, wearing a frilly apron over jeans and a cotton shirt, appeared in the archway to take juice orders. Pausing on her way back to the kitchen, she asked how they'd enjoyed the presentation last night.

They looked at each other. They said it was interesting and Foxy asked if they'd ever had ghosts at the bed and breakfast.

Their hostess smirked and said people occasionally complained of weird sounds, but the banging and popping and clanging always turned out to be the plumbing, specifically, the expansion and contraction of the water lines.

Sounds came from above. Cate and Grace talked as they descended the stairs.

"Honestly, I don't remember a thing," Cate said emphatically.

"I heard you clearly. The word was definitely 'murderer.'"

"Oh, I did not!" Cate looked seriously annoyed.

"What are you guys talking about?" Louise called from the living room.

Cate and Grace appeared startled by their presence. "Grace claims I was talking in my sleep."

"That's because you were." At the bottom of the stairs, Cate held onto the ornate newel post and faced Grace.

Robin knew that look—not at all hostile, but not about to back down. "Hey, kids, no fighting," she said, hoping to lighten the mood, but Grace and Cate were locked in a battle of wills.

Cate threw her hand up. "Okay, but since I don't remember saying it, how can I tell you why I did? Anyway, how can you be sure you weren't the one who was dreaming?" She grinned impishly.

Grace laughed. "You win."

The table was laid with a spring-green cloth and floral dishes, along with a squat vase filled with several colors of ranunculus, giving the general illusion of eating in the garden. Their first course was popovers with honey butter, juice, and a fluted glass of melon balls, followed by a melt-in-your-mouth egg bake, broiled tomatoes, and locally made sausage.

After brunch, they moved outside to a circle of deck chairs to discuss their book. They all agreed the story evoked memories of their own relationships with their fathers.

"Conscientious, focused, and exacting," Louise said of her father. "Lucky for him, his personality and the military were perfectly suited to each other."

Cate leaned forward. "Sounds like an invitation to rebel."

Louise grunted. "Are you kidding? I didn't dare. There wasn't much margin for error. But now—" Her voice caught. "He's less austere now."

When Grace said that was a good thing, Louise gave a quick headshake. "Remember when I told y'all a few months ago how he damaged his car, swerving to keep from hitting a dog?"

They nodded.

"There was no dog." She waited for that to sink in. "He turned in front of a truck, never even saw it, and when the other driver honked at him, he jerked the wheel and plowed into a wrought iron fence. He wants to cover it up by saying he doesn't enjoy driving much these days, but the truth is they suspended his license. Since that car crash, he's fallen twice that I know of. The second time put him in the hospital at Fort Belvoir, where they ran him through a battery of tests. I finally got permission to talk to his neurologist." She picked at a stray thread on the hem of her capris. "I found out my father has known for almost a year that he's got dementia."

There was a collective sigh.

Louise lowered her head as if it were too heavy to hold up. "After all the years he pointed out my failings, he can't bring himself to reveal a single flaw of his own. 'Noticeable atrophy,' the doctor said. He also said Daddy's gone downhill fast since that diagnosis, to the point he's no longer safe living alone."

Robin asked if Louise's mother would take care of him.

Louise snorted. "Take care of him in his dotage? Not a chance. You have no idea what it was like when she finally left him, but it wasn't pretty. Like Sherman's march to the sea, they destroyed everything as they went. She won't even be in the same room with him." Heaving a sigh, she continued. "Honestly, we don't have a lot of choices. It boils down to two: putting him on a wait list for a veteran's home in Virginia or bringing him up here to live with Dean and me."

Grace, who'd been watching a butterfly move from blossom to blossom on a flowering bush, asked about the veteran's home on the Mississippi River bluffs in Minneapolis. "It would be close," she pointed out.

Louise stroked the area over her eyebrow. "I know. We've been talking to them, but they have residency requirements. We're trying to find out how long he has to live in Minnesota before he qualifies. Nobody seems to know."

The silence that followed was full of concern. Louise and Dean had been making plans for their "third act," as she called it. Buying the cabin cruiser had been foundational to their grand plan. Both she and Dean had joined the Power Squadron and taken courses to improve their boating skills. Eventually, they intended to divest themselves of their antique shop and use the proceeds to live on the *Time Out* for a year or so. They would follow the lakes and rivers to the ocean, then take the inside passage north. It meant heading south on the Mississippi and Ohio Rivers, and the Tennessee-Tombigbee waterway in the fall, arriving in the Gulf of Mexico to spend the cooler months in the southern states before they swung up the east coast, chasing the winter away as they went, and then circling back to Minnesota through Canada and the Great Lakes. It was referred to as the Great Loop, a pinnacle experience for boaters.

"My father brought me up to depend on no one but myself. It's tempting to let him live by his own words, but I don't think I can do that." Still rubbing her forehead, Louise tapped the book in her lap. "On the subject of messy relationships, what did y'all think of the father and stepfather in the book?"

Grace blew out the air in her cheeks. "They were each horrible in their own way, but complicated too."

Robin pointed out that life wasn't supposed to go smoothly all the time. "How would we ever build character if it did?"

Foxy tapped her finger on the book. "Did it build the heroine's character to be rejected by her father and humiliated by her stepfather? Hell no! All it did was set her up for a life of failed relationships and years of therapy."

The others nodded.

With her elbows resting on the lawn chair, Louise clasped her hands together. "I'm back to thinking about Bryce Morgan's sons. Do you really think it'll build character to grow up without a father?"

"If Bryce was such a harsh father, maybe they're better off," Foxy said. "At least now they won't grow up living with his disapproval."

They all knew Foxy's moralistic upbringing had left its scars on her, but Robin was taken aback by her vehemence. "I don't agree. At that age, kids love their parents. They don't know anything else. As flawed as my parents were, I was terrified of losing them." And of course she had, in many ways, lost them when she was still little.

Foxy's cheeks had grown bright pink. "You hear about it all the time. Kids get bullied by their fathers for years, and one day they decide they're not going to take it any more."

Cate muttered, "It's a good thing his sons are still young."

Foxy stared at the bird fountain and said nothing.

Grace said, "I guess I was lucky. My dad was a gentle soul. It was hard to get his attention sometimes because his nose was always in a book, like most of the professors we knew. I was shocked when one of his students went berserk after Dad failed him and he lost his scholarship. He actually made death threats. You never know what pushes people's buttons."

Their hostess came out with a tray of glasses and a pitcher of ice water. When she left again, Louise said, "Let's quit tiptoeing around it. We're trying to figure out who had a motive to murder Bryce."

They all admitted it crossed their minds, even though, by all appearances, his death had been an accident.

Robin said, "Based on what you told us, do you think he abused his wife?"

Louise thought about it. "It's hard to tell from one incident. Are you thinking Lexi killed him?"

"Not necessarily," Cate said. "I was thinking about how my own father reacted when I was going through my self-destructive dating stage. He was so quiet and gentle, but he would gladly have killed the guy who hit me, so I lied to him about the bruises. If he was hurting Lexi or his sons, can you imagine her parents standing idly by?"

"Good point." Robin leaned forward, already spinning that possibility.

Louise frowned. "Maybe I'm projecting, but here's what worries me. Now that my father is losing his mind, we'll never have a chance to work through why he was so hard on me. Same with Bryce's kids. With him gone, those boys have lost any chance of getting his approval." She got up and went into the house.

Grace stood, too. "Look, I think we should knock off this nonsense about Bryce. It's all just idle speculation, and all it's doing is stirring up hard memories for Louise."

There was no argument from any of them.

Climbing out of the van with their bags, the women noticed two men on the dock. Louise recognized the one in jogging shorts as Betty Jo's husband, Jack. The other one, wearing the tan uniform of a deputy sheriff, ducked his head to peer into the *Time Out*. She didn't know whether to charge down there and find out what was going on, or get back in the van.

"Hey, isn't that the guy from last night, the ghost hunter?" Robin asked, pointing to a man standing at the edge of the marina parking lot staring out at the water, hands in his pockets.

Simon turned in their direction and raised a hand in greeting. "Just the ladies I wanted to see," he called out as he strode toward them. "Listen, if you have a minute, I'd like to discuss something with you."

"You'll have to forgive me," said Louise. Her eyes were on the deputy. "I think I'd better—"

"Sure, go see what the cop wants. I'll wait."

Leaving them in the parking lot, Louise sidled up to Jack and the man who introduced himself as Deputy Ford. He looked too young to be out of high school. "Just wrapping up loose ends," he said to explain his presence, which was no explanation at all. "I've been talking to your friend Jack."

Louise shifted from one foot to another.

Deputy Ford adjusted the earpieces of his sunglasses. "I understand you both knew the deceased. Would you say Bryce Morgan was a friend?"

Her shoulders sagged. Although she hadn't doubted he was dead, it hadn't been confirmed until now. She told him what she'd told her friends, that they knew each other as boaters, but nothing more.

Leaning with one hand on a bollard, he tried to pin down the time she'd arrived at the marina in Red Wing yesterday morning and if the *Wayward Wind* had been at the dock at that time.

She screwed her mouth to one side. "To be honest, I didn't notice him or his boat, one way or the other. He could have gone out before me or after me, I just couldn't say for sure. The first time we spotted the *Wayward Wind*, she was zigzagging all over the place and I knew right away she was in distress." She told him about her attempts to raise the captain on the radio.

He consulted his notes. "When did you call for help?"

"The *River Rat* actually called in first."

"Uh-huh. Jack here says you motored your dinghy over and lassoed the thing."

"I was afraid if help didn't get to the sailboat in time, it might crash into another boat, so yes, I threw a towrope on it."

He bunched his lips. "Did you go aboard?"

Louise's mouth went dry. If she were to tell him Robin had actually climbed on board for a closer look, he'd want to know why neither of them had offered aid. She didn't want to get into ancient history of her mother's role in Bobby's death. She'd taken CPR recently, and yet confronted with a grievous head injury, she'd fled the scene. Judging by Robin's description of blood and brain matter, anyone would have concluded there was nothing she could have done.

The deputy repeated the question.

"No, I never boarded the sailboat. I'd left my inexperienced crew long enough."

Jack laughed. "It's not like you need experienced sailors. You got a stinkpot."

She'd heard sailors use this derogatory term for powerboats, and talk as if sailing was more demanding, more cerebral. She wasn't going to take the bait.

Deputy Ford asked her something, but her attention had shifted to the open section of her boat's lifeline. Each time the boat rocked, the dangling clasp clanged against the stanchion. "Did you open that?" Louise asked the men.

"No, ma'am," said the deputy.

Jack looked sheepish. "Betty Jo might have." He explained that his wife had stopped by that morning to check up on Louise. Jack and his wife had to know it was poor boat etiquette to set foot on someone else's boat without permission. It would be the same as opening the door to someone's house and walking in.

Before leaving, the deputy jotted down Louise's contact information. Closing his notebook and replacing his pen in his shirt pocket, he sighed. "Those boom accidents are nasty business."

"It's such a rookie mistake," Jack said with disdain.

"Damn shame."

Jack wanted to know what would happen next.

"We like to expedite things. I got my report to file and then the doctor fills out a Pronouncement of Death form before the wife's free to make burial arrangements. We're not like the big city. Those people like to bury you in paperwork over a garden-variety death." He chuckled at his own joke as he strode down the dock to his vehicle.

* * *

SIMON ASKED IF SHE'D picked up on any paranormal activity at his presentation last night.

She said she had not.

"How about any changes in the temperature? Or maybe you sensed something out of the ordinary."

She recalled the sudden chill in the room just before she saw Cate descending the stairs last night. Now, in the light of day, she wondered if she'd imagined it. "No, not really."

Grace explained, "Simon's partner thought there was a ghost hanging around us last night." She looked to Simon to continue.

"Actually, Angie's a volunteer," he corrected, emphasizing the demotion. "She said there was a presence hanging around your group last night toward the end of my program. Angie claims to see auras, ghosts, entities, that kind of thing. Not me. I just take down people's accounts and measure activity with my equipment. It's all scientific."

"An entity? I don't like the sound of that." Cate clung to her turquoise pendant, a sure sign she was trying to catch a psychic whiff of what was going on.

He shifted uncomfortably. "She didn't say 'entity.' The word she used was 'presence.' See, I had the volunteers positioned at the back corners of the room, and from where Angie stood she saw a presence or a spirit hanging around your group." He cleared his throat. "She said it seemed to be connected to the woman with, uh, platinum hair. "

Cate looked crestfallen.

Robin elbowed her. "Come on, Cate, don't tell me you're insulted that the spirit chose Louise over you."

Cate's tone was sardonic. "I'm devastated. You know how important those otherworldly popularity contests are to me."

The paranormal investigator scratched his head and continued, "Angie said the presence felt male, perhaps some kind of father figure."

Until now, Louise would have reacted to that line with suspicion. She'd derided television mediums who spoke to grieving people in riddles, using initials or numbers or inexact phrases like "mother figure," all designed to gain trust so they could fish for information from the living.

She knew she was supposed to say something, but her mind was elsewhere. Running her tongue across her lips, she reached into her pocket, pulled out her cell phone and poked a button. "Dead," she pronounced.

Foxy gasped. Grace put her hand to her forehead.

"Oh, come on, girls. My phone is dead, that's all. I forgot to recharge it in the room last night." She held it up to show the black screen.

"Dean would have called one of us if he couldn't get hold of you," Grace said, pulling out her cellphone. The others checked theirs for voicemails.

Louise didn't catch what Simon said, but Robin referred the question to Cate. Cate's response was to throw her hands up. "I got nothing. Not about the boat. Not about the guy who died. Not about any spirits following Louise. Nothing." Cate had often voiced frustration about the way her intuitions came to her on their own timetable, presenting themselves in obscure and baffling ways.

Simon bit the insides of his cheeks. "By the way, I thought you'd be interested. We followed up with some of the people who had stories to tell last night. That couple whose grandkids thought they saw a drowning person—well, their report is consistent with a smattering of sightings over the years, always about a drowning woman. I asked the grandmother if the kids liked to make up stories, but she insisted they were plenty upset and believed with all their hearts in what they saw."

Cate's brows puckered. "But did you actually talk to the kids?"

He nodded.

"Did you ask if they could tell whether it was the ghost of someone who's already passed, or a prophetic vision?"

A flash of amusement tugged at the corner of his mouth. "Not in those words."

Cate bristled. "Of course not in those words."

He shifted his weight back and forth, his eyes focused on something in the distance. "The girl was very definite. She said she saw a girl or a woman with long black hair."

Cate, who'd been twirling a strand of her own dark hair around her finger, stopped mid-twirl.

On their way to Red Wing aboard the *Time Out*, the women began to slip back into the lightheartedness they'd shared at the outset of their trip. The humidity had lessened overnight. Small clouds dotted the sky to the south and the breeze was pleasantly warm. Spotting an eagle's nest in a massive dead tree, Robin grabbed her camera and immersed herself once more in this pastime-turned-job of nature photography. Cate, tired from a poor night's sleep, sprawled out in the berth belowdeck while Grace and Foxy kept Louise company in the cockpit.

Throughout the day, Simon's words would pop into Louise's mind, and then she would compulsively check her now charging cell phone for messages about her father. So far the only message had been from the assistant at their antique store, asking permission to discount the price on a porcelain mantel clock for a cash customer. Louise texted Pam back saying she trusted her judgment. She sighed, knowing every relinquished decision propelled her one step closer to retirement. But just as she'd once dreamt of owning an upscale antique store, she now felt the call of the boating life. She and Dean wanted to spend chunks of time on the *Time Out* this summer, fine-tuning their relationship skills as well as their boating skills in preparation for the Great Loop. Now her father could change all that.

It was mid-afternoon when the *Time Out* was safely docked at the Ole Miss. Only then did Louise call Dean, using the speaker mode while she tidied up things in the galley. His deep, resonant voice filled the enclosure.

"I talked to your father today," he told her. "He can be a stubborn old cuss, but I got him to agree to come up here for a long visit. I'll start checking out flights, if that's okay with you. Once he gets here we can ease into the other discussion." He didn't have to say "the other discussion" involved a permanent move that entailed such indignities as her father relinquishing his driver's license and signing over power of attorney to his only living offspring.

"He'll be suspicious. It's not easy to fool Colonel Trenton," she said, using the rank that brought up images of authority and a will of steel. "Trust me, I've tried. You know what I got by with as a teenager? Absolutely nothing!"

"The colonel is slipping, Lou. I mean noticeably, just in the last couple months." He paused for her response, which did not come. "I think it might go more smoothly than you think, especially now that his sense of time has gotten skewed. I figure we can just keep extending the visit, and by the time he's figured out how long he's been with us—if he ever does—maybe he'll have lived in Minnesota long enough to satisfy the residency requirement."

Louise wiped the sink with a rag and swept the small galley floor. "It's the next move I worry about. I mean, can you picture how that conversation will go? 'Guess what, Dad, we're putting you in assisted living. It'll be fun. You'll make new friends and play bingo, maybe even make some macaroni art.'"

He chuckled.

"I just want to stay on the boat and pretend it's not happening." Her lips began to tremble.

Dean cleared his throat. "Listen, why don't you stay on the boat a couple more nights with your friends? Pam and I can manage the shop."

She was torn. "You're a sweetie, but no, I'll come home. I'd be all alone here anyway." She was embarrassed to hear how petulant that sounded. Taking the garbage bag and her phone with her, she climbed above to join her friends, who were happily chattering on the deck.

"When did that stop you? Stay by yourself," Dean told her. "You need your happy place to rest and recharge before your father gets here. Once the real fun starts, you'll wish you'd stayed."

"You'll need a break too, love, trust me. The colonel's not easy to live with."

He gave a dry laugh. "I can deal with him."

She grimaced. "You're right. If he listens to anyone, it'll be you."

"What can I say? I'm a charming fellow," Dean said, his soothing voice taking the sting out of her father's frank preference of Dean to his own flesh and blood. "In fact, I'm thinking if I can get a few things squared away here, I'll drive down for a night of wild abandon on the boat. I promise to charm the pants off you." His chuckle was seductive.

Louise dampened the speaker, but it was too late. She looked up to see the amusement on Grace's and Foxy's faces.

Doing her best to ignore them, she abruptly changed the subject, giving Dean the Cliff's Notes version of Bryce Morgan's death, avoiding the part where she conscripted her rookie crew to tether the boats together until help arrived.

He said, as so many had, that it was foolish for Bryce to sail alone, and then, just as Betty Jo and Jack had done, he brought up the night they'd witnessed the Morgans' spat that ended in Lexi's shoes being used as projectiles. "You were kind of hard on the guy, Lou. I mean, he had a point about the candles being a fire hazard."

"He could have been gentler."

"He's a lawyer. He's used to being direct."

"She wasn't his client, Dean."

"No, but you have to admit her reaction was immature. Way over the top, if you ask me."

Louise sighed. She dearly loved the man, but sometimes he could be so dense. Slipping the phone into her purse, she saw Foxy, Grace, and Robin piling their gear on the dock, ready to take off.

Cate, however, lounged on the aft cushion, wearing an enigmatic smile. "I'm staying," she said. "At least until Lover Boy gets here."

Louise hung her head. She wasn't going to get by without a little friendly ribbing. "You don't have to. I'm a big girl."

Cate shushed her, saying her mind was made up.

Louise warmed to the idea, "Okay, then. But I don't think I can promise as much drama as you're accustomed to."

"Yes, but you can't promise *less* drama either." Cate's expression was earnest but her eyes danced.

In the parking lot, they all hugged. The two that remained watched their departing friends until they were out of sight. Turning to Cate, Louise said, "I think we'll err on the side of sanity and not take the boat out again."

"No argument here."

"And we'll have to eat out, because we're down to a couple bottles of wine and some limp celery."

"Hmm, if there's enough wine, maybe it won't matter that the celery's limp."

Louise put an arm around her. "I'm so glad you stayed." Suddenly she had an urge to bring the other three back, hold them tight and tell them—Tell them what, exactly? And then she knew. She wanted to tell them when the five of them were together, they were damn near invincible.

14

fter retrieving Bryce's wallet from the sheriff's office, Lexi had her sister drop her off at the marina to pick up Bryce's car. Zan offered to stay around and follow her home, but Lexi wanted to be alone for this. As she made her way down the dock, she pictured herself a condemned man being forced to walk the plank. Staring at the sailboat, she felt only revulsion for it. The *Wayward Wind* looked no different from when Bryce had first brought her here. It had been a hot summer day just like this, and just like that day, she had caught a whiff of diesel mixed with a slight fishy smell, only today it made her stomach roil. She popped a lemon drop into her mouth, sucking on it until the nausea passed.

All she had to do was unclip the lifeline and step through the opening, then put one foot on board, followed by the other. Her reluctance turned to paralysis. She had only two choices. She could stride forward confidently, or she could turn and run. She wavered and felt the slightest pressure on her back, between her shoulder blades. Alarmed, she jerked her head around. No one there. Gulping hard, she felt prickles of ice running down her neck. She told herself she was overwrought, possibly hallucinating, yet she still couldn't shake the sensation of that cold hand pressing her forward.

With one hand gripping a wooden post and the other on her belly, Lexi breathed through pursed lips, as she'd done in Lamaze classes. "No such thing as ghosts," Lexi told herself, timing the words to her breaths. "You just have to get back on the horse." Suddenly Lexi began to laugh. "Why on earth would I want to get anywhere near a horse that—?" Mid-laugh, she clamped her hand over her mouth. For a fraction of a second, she'd thought someone was lying on the deck. Closing her eyes and opening them again, the image was gone.

The deck was shiny and clean. Of course, she realized as the nausea rose once more, they would've had to hose it down after . . . the accident. The accident. She inhaled deeply, averted her eyes from the deadly boom and stepped onto the deck, painfully aware that her sandals were smooth-soled and could easily cause her to slip. Although she would not be hearing Bryce's proper footwear lecture again, she tensed automatically.

Picking her way around the lines and cleats toward the companionway, she backed down the ladder as Bryce had taught her, holding onto the rails on either side. Once below, she set to filling a canvas tote bag with the few toiletries Bryce kept on the boat. She unloaded the little refrigerator into the red cooler and snagged a box of saltines and a couple of soup cans from the galley locker. There were no dirty dishes in the sink. Bryce believed in leaving things ship shape. Hauling his empty gym bag from a locker, Lexi stuffed it with the few items of clothing he kept there—a yellow rain jacket, underwear, tee-shirts and nylon zip-off pants. She found his car keys on a shelf above the V-berth.

This wasn't the first time she'd gone through the boat in his absence. It was embarrassing to admit, even to herself, but on more than one occasion, convinced her husband was having an affair, she'd checked up on him—all those nights on the boat, all those clients he couldn't discuss—but never once had she found evidence that he was fooling around. Not a shred. Once a friend stayed with the kids and loaned Lexi her car to follow him. That was the time he'd gone to the Indian Affairs office in Bloomington and after seventy-two minutes, he'd come out and driven to the gym. Two hours later, he was home. Another time, after one of his weekends on the water, she'd driven to Red Wing to go through the *Wayward Wind* looking for signs he'd entertained a woman on board. Not so much as a lipstick print on a glass or a toothbrush. No tampons, hair clips, or nail polish. No jewelry, no lacy underwear.

But when all was said and done, she'd learned nothing from these little excursions. As Bryce was fond of telling people, it was almost impossible to prove a negative. Considering her husband's innate caution, discretion, and attention to detail, Lexi knew he'd have been too meticulous to leave traces of an affair.

She made two trips to the car with Bryce's belongings. Then, returning to the *Wayward Wind*, she went below once more, where she cast her eyes about the sole of the boat, looking for anything she might have overlooked. Back in the sunlight, she walked the length and breadth of the boat, scanning the deck. At the stern, she opened the lifeline gate and peered down, unable to bring herself to set foot on the swim ladder. Taking deep gulps of air, she stared down at the water until her head cleared.

Pulling away, she forced herself to go through the boat checklist and put things to order, hopefully for the last time. The mainsail cover was already on. The winch handles were stored in their pockets. All the electronics were turned off and the forward hatch closed, as was the smaller hatch that provided ventilation for the head. She closed and locked the companionway. Halfway up the dock, she threw a backward glance at the *Wayward Wind*, trying to fix in her mind that her life with Bryce was truly over.

She had one more thing to do. The local sailor who'd refused payment to ferry the boat from Lake City had told her all about the women who'd first noticed the sailboat was in trouble. She scoped the marina until she spied two women on the *Time Out*.

They looked away, pretending they hadn't been watching her.

Lexi passed a hand over her sweaty forehead, swallowed down her rising panic and headed in their direction. She recognized one of them as the boat's owner. She vaguely remembered talking to Louise a few times and thinking it would be nice to get to know her. Even though they'd exchanged phone numbers at some point, they'd never gotten around to meeting for lunch in the Cities. The truth was, after that ugly fight in the marina, Lexi hoped never again to see the people who'd sat and watched the whole mess from their deck chairs. If she could wave a magic wand, that memory would be buried along with her husband.

Voluminous hair barely moving in the breeze and lips parting in a warm smile, Louise came to meet her on the dock.

"I just wanted to thank—" The words died when Louise engulfed her in a hug. Because she didn't want to cry, Lexi diverted herself as she often did by casting herself in a play that closely resembled her life, her own little twist on "fake it 'til you make it." She slipped into the role of news reporter. "I don't think I'll be at peace until I walk myself through what happened after he left the house," she explained before peppering Louise with questions about what they knew of Bryce's activities leading up to their discovery of him.

She claimed to know very little.

"You don't think anyone was with him yesterday, do you?" Lexi asked. She held her breath.

Louise tilted her head and sharpened her eyes. "I have no reason to think anyone else was on the boat."

She nodded. Even though Lexi had said she wanted to know everything, Louise talked about finding the boat, in more detail than Lexi wanted to hear. As she talked, Lexi noticed Louise talked with her hands and showed a flair for drama. It made her think of an exercise they did in her improv class. Lexi was supposed to be someone with a dirty secret going to a neighborhood cookout. Exaggerated gestures and avoiding eye contact were keys to the body language of deceit, and she'd done it well. She wondered what Louise was hiding.

Louise had stopped talking and was looking at her oddly. "I don't think you need to hear all of this. It won't do you any good to picture it over and over because you can't change a thing. What you need is time."

She might have stayed longer and asked more questions if that other woman, tall and lanky with long dark hair like her own, had not appeared. She stepped off the *Time Out* and introduced herself as Cate. Although Cate smiled, Lexi found her unsettling, as if the other woman were not only memorizing her face, but peeling off the layers to reveal hidden thoughts and emotions.

Suddenly Lexi was anxious to get in her car and get away.

15

Wow, she really didn't like me," Cate said as they watched Lexi rush to her car and drive off.

"Even I picked up on that." From the moment she'd seen Lexi step aboard the *Wayward Wind*, Louise had wondered what she was looking for. "Want to take a little walk with me?"

Cate nodded and followed her without question. She didn't appear the least bit surprised when their walk led in the direction of the *Wayward Wind*.

The closer they got, the more her apprehension grew. She realized it had something to do with a sound coming from the sailboat that resonated with something in her memory—a soft, repetitive clank of metal against metal. Scanning the vessel for the source, her eyes fell on the stern of the boat. The aluminum lifeline gate swung open and clanged shut, open and shut.

"Dang it all to hell!" she said. Snatching her phone from her pocket, she punched in a number. As soon as the connection was made, she lowered her voice to little more than a whisper. "When we got to the boat, was the gate open?"

"Who is this?" Robin asked.

"Sorry, it's Louise! I just need to know, was the gate open?"

"Is everything okay?"

"I'm talking about the gate on the back of the sailboat. Was it open or closed when we first got to the *Wayward Wind*?"

"Gate?" Robin echoed.

Louise squeezed her eyes tight, took a deep breath and started over, more slowly this time. She explained that she and Cate were standing on Morgan's sailboat and she was having a moment of déjà vu. "I need you to think about this. You're standing on the swim ladder of the damn sailboat and you're about to climb those couple of steps to get on board. Can you picture it?"

There was a pause. "Okay, got it."

"The lifeline circles the boat and to get on the boat, you have to open a gate. Do you remember unlatching it?"

"What's going on?" Cate mouthed, but Louise waved her off.

When Robin answered, her voice was croaky, as if she'd just been awakened. "Oh, damn, Louise, I don't remember. Is it important?"

"It might be. Take your time. Think it through." She waited. From the look on Cate's face, the importance of this detail was becoming clear to her.

Finally Robin spoke again. "I wish I could tell you for sure. I do remember when we were leaving, you told me to close it."

"What about when we first got there?"

"I may have opened the gate, in fact I think I did, but for the life of me I can't say whether or not it was latched . . ." A couple of heartbeats later, she gave a little gasp. "Oh!" she breathed.

"Uh-huh, exactly what I'm thinking," Louise answered. "If that gate wasn't latched when we got there, it should've been."

"Bryce could've left it open."

"Possibly, but boaters are picky about such things. He wouldn't set sail with it open. The clanging alone would've made him check it out."

"Okay."

"It means he may not have been sailing alone."

Cate, standing over her shoulder, spoke so they could both hear. "Maybe his killer escaped by climbing down the swim ladder."

"That's a lot of dots to connect, Cate," Robin said.

16

They walked an easy mile to the Veranda, one of three restaurants at the St. James Hotel, which boasted a panoramic view of the Mississippi. On the way, Cate grilled Louise with questions about the boat rescue and the Morgans' marriage. "The more details, the better chance my intuition will kick in. Do you really think someone else was on the boat with Bryce?"

Louise said, "Let's say someone was. I mean, you called someone a murderer in your sleep."

Cate frowned. "Some little memory just flitted through my brain, but I lost it."

"Well then, keep thinking."

They turned up Broad Street. Cate stopped to shake a pebble out of her sandal and was bending over when a car horn caused them both to jump. Cate staggered a couple of steps before recovering her balance.

The car pulled up next to them. A man leaned across the passenger seat, calling to them through the open window.

Cate put on an attitude as she ambled over, leaned her forearms on the window frame and looked him in the eye. "Are you stalking us?"

His laugh was uneasy. "Uh, I thought I recognized you."

She raised an eyebrow. "You recognized me bending over?"

"No, no, I mean, I saw you two and I, uh . . ." he stammered.

Cate put him out of his misery with a bubbling laugh. "I'm kidding."

"Well, if it isn't Casper, the friendly ghost hunter," Louise said, squinting into the car's interior.

Simon pushed his sunglasses to the top of his head. His eyes were bleary, as if he hadn't slept in days. "I'm sorry. I just, y'know, I was looking for a place to grab a bite and well, I really don't like to eat alone, so I—"

"Will you please join us for dinner?" Louise drawled. "We're heading over to the St. James."

He gave them a lopsided grin and bobbed his head up and down. "I'm actually hoping they'll let me do some recording there."

Cate noticed the collection of electronic equipment in the back seat of his little Honda. She suggested meeting in the hotel lobby.

He grinned. "That would be nice. I like Jimmy's."

"Yes, Jimmy's," Louise said. "Perfect." After he drove off, Louise explained that Jimmy's, a British-style pub, was just upstairs of the Veranda. "It's nice, too."

When Cate spied him in the lobby, Simon was considerably less flustered. Riding the elevator with them to the top floor, he didn't mess around with small talk but dove in with what, in his line of business, might be considered normal conversation. Turning to Louise, he said, "I think you have an idea who your ghost might be. Am I right?"

Her laugh was dry. "You saw my reaction."

He nodded. "Sorry. Sometimes I'm too blunt."

"Blunt I can handle. It just caught me off guard. I'm usually a skeptic, but when you said it was a father-type presence, my first thought was Daddy must've died. He's been ill, but he's not a ghost yet, although at some point he'll surely be more ghost than real."

He looked at her quizzically.

"Dementia," she said.

"Ah," said Simon. "So it's not him. Can you think of anyone else, some father figure who's passed?"

"He's the only father I've got."

The elevator doors opened and they seated themselves in the pub, with its leather upholstery and rich wood. A waiter came to take drink orders, drawing their attention to the list of craft beers.

Cate looked through the selection and chose a local brew called Surly Furious.

"I'm a scotch man myself," Simon said.

Louise said, "So am I. I'll have a Glenlivet, neat."

"Make that two," he said to the waiter. Then he turned to Louise with a devilish expression. "Scotch man? I could have sworn you were a woman." It came off as brotherly teasing rather than flirtation.

Louise responded by batting her eyes and saying, "Why, of course I am. But the truth is, I was raised a boy."

Simon sat back, nonplussed.

Cate watched the interplay and raised an eyebrow. She wanted to hear Louise's explanation.

"Not anatomically male, of course. It's both more and less complicated than that," she said. "You see, my daddy wanted a son. He had one, actually, his fair-haired boy. I was too young to remember how he treated me before Bobby died. All I know is I grew up different places in the South, where all the girls did the whole beauty pageant thing. I, on the other hand, wore pants and got toy trucks and fishing poles for my birthday. Daddy taught me to shoot a gun, and the way he talked, I was expected to grow up and carry on the Trenton family tradition by serving in the Army. The closest I got was when we even did Civil War reenactments together."

The more she talked, the more southern her accent became. Cate knew some of Louise's background, but it still surprised her to hear it now, in this detail, in this setting and in this company. She listened as her friend shared some of her most private history with a relative stranger. She described a childhood that was a battleground created by her parents' grief and differing expectations of their only daughter. She marvelled at the fact Louise had turned into this warm, vivacious, and decidedly feminine woman.

"My mother did her damnedest to instill in me the graces of a Southern belle," Louise said, "but I spurned all that to please Daddy. I guess it took a while to figure out I'd never be more than a poor substitute for a son."

Listening, Cate thought it should come as no surprise that her father's health problems were dredging up old conflicts.

They ordered a second round of drinks and bar food.

Cate caught Simon looking over the top of his nearly empty highball glass at her. "Does that necklace have special significance for you?" he asked.

She hadn't realized her fingers were curled around her turquoise amulet. "My father was Cherokee. It belonged to him."

"Ah!" He leaned over to get a better look as she held it out to him.

She noticed his eyes kept flicking up to her face, looking for signs of her Native ancestry. She was used to this reaction. She'd inherited the long narrow nose, high cheekbones, and straight dark hair of her father's people, but until strangers heard her full name, Catherine Running Wolf, they more often guessed her to be Italian, Jewish, Greek, even Scottish or Irish. Having lived, for the most part, in the world of her mother's northern European background, she felt compelled to speak now and then to her native ancestry. "We believe turquoise has healing energy. Many of my people believe it gives them protection. In fact, I've heard of people finding a crack in their turquoise after going through a life-or-death ordeal and saying the stone took the blow for them."

He sat back with a *humph*.

"Is that what you believe?" Louise asked her.

Cate grinned. "I've put myself in a fair amount of danger and it hasn't cracked yet. Turquoise is also supposed to enhance prophetic abilities."

Simon cocked his head. "I haven't heard that. Tell me this— do you ever see things before they happen?"

Even though her father had taught her to view her intuitive abilities as a natural gift, her second sight had certainly set her apart as a child. She still remembered how her best friends shunned her when she warned them about an older boy on the playground who did bad things to animals. She'd seen it in her head. Louise and Simon waited for an answer. "For me, fidgeting with my necklace is soothing, just a way to clear my thoughts, kind of like a worry stone."

Simon adjusted the bows of his glasses over his ears. "What are you worried about?"

Worried? Her senses were on alert, but she hadn't thought she was worried. She laughed off the question.

Their food and drinks arrived. Cate suggested the "male presence" might be Bryce Morgan's ghost, and Simon instantly latched onto the idea. "He's just passed, so his energy may very well be lingering. I don't mean to alarm you, but it's possible he attached to you."

Louise tried to make a joke of it, looking behind her and brushing something invisible off her shoulders, but Cate saw her nervousness.

"He may not even know he's dead yet," Simon continued. "Sometimes spirits remain earthbound because they can't comprehend what's happened to them."

Cate, who'd spent years learning about clairvoyance or intuition or the Sight, or whatever the heck people called her abilities, said, "I've heard they hang around sometimes, waiting for a loved one to join them."

"I believe that. Or sometimes they don't want to cross over because they think they'll be punished for whatever they did when they were alive," Simon said. "Then again, some people simply aren't ready to give up their material possessions."

"Why on earth not?" Louise asked. "They're already dead, so that's not really an option, is it?"

He chuckled. "I like that. 'Why on earth not?' Good one. I might have to work that into my program." He bit into his sandwich and continued to talk with his mouth full. "There are lots of reasons to hold on. Maybe they have unfinished business and they try to communicate with the living to finish it for them so they can be at peace."

Cate leaned her elbows on the table and dabbed at her mouth with a napkin. She locked eyes with Louise. "I think we need to consider the possibility that Bryce is trying to tell you something. Maybe there's something about his death he wants you to know."

Louise kicked her under the table.

"Ouch!" Cate yipped, then continued undeterred, "No, seriously, it wouldn't be the first time a murder got passed off as an accident or a suicide. We should know that as well as anyone."

On their walk back to the boat, Cate told Louise about the snippet of dream she couldn't remember earlier. After she and Louise had talked in the night, Cate had returned to bed. And to her dream. This time the trees that were actually people had formed a circle and were looking down at something in the middle. Cate said, "When I looked harder, I saw it was a body and knew one of the tree people did it."

They'd just finished the opening hymn when Robin saw Grace slip in. She sat across the aisle fanning herself with a church bulletin. It was typical for both of them to attend church without their husbands. Grace's Fred coveted his weekends when he could sleep in, and Robin's Brad had gotten in the habit of lounging around at home on those Sunday mornings he wasn't out delivering babies. Robin figured he was sitting in his underwear at this very moment, drinking his third cup of coffee and reading the *New York Times*. There was no need for either of them to rush home.

As soon as the worship service ended, Robin rushed over. "Do you have a few minutes?"

Grace removed her reading glasses and put them in a pocket of her purse. "For you, I have more than a few minutes. Want to grab breakfast? Maybe we could go for a walk. I have sneakers in my gym bag."

Robin was already wearing her Birks.

It was a short drive to Fiftieth Street, where they parked and crossed the street to the path that ran along the Minnehaha Creek.

Falling into step, they talked about making Sunday strolls a habit. Robin suggested they might take up tennis or golf.

"I'm horrible at both of those. Let's figure out a sport we both like."

They passed other walkers—mothers power-walking with strollers, families with dogs, bare-chested men on skateboards, youth playing Frisbee—plus a few bikers and picnickers.

"Wow! I guess I shouldn't be surprised," was Grace's response when Robin confessed she'd climbed aboard Bryce Morgan's boat. "We just never leave well enough alone, do we?" She hastened to say she would've done exactly the same thing.

Robin recapped the phone conversation with Louise. "It's driving me nuts that I can't remember about the latch. If someone else was on that boat, it must have been murder, because if it was an accident, they would've called for help and stayed with him.

"Unless that other person shouldn't have been there in the first place. Maybe Bryce was having an affair and she, or he, for that matter, couldn't risk being found out."

It had crossed her mind, but hearing her say it, it sounded more plausible. "I don't know what to do, Gracie. If it really was murder, it's possible I destroyed the only evidence."

Grace wondered aloud if they should tell the authorities, then immediately answered her own question. "Like you said, if there was ever any evidence, it isn't there anymore. All we've got is a faulty memory and conjecture. No smoking gun."

"Doesn't intuition count for something? We've been right before. Louise thinks there's more to it. And what about Cate's dreams?"

"Cate has a lot of dreams. She says herself she doesn't know how to interpret them. And sometimes she's just plain wrong."

Robin smiled. "You're right."

"Naturally." Grace smiled back. "Besides, if we get involved in one more suspicious death, how long is it going to take authorities to slap the cuffs on us? Think about it."

"I've thought of little else. Gracie, do you remember when we first started to call ourselves No Ordinary Women? It didn't really mean that much to us until we found ourselves investigating a real murder instead of just reading about them."

Grace agreed.

"When did we decide it was okay to muck around where we don't belong? Do we think we're so clever the rules don't apply to us?"

"We *are* clever."

Robin said, "Speaking for myself, I think I took too much pride in playing detective."

Grace kicked a pebble off the path. "It wasn't just you, you know." They halted when a dog crossed their path to catch a rubber ball. "Isn't it beautiful here?"

Robin agreed. In fact, next to Lake Harriet, this was her favorite place to walk. Sun shone through the trees, dappling the path, and just feet away, water in the creek burbled its way toward Minnehaha Falls, where it would plummet into the Mississippi. "The thing is, the more I try to remember about the gate, the more confused I get. I can imagine it open, and I can imagine it latched—both pictures are equally clear in my mind."

"Pictures!" Grace said, stopping in her tracks. "Weren't you taking pictures when you saw the sailboat?"

Robin's eyes widened as she realized what Grace was suggesting. "I bet you caught something on camera."

"I just started working on them last night." Robin's pulse quickened. "I took all those shots of eagles and was still looking through the lens when I saw the boat."

"Problem solved," Grace said. "All you have to do is develop the film and you'll know once and for all whether or not the gate was latched. "

Robin hoped that was true. It would be the best possible outcome if she could prove two things to herself and Louise—that they had not altered a crime scene, and that there was actually no crime scene to mess up. Despite the beautiful summer day, she was eager to get home and spend the rest of the day in her darkroom.

Turning back toward the car, they picked up the pace. "Did it just get a lot warmer suddenly?" Grace asked, adding, "And no, it's not what you're thinking. I'm done with hot flashes. It's just plain hot."

At the exact same moment, they both mopped their hands across their foreheads.

"I think we found our sport," Robin said. "Synchronized sweating."

18

From a cursory glance at the developed film, Robin couldn't find one that clearly showed the stern of the *Wayward Wind*. Without that evidence, she had no reason to believe Mr. Morgan's death had been anything other than a fatal miscalculation. No mystery, just a garden-variety boating accident. With a less troubled conscience, she remained in her basement darkroom, working in a mindless way to finish processing the film from their boat trip. As she plucked photo paper from the last bath, she clipped the pictures one by one to a drying rack.

Switching off the infrared light and switching on the overhead fluorescent, she moved in for a closer look at the prints she'd finished last night, already displayed on the corkboard. In this batch she'd gotten a series of action shots of a single bald eagle soaring overhead, then dropping from a height, talons outstretched to catch its meal. She'd gotten several shots of three adult eagles wheeling, each on its own updraft, displaying a curvature of wings that changed in each successive shot. She was pleased with the results.

Following the publication of her last coffee table book of photography, Robin had made the tough decision to take a break from that format. Although it had been fun producing five books of her photos, she felt like it had run its course. The production cost was higher than for other books, and she suspected hers were often bought because the cover photo matched the buyer's décor, then carefully positioned on the coffee table, never to be opened again. It had taken time and effort to arrange book signings, and then sometimes a mere handful of people showed up. So at least for now, she'd turn her photography into framed photos and reprints to sell at galleries and art fairs and to her small but loyal clientele.

She checked the notepad where she recorded details about pictures she'd taken, such as speed, aperture, filters used, subject, time, and location. Running her finger down the last list she saw, just as she recalled, several minutes had elapsed between the series of eagle photos and those of the *Wayward Wind*. If she'd followed the trend to go completely digital, some of that information would automatically be attached to the photos, but she enjoyed doing it "old school." She hadn't made the transition to electronic books, either. For Robin, developing her own film held the same kind of mystique as the slow unfolding of a good murder mystery. The developer, stop bath, and fixative were as essential to her craft as plot, pacing, and setting were to a book. Photos told stories, too, and sometimes they didn't have a happy ending—like the voyage of the *Wayward Wind*.

Looking at the clock, she unclipped the latest prints from the drying rack and tacked them to the board. Her eyes darted from one to the next, and like the cartoon flipbooks she'd made as a kid, these images, placed in the proper order, created a movie. The problem was she'd walked into the middle of this movie. Bryce was already lying dead when she started shooting and no one else had recorded how that had come about. She could make up any beginning or ending. Occam's razor said the simplest explanation was usually the right one. One more reason to believe his death was an accident.

It was preposterous to think someone had whacked him on the head, dropped the murder weapon in the water, set the scene to make it look like the boat itself had done him in and then escaped in the dinghy. But no, she remembered the dinghy was still tied to the sailboat. Could another boat have come along, driven by an accomplice? There was no way to tell, of course. It wasn't like you could check the water for footprints.

She leaned closer. Right next to the boat, nothing unusual was happening. She checked farther away. In one of the photos, she spied a dark spot in the water closer to shore, almost indistinguishable from the hanging branches and shadows. It was too small for a boat or even an inner tube. Grabbing the magnifying glass from the pegboard, she zeroed in on the mysterious object, remembering how Louise's hat had kited across the water before sinking. Maybe Bryce had lost his hat in the wind.

She looked through the other photos for the same detail and when she found two more, she rearranged the photos so the spot moved and then disappeared. A wayward hat from the *Wayward Wind?* Or maybe a water bird or a submerged branch . . . a small beach ball.

She pinched the area between her strained eyes, sat back and looked again, this time without the magnifying glass. Zooming in, zooming out—it was a method she used when she couldn't get clarity. Should she delve into Simon's world of the supernatural and consider the possibility of that dark shape being the ghost of someone who drowned? Or perhaps it was Pepie, a kissing cousin of Nessie, the Loch Ness Monster.

She laughed out loud at how easily her imagination could lead her astray, obsessing about what was probably just a shadow in the water. She began to clean up her workspace. A person could only conjecture so long. She hung up the magnifying glass, and once more her eyes fell on the two prints and she picked them up. Suddenly she knew without a doubt she was staring at the bobbing head of someone swimming away from the scene of a crime.

There was no way to explain what happened next. Fear gripped her as she felt icy fingers touching her wrist. She dropped the photos and fled the room.

19

Feeling like she was entering the *sanctum sanctorum*, Lexi hesitated to step into Bryce's office, but his partner Delroy urged her forward. Handing her a pair of bank boxes, he told her to take everything from the top desk drawer. She was allowed to remove what she wanted from the credenza and the bookcase, too, but not, of course, from the cabinets where he stored files of cases he'd been working on, and those they'd declined representing. That all belonged to the firm now.

Her eyes swept the framed diplomas and awards on the south wall, and the photographs and newspaper articles on the west wall. One article dealing with arrest rates of minorities had a sidebar in the form of a pie chart. If Bryce's life had been a pie, she thought, work would have eaten over half of it, the boat would get a large piece, à la mode, and Lexi and the boys would have shared a single slice.

She noticed how his desk chair tilted to the right. She could see him sitting there, leaning on the arm of the chair as he listened intently to the person on the other side of his desk. In contrast, his recliner at home had a round dent in the headrest where he lay back with his eyes closed, tuning out the world around him.

Seated in the side chair, Delroy knit his long, brown fingers and watched her, his expression neither unkind nor overly kind. He was powerfully built, with a broad face, closely cropped hair, and unreadable eyes. She resented him staying in the room, watching her movements as if she couldn't be trusted. She wanted to ask him why he'd never really warmed to her, but was afraid she wouldn't like the answer.

She suspected Delroy had sensed her jealousy from the beginning. He and Bryce had been in law school together and it was she who had been the newcomer, the interloper. The two men worked and played hard together. They had the same interests, knew the same people and spoke the same legal jargon. Over the years, she'd heard them gossip about prosecutors and judges she didn't know. They'd talked about everything from federally recognized tribes, protected classes, and marriage equality to paternity leave, pediatricians, and potty training.

Sitting in her husband's chair, she peered into the center desk drawer. It held nothing but paper clips, rubber bands and pens, an unused pocket calendar, a nail file. A handful of wrapped mints, a bottle of ibuprofen, business cards. A curl of postage stamps, sixty-two cents in change, and tossed in with the memo pads, the only personal item, a small family photo they'd used for last year's Christmas card.

"His death is not just a loss to the firm, but to the community," Delroy said, stroking the contours of his mustache with thumb and forefinger. "It takes time to make the connections he had and earn the trust of all the different civil rights groups."

"Not to mention the loss to his wife and children," she said, thinking a lawyer devoted to upholding the rights of others should be more compassionate. She swung in her chair to face the credenza. Among the books were two photos. Standing, she picked up the candid, full body shot of her, and made a face. Bryce knew it wasn't her favorite, with her hair hanging lank on either side of her head and her ears sticking out. He said he liked her smile in it. The larger frame held a professional photo of the boys from a couple of years ago.

"Bryce loved you, you know," Delroy said gently. "You and the boys. You were his whole life. Except for this." He made a hand gesture to encompass the office. "He was good at what he did, Alexis, including caring for you financially."

"He said I'd be provided for if this day ever came."

He tented his fingers. "He wanted to do the right thing."

Something in his tone alerted her. She set the picture down and turned to face him.

Delroy held her gaze. "Your husband talked to me about something I want to discuss with you. I'm afraid it may come as a surprise to you."

Her back stiffened. "He was having an affair?"

He looked at her with pity. "No, Alexis, he was not having an affair. As far as I know, he was always faithful to you, and we talked about a lot of things."

Clinging to the back of the chair, her fingers dug into the fabric. "I'm fully aware he talked to you about us . . . about me."

He blinked, removed his glasses and polished them with his tie and gave her a white-toothed smile. "He talked about you often. As I said, he loved you."

Why did he keep reassuring her about Bryce's love? There was something he wasn't saying. "He loved me, but . . . ?" she prompted.

"Because he loved you, he was troubled that he'd misrepresented something to you."

"Do me a favor and don't sugarcoat it. He lied to me."

A slight nod of his head accepted her words. "Of course you know about his daughter, Courtney."

She hadn't expected that. "I know she exists, if that's what you mean." Then, sensing she knew where he was headed, she said, "And I know her mother refused child support from him."

He was not looking directly at her, but at his own hands, which were still tented. He interlaced his fingers, then drew them to the sides, like duplicated strands of DNA pulling apart. "That was true in the beginning. Mallory was young. I think she sincerely wanted to prove her independence, but after a while the realities sunk in and she reconsidered."

Lexi kept a poker face.

"It was years ago, long before he knew you. Maybe it was just that she'd found out it was hard being a single mother, or maybe she really did love him, but the thing is, she begged him to give it another try with her, as a family. Maybe even have another child."

Her left hand went to her belly. "What are you saying?" The world tilted and she dropped into the chair.

"No, no, nothing happened. He turned her down. Water under the bridge and all."

"Oh."

"But he felt guilty about the way things had ended and so he started sending Mallory money to help with expenses. Not a lot. A couple, three hundred a month, always in cash. I think they were both comfortable with the arrangement, at least for a while. She didn't have to declare it as income, and he knew he was getting off easy. You know, she could've taken him to court and gotten a lot more."

She clutched her hands in her lap to keep them from shaking. "He never told me."

"No, no, he did not. And it gnawed at him. When Courtney was a senior in high school, Mallory paid him a visit here at the office. I was across the hall and actually heard most of it. She looked around the place and commented that he must be bringing down a good income. She asked him to pay for their daughter to go to college. She was very careful in her wording so he couldn't accuse her of blackmailing him, but later he asked me it I thought she was scheming to break up your marriage."

"Was she?"

He shrugged.

Lexi realized she'd been holding her breath, waiting for the blow. "How much did he give her?"

Delroy smoothed his mustache before answering. "You know Bryce. He wasn't about to dole out money without some terms. He'd had very little to do with her upbringing, and he figured if he was going to pay for her education, he wanted to be part of her life."

She snorted. "Well, she must have turned him down, because I don't think we got so much as a phone call on his birthday."

"Actually, she agreed and they did see each other, but on her terms." He chuckled. "Bryce said she was a shrewd negotiator. I think he was kind of proud of that. She'd never really known him, not the way BJ and Brian know him, and she told him she wanted to have him to herself, spend time together, one on one."

She stared at him. "He went along with that?"

"He talked to me about it and I told him I thought he should've stepped up long ago. I told him what he already knew, that her request was not unreasonable."

Lexi waved her hands in front of her to make him stop talking. She would have been better prepared to find out he had been having an affair. But sneaking around with his daughter? It was just crazy.

Delroy leaned forward. His expression softened. "He understood, I think, that she felt neglected all those years. He wanted eventually to integrate Courtney into your family, and I think she wanted that too, but they needed to build each other's trust first, you see. And at the same time, he was firm in his belief that he shouldn't give her everything her little heart desired. He wanted her to work for it, have skin in the game, you understand? Her grades weren't the best, and he set some high standards."

She sighed. "That sounds like Bryce."

"He paid her tuition for her first two years at Madison, saying that was time enough to prove she was serious about her education. He made a bargain with her that if she could raise her grade point average to a 3.5, he would pay for a third year.

Lexi raised her eyebrows.

"I'm in no position to judge how hard she tried, but suffice it to say, she didn't meet his expectations. He talked about it like a business contract. We had our differences about it, he and I. He acted like he was off the hook when it came to Courtney. I hoped, given time, he'd relax his position."

Given time. Her eyes stung with tears.

"Courtney took a semester off to figure out what she wanted to do with the rest of her life. She took a job. One semester became two and, so on. That was almost three years ago. She came back to him, asking for another chance, and Bryce gave her another challenge. He said if she could save enough to pay for her third year of school and improve her grades, he'd pay her back that money on top of funding her fourth year. He gave me the impression he'd underwrite the rest of her education, even grad school, as long as she was serious."

She couldn't hold it back any longer. Her breathing was ragged. Her lips pulled back and she didn't care if her anger showed. "I'm the one he should have talked to, not you! I'm his wife! It's my money, too, my future, the future of my children."

Courtney sat on the edge of the bed, curled forward and rocking, her hands pressed between her knees. Sun streamed through the window of her small apartment, laying a strip of light across the denim blue bedspread and her tanned thighs. "I don't know what to do," she mumbled.

Balanced on the edge of her dresser, his legs dangling below him, Devin said, "Yes, you do. You go right out and get an even better job." He ran a hand through his thick, freshly cut hair.

"You make it sound like it's no big deal, but it's not like I can just make a wish like . . . like a genie."

"Genies don't make the wishes. They grant them."

"Oh, go to hell!" She threw the Kleenex box at him.

Devin laughed and caught it. Hopping down from his perch, he handed her the box. "Here, your nose is running." She blew her nose loudly.

"Pull yourself together, panda bear."

"Don't call me that."

"Have you looked at yourself lately?" He sat next to her, took her chin in his hand and swiped a thumb across the mascara smudges under her eyes.

"I hate it when you make fun of me."

"I hate it when you feel sorry for yourself."

"Don't you think I'm entitled? My father is dead. I'm unemployed and if I don't come up with rent in two weeks, I'm out of here."

"So put on your big girl panties and go look for another job. Madison's a big place." He kissed her shoulder and slid a finger under the strap of her tank top.

She swatted his hand away. "Yeah, but the good bartending jobs are taken."

"So find something different. I'm sure there are better gigs out there than tending bar. Better hours, too."

"The college kids get all the entry-level jobs. I'd never get tips like that at a burger joint, anyway."

"I bet you could if you showed a little cleavage." He poked her in the ribs. "Right, baby lips?"

She narrowed her eyes at him.

His grin broadened. "Snookums?"

"You can be such a jerk."

He pulled away, pretending to be offended. "Hey, you got the wrong guy. I didn't make you late for work. I don't make you put in overtime with no notice, and I'm not the one who fired your ass. It's your boss who's the jerk." He put his arm around her, drew her close and kissed the top of her head.

Huddling against him, she let him rock her. For a whole minute she felt loved and protected, but then old resentments bubbled to the surface. How could Devin understand? He'd never had to worry about money. His father made a killing in Silicon Valley before moving the family to Milwaukee—actually to River Hills, definitely the zip code of choice. Devin went to a prep school, golfed at the nearby country club, and learned to sail on Lake Michigan. He backpacked in Costa Rica and scuba dived in the Barrier Reef, and when he was done with school, his parents bought a condo for him to live in during his unpaid internship at a tech company.

Her leg jiggled when he patted her thigh. "C'mon, let's take a look at your résumé. Nobody cares you got fired. Just say your boss hit on you and you turned him down. Then it's just a he-said/she-said thing."

"I got fired from the fitness center, too, in case you've forgotten."

"That was bogus. They didn't care about a few free meals. They were just making a point about fraternizing with members. You have to understand that about the country club set. They pay a lot of money to feel superior to the help. It's just elitist bullshit."

Her chest felt tight. "Well, you should know. You were the elitist I was fraternizing with."

"C'mon. Maple Bluff isn't exactly Milwaukee or North Shore. I mean those clubs—"

"What does that have to do with anything? Here's what they'll ask in interviews. Why did you leave that job? How about that one?" She threw herself back, covering her face with her hands.

He lay on his side next to her, propped on one elbow. He smelled like Armani and the hummus they'd had for lunch. Peeling her hands from her face, he kissed her forehead. "It'll be okay. I promise."

She thought about what her mother had said the first time she met Devin. "That poor boy is smitten. If you play your cards right, baby girl, your life could be real sweet." It was an odd sentiment, coming from the woman who drove away men with her cynicism. Maybe deep down she'd regretted losing Bryce. At least he would have been a good provider.

When Devin dipped his head to kiss her, he got that dreamy look, probably the same one that prompted her mother's comment. He swung one leg over hers, and pressed himself against her. Their lips met and she wanted the rest of her life to disappear so she could spend her days like this. *Your life could be real sweet,* her mother's voice said in her head.

Slipping a finger under the waistband of her shorts, Devin said, "It's going to be fine. Don't worry."

His words broke the spell. With her hands on his chest, she resisted his attempt to kiss her again. "How can I not worry?" Her lips quivered. "I'm scared."

"I know, babycakes." His eyes were heavy-lidded and full of desire.

She decided to go for broke. "I could move in with you while I figure out what to do."

He pulled back. "Or you could just get another job."

"I've already been late with the rent so many times I don't have a grace period any more. Can't I stay with you until I can work something else out?"

He inhaled through his nose and pressed his hands into the mattress, ready to launch off the bed. His dark eyes had gone from sensuous to guarded. "It's not going to come to that." His eyes flicked to the door.

Clinging to his arm, she pled with him. "You can't leave me now."

He looked away, shaking his head.

"Seriously, you're just going to abandon me? First my father, then my boss, and now you?" She sprang to her feet and raced across the living room to throw open the front door. "Go ahead, then. Leave. That's what everyone does."

He got up slowly. Steeling herself for him to blow past her and down the hallway, she glowered at him. Instead, he shut the door and drew her into an embrace. "Come on, Courtney, don't be this way."

Her words were muffled against his chest. "What way?"

"You know what I mean. You're blowing this way out of proportion, like you do."

She struggled to pull away. "Like I do? What the hell, Devin? I might be out on the streets and you won't even let me stay with you."

Throwing his hands out in a helpless gesture, he said, "C'mon. It's not like that. I don't want you to just give up on looking for work. How is that going to help in the long run? And besides, you know the drill about my place."

Indeed she did. As long as his parents technically owned his condo, they reserved the right to dictate who could or could not live there, and although Devin disagreed in principle, he went along with it, demonstrating over and over he wanted the comforts they had to offer more than he wanted her. "Oh, I haven't forgotten your mother specifically banned me from living there. According to her, I'm not good enough for you."

"You know I don't feel that way."

"You don't stand up to them. Maybe you're the one who needs to grow up and get a place of your own," she goaded him.

But instead of getting mad, he laughed. "Fair enough." He pulled out a kitchen chair and told her to sit. Seated across from her, he leaned back, folding his hands across his taut midsection. "Let's try this a different way. What do you like about bartending?'

She shrugged. "I don't mind the work but what I mostly like is talking to people. A few are real pains in the ass, but the tips are good.

"A ringing endorsement." He rolled his eyes. "What do you love? What do you want in a job?"

"Money. Duh."

He chuckled. "Besides that. Think outside of the box. Do you want to inspire people, make a difference in their lives? Maybe you just want summers off so you can travel. Nobody works for just the money. They care about what it stands for and what you can buy with it, like education, travel, a house, supporting a charity you believe in, starting a small business. What's your carrot?"

Nobody had ever asked her that, not even her father. All he cared about was that she fit into his mold by finishing college and making serious money. Never once had he mentioned joy. Any talk about her future had been about ambition and prestige, and she always felt like he was sucking the life out of her. "I want respect, appreciation. And I want to be paid well. I want to be treated like an adult, someone with a brain. I want to be part of something bigger." The harder she tried to answer his question, the more she suspected Devin had a right answer in mind. Finally she said, "Fine, I don't have a clue what I want, okay?"

His brows pulled together. "Okay. I get that. But you still have to do something. Don't limit yourself to what you've always done. There are all sorts of opportunities out there if you just look."

"Like what? And before you answer, keep in mind they're all going to check references, including my last three bosses who canned me."

He grimaced and rubbed the back of his neck. "You can't let that defeat you, Court. Look, a few years back my sister was exactly where you are. She quit school, took part-time jobs and didn't know what she wanted to do with her life, either. I lost count how many times Amy got sacked. When she finally got sick enough of that life, she went back and finished her business degree, and look at her now. She's pulling down well over six figures."

Not even trying to disguise her contempt, she said, "Lucky her. Trouble is, I don't have anyone paying for college, remember?"

He snorted. "Neither did she. Not after the first two times, anyway, when she didn't even bother showing up for classes and my parents lowered the boom."

She flinched.

"What? What'd I say?" He groaned when he realized his mistake. "Aw, shit, I'm sorry. Bad choice of words."

She pressed a fist to her mouth and managed to hold back the tears.

"I'm so sorry, really. I just wanted to say Mom and Dad didn't give up on her, but they did kick her lazy ass out. Tough love, you know."

That was news. "What did she do?"

"She landed a job as a live-in nanny. Not her life's ambition, but if you count her room and board, insurance, use of a car, that kind of thing, it was damn good money. She recognized it was a stepping stone to something better. Now she has her own nanny who earns a lot more than Amy ever made in those other jobs."

She felt the first stirrings of hope. "How did she find the nanny gig?"

"I think it was somebody my dad worked with." Pressing his palms together, he chopped the tabletop with the edges of his hands. "But that's not the point."

"Oh yeah? What is?" She wished she hadn't asked.

"The point is, it's time to get real. You have to quit feeling sorry for yourself. I can't do all your thinking for you."

Anger and shame reddened her face. Who made him God?

He sighed heavily. "Listen, damn it, I'm sorry you lost your father. I know it was a huge loss for you, but you can't expect a job to fill that void. Family is family. Work is work. And you either have a work ethic or you don't. Sorry to be so blunt."

"Blunt is blunt and being an asshole is being an asshole."

He continued as if she'd said nothing. "Listen, you don't have the luxury of holding out for your dream job. You call your contacts, put your résumé online, drive around looking for "Help Wanted" signs. Wait tables, flip burgers, pull weeds, whatever, and start thinking about a long-term goal, and then do things that take you closer to it."

Her answer was steeped in sarcasm. "Can I at least wait until after I bury my father?"

Devin had more patience than any guy she'd dated, but she could see she'd pushed him too far. He stood, fists clenched at his side. "Maybe you'll get lucky and your father will have left you a fortune. Then you can spend the rest of your life pretending you're actually going to finish school."

He might as well have ripped out her beating heart. Her face was burning. "No such luck. I'm not in his will."

"You don't know that."

"Are you kidding? Mom's first order of business was to find out. His partner said my father never bothered putting me in his will."

Devin's eyes widened. "That's cold." Muttering under his breath, he called her father a few choice names before coming to wrap his arms around her. "I'm sorry. He really was a bastard."

21

ouise scanned the room while she waited for Cate. She recognized several people at the visitation—the Minneapolis police chief, a couple city councilmen, plus civic leaders from the African American and Native American communities. Picking up on snippets of conversation, she assumed some of the civic leaders were using this opportunity to schmooze and petition and coerce. Politics as usual.

Her dress shoes pinched her toes, the way they always did in hot weather. She checked her phone for messages and saw Cate's text saying she was running late. Louise decided she didn't need Cate with her to pay her respects. Bryce's young widow was more composed than she would have expected. Greeting her with a cool handshake, Lexi introduced Louise to her mother-in-law and sister-in-law. Despite their obvious grief, they were attractive in the way women are sometimes described as handsome. Judging by their physical distance from Lexi and their stilted manner of speaking to her, Bryce's family and his wife had no great love for one another.

With those introductions over, Lexi drew Louise aside to introduce her to her own family, her parents Alice and Phil, and a sister named Zan, who was a slighter, more delicate version of Lexi. Hands were shaken and condolences offered. Louise's instinct told her these were good people.

"You remember my boys," Lexi said, gesturing to two little fellows wearing vests over their long-sleeved shirts, dress pants, and oxford shoes. They were crowded together on a club chair, looking hot and miserable.

It had to have been at least a year since she'd seen them. "They're just as adorable as I remember," Louise told her.

Lexi's smile was sad. "At the moment. But when they're not being adorable, BJ and Brian are just a whole lot of work. They can be little hellions."

They looked less like hellions and more like they were in Kid Hell, denied comfortable play clothes, and having to sit still with nothing to do. The older ran two fingers along the welt of the upholstery and chewed his lower lip. The younger one had his arms wrapped snugly across his middle. Both mouths turned down at the corners.

Just then a pretty girl—a young woman, Louise saw on closer inspection—came and handed each of the boys a lollipop, which they immediately unwrapped and jammed in their mouths. When she tousled their hair they looked at each other and, with twin lollipop sticks poking out of their mouths, smiled identical smiles.

Lexi's mother Alice sidled away from her daughters and spoke to Louise out of the corner of her mouth. "See that girl with my grandsons? That's Courtney, Bryce's daughter. She's from a previous relationship. Obviously. I mean, she's not much younger than my own girls. They scarcely know each other, but look at them."

"They certainly seem enthralled by her."

Alice tugged Lexi by the arm, drawing her into the conversation. "That girl's been a godsend today."

"Hmmph," Lexi said, furrowing her brows.

Bryce's daughter Courtney was medium height, with an athletic build. She wore her blonde, almost white, hair in a flattering pixie cut. When she bent to say something to the boys, they nodded soberly and slid off the chair. The younger boy tucked himself against her leg. There was something so natural about the way her hand slid down and cradled his head.

Louise studied the three of them together, the dark-haired little boys and their fair-haired sibling. On first impression they did not look much alike, yet they still managed to look like family. "She likes them, doesn't she?" she commented to their grandmother.

"I have to admit I'm pleasantly surprised."

Courtney now had one boy hanging onto each hand as she walked with them to the bank of flowers. They stuck their noses into the lilies and bubbled over with laughter when they saw the other with orange pollen on his nose. Pulling a tissue from her pocket, Courtney brushed their little noses before leading them around the room, all the while talking to them. She appeared to be coaching them, and they appeared to be a rapt audience. Together the three of them wended their way through the crowd, shaking hands with those who had come to offer condolences. Like junior politicians, the boys worked their way around to Louise and their maternal grandmother. The older boy approached with an outstretched hand. "Thank you for coming," he said to Louise. "My name is Bryce Junior and this is our sister Courtney."

"Her name's Courtney," Brian repeated. "She's our big sister."

They beamed when Louise complimented them on their manners.

Brian turned to Lexi's mother and stuck out his hand.

Alice leaned down and looked into his eyes. "So glad to meet you. What did you say your name was?" When he told her, she said, "Oh, aren't you just the perfect little gentlemen!"

Brian's earnest expression cracked and he bounced on the balls of his feet, chanting, "Gramma, gramma, gramma." His older brother rolled his eyes theatrically and groaned.

Lexi's mouth tightened. "You need to stay with me now," she told her sons as she snagged them, once in each arm. They wriggled in her grasp. "Thank you for watching them," she said to Courtney in a manner that made it clear she was being dismissed.

Tears glistened in the young woman's eyes. Louise, Lexi, and Alice watched her retreat to the back wall. "I raised you better, Alexis," said Alice. "By all rights that girl should be standing right here with us."

Lexi's eyes flashed. "Why are you being so nice to her, anyway?"

"Because you're not! I don't give a rat's behind how you feel about her mother. That girl doesn't deserve to be treated like the hired help."

Louise backed away, intrigued, yet embarrassed by witnessing this interchange. She wandered through the crowd and wound up at Courtney's side. "This must be so hard for you," she said.

Courtney pressed her lips together and stared at the ceiling. "Thanks. Everybody else—" She choked on the words.

Louise glanced back and saw Lexi watching them.

"Here, I'll show you." Courtney motioned for Louise to follow her into a smaller adjoining room, where a few people looked through photo albums and pointed out pictures hastily affixed to foam core boards.

Hadn't anyone else acknowledged the girl's loss? Louise wondered. Judging by what she'd overheard and by the way Bryce's daughter drew her into her confidence, she may well have been the only one to reach out. She studied the photographs, and pointed to a single snapshot lying on the table. "Is this you?"

Courtney looked surprised and picked it up. "Mom must've brought my baby picture, otherwise I wouldn't even—" Again, the words stuck in her throat. She extracted a picture from her pocket and showed it to Louise.

"Is this . . . Lexi?"

"You'd think so, wouldn't you?" Courtney's smile was triumphant. "That's actually my mom."

Louise did a double take. She looked from Mallory's picture to Lexi's and back. "Wow."

Courtney bobbed her head. "I guess you could say Dad had a type—skinny, dark hair, long legs."

"They could be sisters." It did not escape her notice that when Courtney dropped the photo, it landed on the open page, effectively replacing Lexi with Mallory in their wedding album.

"I know, right? My mom's probably, like, twenty years older, but she's in really great shape. I mean, look at her." Courtney pointed to a woman sitting by herself toward the back of the room.

"She's here?" Louise didn't even try to mask her surprise.

"In body only," Courtney said. "I begged her to come. She's pissed. Can you tell?"

"She doesn't look too comfortable with all of this."

"I didn't realize it would be so hard for her. Lexi's not real thrilled, either. I don't think they've ever been in the same room together."

Beyond their other physical similarities, Courtney's mother and Lexi had chosen to wear sleeveless sheath dresses that showed off shapely legs and well-muscled arms and shoulders. Louise tried to imagine how each might feel about this remarkable resemblance. It would be understandable if Courtney's mother felt like she'd been traded in for a newer model of herself. With Lexi, it was less obvious, but Louise thought the young wife could be insecure, never being certain if Bryce had chosen her for herself, or as a stand-in for his first love.

Courtney jerked her head in Lexi's direction. "Look at all those people coming to comfort the grieving widow, like she's the only one who lost someone." Bitterness tugged at the corners of her mouth. "Don't tell me people here don't know who we are. They might sneak a peek at us now and then and gossip, but that's pretty much it. See that skank with the pink Armani bag? She pointed out my mother to her friend and said my father had, and I quote, 'a regrettable one-night stand with her.'"

In her mind, Louise said, *Well, bless her heart.* Out loud, she said, "What a despicable thing to say! Don't pay her any mind."

Courtney sniffled and swiped the back of her hand under her nose. "It wasn't a one-night stand, you know. He and my mom were seriously into each other in college, and I don't just mean sex. They met at a Gulf War protest. Did you know that?"

Louise shook her head and took another look at Courtney's mother, imagining her and Bryce two decades ago, full of righteous outrage, their attraction to one another kindled by political activism.

"Want to meet her?" Without waiting for a response, Courtney took off toward her mother. Louise tagged along, wondering what the hell she'd gotten herself into. It appeared she was being drawn deeper into more drama surrounding Bryce Morgan. His family dynamics were prickly, to say the least.

The woman looked up, startled, as Courtney introduced them. Her smile did not extend to her eyes, even when Louise offered sympathetic words. "How did you know Bryce?" Mallory demanded to know.

Louise hadn't prepared for this. She said she and Dean had known the Morgans from the marina. "We didn't know them well, but we're all boaters. We talked from time to time."

Mallory managed to look both bored and vexed at the same time.

Louise kept talking, as if compelled to fill the silence between them. "We, uh, my friends and I saw the boat that day. It was floundering in the water and we knew something was wrong.

Courtney inhaled sharply.

Mallory appraised Louise. "So you're the ones who found him."

Louise nodded. There was more she could have said, but Courtney's discomfort was obvious. "I'm going to check on the boys," Courtney said and wandered off.

Louise tried once more to make conversation with Courtney's mother. It was stilted at best. Mallory was not an easy person to talk to. She was guarded and aloof, as perhaps anyone in her situation might be, but it went beyond awkwardness. Louise got the impression she relished her outlier status, and then she remembered Mallory and Bryce had met at a war rally. In her experience, some protesters were never happier than when they had something to rail against. Being disgraced and having one's child be unacknowledged was cause enough to explain her attitude. "You and your daughter must be devastated," Louise said.

Mallory inclined her head. "Bryce's death was . . . a complete surprise." She paused and frowned. Her sentences were halting as she chose her words with care. "You needn't be so . . . solicitous with me, since he and I had not been . . . friendly in years. Courtney and her father were estranged for some time, though they had recently begun to make amends." After a long and uncomfortable pause, she said, "It has been quite . . . traumatizing for Courtney, actually."

Louise couldn't come up with the right words.

"She and I have gotten along quite well without him all these years. Personally, I can't think what's changed to make her grieve this much."

What? She wasn't supposed to grieve her father's death? Louise hoped her reaction didn't show on her face. "Everybody handles grief differently." As she spoke the words, she wondered how she would grieve when her own father died. Dementia was already stealing bits of him away. Maybe by the time his breathing stopped or his heart quit beating, she would have done all her grieving.

"It was kind of you to talk to us. Thank you." To Louise, Mallory's words sounded like a dismissal, delivered in the same manner her mother employed whenever she spoke to the army wives of lower-grade officers.

The thought had not taken shape in Cate's mind the day Lexi showed up at the *Time Out*, ostensibly to thank the No Ordinary Women for discovering her husband. The impression she'd gotten that day was one of mistrust, but whether that meant Lexi was suspicious of the book club women, or feared they might discover some secret of hers, Cate couldn't discern.

In the days since then, Cate wondered if she'd missed some clue. It had niggled at her as she was drifting off to sleep last night, and was on her mind on waking. She hated to admit it might be more a subject of curiosity than sympathy that induced her to go to the visitation.

It was after four o'clock when she hopped onto I-94. Traffic was always heavy on this stretch, and people always drove too fast to be tailgating as they always did. As soon as she merged onto 35W, she took the first exit, hoping to make better time on side streets, but even there she had to slam on her brakes, once when a taxi zoomed around her and slowed to make a turn, and again when the driver ahead of her braked suddenly to back into a parking space.

Arriving late, Cate bustled into the building, her filmy scarf streaming behind her. Almost from the moment she entered the room she felt disoriented. Lexi stood composed and erect, her features frozen into a polite smile as she shook hands. Next to her stood a women of similar stature and coloring who obviously shared genes with Lexi, a sister, most likely. Cate wondered where she'd seen her before. Her head felt swimmy as she took her place in line. She shook hands with Bryce's mother and sister, a grim-faced duo. Zan introduced herself as Lexi's sister. Despite her willowy and delicate appearance, her hand-shake was surprisingly firm. Zan hovered next to her sister, occasionally exchanging a look that made Cate think of shared secrets.

Lexi had bluish circles under her eyes and signs of strain showing in the tautness of her smile. She swayed a little on her feet and Zan clutched her sister's arm, helping her slip through the crowd and into the hallway.

Puzzled, Cate watched them go. The linked arms, the swaying. They reminded her of something. Her eyes fell on Louise standing not far away, talking to—She stopped. If she hadn't just seen Lexi and Zan disappear into the hall, she would have thought Louise was talking to one of them. Perhaps this one was another sister.

Weaving toward Louise, she looked into the face of the slender, dark-haired imposter. She remembered a shred of dream, and then suddenly she was in the dream, frightened and trying to catch her breath, her hair sticking wetly to the cleft between her shoulder blades. And then she was herself again.

Louise beckoned to her. She introduced Cate to Mallory, the mother of Bryce's first child. Mallory regarded her with a single raised brow.

She felt her own eyebrow twitch in response. It was completely involuntary. Trying to ignore the scarcely concealed hostility of this complete stranger, she turned to Louise and apologized for keeping her waiting. "I hate rush hour," she said. "How on earth do people drive in that traffic five days a week?"

Mallory looked at her with disdain. "Excuse me. Maybe you have the option to drive at your convenience, but most of us get caught in traffic because it's part of getting to and from work."

Cate sucked in her breath. "I'm sorry. That was terribly insensitive of me." It was not the first time Cate had offered an opinion without adequate thought for how her words might fall on others.

Mallory did nothing to put her out of her misery. In fact, if this were a staring contest, Mallory would be the clear winner.

"Can we start over?" Cate asked.

"Actually," she said, touching a hand to her throat, "You'll have to forgive me. I need to sit down." She sauntered off without so much as a backward glance.

When she was out of earshot, Cate turned to Louise for absolution. "Was it just me or did that woman not like me?"

Louise laughed out loud, then quickly covered her mouth.

"Seriously, I had the creepiest feeling when I saw her." Cate tried to explain the sensation of dream and reality coexisting for a brief moment. "Look, I know I just got here, but I'm ready to go."

Louise gave her a funny look.

Escaping into the sultry air, they stood near the main door. Cate said, "The unspoken thoughts in that room were way louder than the spoken ones. What was that all about?"

Louise jerked her head to indicate other people milling around. "This isn't the place to talk about it."

"Do you think they could tell we were on a surveillance mission?" Cate persisted.

"Surveillance? Is that what we're calling it?"

"Okay, fine, we were snooping."

Louise gave a throaty laugh. "Honey, you make that sound like a bad thing."

Twice on the short drive to Victor's Café, Cate reached for her phone to call Robin, then remembered Robin and Brad were out for the evening. Pulling to the curb, she powered her windows up and saw Louise gliding into the space right around the corner. The temperature had dropped into the mid-seventies, pleasant enough even with the abundant moisture in the air. Wonderful aromas wafted from the Cuban café. They had to wait only a few minutes to get a table in the small patio area, separated from the street by flowering vines, potted plants, and brightly painted fences that doubled as flower boxes. It was a busy intersection and they had to raise their voices to be heard.

Looking over the top of her wine glass, Cate said, "I'm dying to do a post mortem on the visitation."

"Really?"

"Well, sure, don't you want to?"

With a wry smile, Louise said, "No, I mean how long did it take for you to come up with dying, post mortem, and visitation in the same sentence?"

"Thanks, I kind of liked that, too." Cate wiggled her eyebrows. "Well, what'd you think? Who did you talk to? Did you find out anything about his family? Anything strike you as suspicious?"

"Hold on, counselor!" Louise laughed. "My brain doesn't work that fast." She splayed her hands on the table, tapping her fingernails as she thought. "I have to say my biggest impression was how well the children behaved. I can't get over how sweet his daughter Courtney was to those two little boys."

Cate might have entered the conversation at a different point, but she responded to Louise's comment. "Did you talk to her?"

"I did. She's an interesting young woman." They paused when the server came with salads. Louise speared a slice of avocado and savored it. "I get the impression Bryce wasn't around for her when she was young. I thought she showed a lot of grace considering she was probably shoved aside, especially after his sons came along. I think Courtney and her mother are practically outcasts."

Cate nodded, deep in thought. "You'd expect her to have a lot of animosity, wouldn't you?"

"Of course. If I were her, I'd wonder if he didn't like me because I'm a girl."

"It's possible. I'd be amazed if she didn't resent the boys. It's hard to admit sibling rivalry at my age, but do you remember how threatened I was when I found out I had a brother?"

A pair of motorcycles drowned out conversation for a bit, then Louise said, "As for me, my sibling rivalry was with a ghost."

"I can't imagine. Bobby's death must have been devastating."

"It was never the same," Louise said. "I don't think my folks ever knew how hard it hit me. If they said it once, they said it a hundred times—kids are resilient. It never crossed their minds I might feel like a consolation prize. Bobby was forever adorable. I, on the other hand, passed adorable somewhere back in my single digits. I tried so damn hard to be a good son."

Cate tilted her head and smiled. "I hope you're done trying to be a boy. You're a beautiful woman. You know that, right?"

Louise got a faraway look. "I can't believe how long I passed myself off as a boy. I was always a tomboy, but then my father started taking me to Civil War reenactments. It was fun, you know, just something I did with him. I felt special. For a long time I was the youngest one there. In the beginning they had me play a messenger or a drummer. My father was so proud of me dressed me in that Confederate uniform, and when I put it on, it never occurred to me I was anything but a boy."

"Sorry, I have trouble picturing it."

"I did it for years, getting bigger costumes, being promoted to the infantry." She took the last sip of her wine. "And then I grew breasts."

Cate grunted. "Oh, Lord. Not that puberty is easy for any of us, but growing up with all that gender confusion . . ."

"I wasn't confused, but I surely was dismayed. I didn't want to give up those weekend reenactments with my father, so I came up with a solution. I got myself some big ol' Ace bandages and wrapped myself up 'til I had a double chin."

Cate started to laugh, then sobered. "You bound your breasts?"

"It hurts, just in case you wondered."

"How long did you get by with that?"

Pushing herself back from the table, Louise crossed her legs at the ankles, and folded her hands in her lap. "I wasn't outed, if that's what you're asking. Who knows how long I could've pulled it off, but then something happened the summer before my fifteenth birthday."

Cate leaned on her elbows, face in her hands. As long as she'd known Louise, it appeared there was still plenty to learn about her.

"The weather was fearsome hot that day and the other men were opening their uniform jackets, but of course I couldn't do that. We were in a gulley, ankle deep in mud, when it started to rain. I was slippin' and slidin' all over the place trying to get up the hill with the rest of the troops. Some old coot offered his hand. He pulled me up a ways, but by then it was just the two of us, cut off from the others. His foot slid, and before I knew it we were down in the mud together. Then all of a sudden I feel the slimeball's hand slippin' and slidin', trying to burrow under my uniform pants. I pushed him hard and he wound up flat on his back in the aforementioned mud. Well, the long and the short of it was I threatened to skewer him with my bayonet if he ever tried that again." She went on to say she was certain her cover had been blown, but when the battle was over, she hid in an old shed, where her father found her. When she told him what the creep had done, he wasn't overly surprised. "I told him he ought to kill the sumbitch. You know what he said?"

Cate shook her head.

"He said, "Yeah, that's just Old Siler. He always did like boys, the younger the better."

Cate was speechless.

"Yes, indeed. I was outraged for days and when I confronted him again I said he was a piss poor protector. I actually used those words. He looked at me hard and he said 'I no longer need to protect you. I raised you up to protect yourself.'"

"How can you even think of taking . . . that man into your home?" Cate sputtered. "I'm sorry, I didn't mean to say that out loud."

Louise exhaled loudly. "What else am I going to do? He's not the man he used to be. Just as ornery, maybe, but now he's like a toothless Rottweiler. He can bite, but so what?"

"That doesn't keep him from saying horrible things."

"True. But here's the funny part. It turns out he was right. I actually did know how to protect myself back then. In fact, I took some pride in it."

"Did the old goat try anything with you again?"

"Siler? Naw, I never went back. I gave up reenactments and I gave up trying to be Bobby. It was liberating, to tell you the truth.

Being the best son wasn't a contest I was ever going to win, anyway." She fluffed her bouffant hairdo and flapped her eyelashes. "I decided to be a girly girl. One who can take care of herself."

"You're all of that," Cate said. "Families are so messy,"

"I'll drink to that," Louise said, lifting her second glass of wine. "The Morgan family sure has some odd dynamics, don't they?"

Cate remembered the woman's withering expression. "Mallory's something else."

"A real piece of work. Before you got there, I went out of my way to talk to her and Courtney. I made a point of acknowledging their grief and tried to strike up a conversation. Two seconds in, it was like I stepped in horse dookie."

Cate laughed. "I wasn't imagining it, then."

"What do you suppose she has against us?"

Cate said she had no idea.

"Did you talk to Lexi?"

"Uh-huh. Her reaction wasn't hostile, but I thought she was uncomfortable talking to me. She didn't meet my eyes at the marina and she didn't tonight."

Louise shrugged. "Maybe the heat was getting to her. It was suffocating in there. It was beastly hot when Bobby died, too. Mom and Dad were destroyed by his death, but they still had to call people, make arrangements, that kind of thing, and then they stood in that horrible stuffy funeral parlor shaking hands and pretending to smile."

"You can be sure it's a strain on Lexi. And then she has to get up in the morning and go through the whole rigmarole again for the funeral." After a moment Cate said, "I suppose stress has a lot to do with it, but it's hard not to take it personally when she takes one look at me and says she's woozy. Next thing I'm standing there while her sister rushes her out of the room."

"I guess I didn't notice. I doubt it had anything to do with you."

Cate had spent a lifetime trying to hide her perceptions from others who didn't understand. She felt herself shutting down in the face of Louise's doubt.

"I'm sorry. You think there's more to it, don't you?"

Cate tipped her head back, gazing up, as if the answer were in the sky. "Maybe it's nothing, but when I met Lexi at the marina, I thought I might have met her before. It occurred to me she might be the woman with long dark hair I dreamt about. Then I met Zan and Mallory and . . ." Her voice trailed off as she struggled with an old childhood fear.

"What's wrong?"

She tried to laugh it off. "I used to think if I dreamt about someone, they'd remember it, because they were there, too. It took me years to figure out it doesn't work that way."

"You mean two people having the same dream?"

"Some people believe the dream world is its own reality, and people can actually meet there." She frowned. "I don't know if I believe any of this, but it makes me really uncomfortable to think I could be sharing some other reality with people I don't know in this one. All I can say is this: when I met Lexi, it felt almost like she thought I might have overheard—or overseen—something she wanted to keep secret."

Returning from an early dinner to celebrate their anniversary, Robin and Brad sat side by side on the front porch, facing Lake Harriet. Across the street and down the hill by the lake, the evening strollers were out. A lowering sun cast a swath of gold on the water's surface. The air was redolent with flowers Robin had planted in beds and pots and hanging baskets.

In the early years of their marriage, a romantic anniversary dinner almost by definition included gifts and roses and what Brad called the three C's—candlelight, cocktails, and carnal knowledge. More often these days, the third C stood for cuddling, which she'd come to value as being just as intimate.

Brad, an obstetrician much in demand, had ended his workday with a difficult and protracted birth ending in a caesarian section, and would rise early tomorrow to do hospital rounds. On the darkening porch, they reminisced about milestones in their marriage. His voice thickened as he talked about the year he'd thought he might lose her to cancer. Snuggling against him, they both began to nod off and decided to call it a night.

Passing through the kitchen, Robin saw the weariness in his still handsome features as he said, "Stay up if you want. It's not even nine o'clock." Before heading upstairs, he threw an arm over her shoulder and kissed her on the cheek.

"Is that the best you can do?" she teased. "A one-armed hug and a peck on the cheek?"

He scooped her to him and kissed her full on the mouth. Finally he released her. "That's all I've got in me tonight. Sorry." Yawning, he turned away. He was halfway up the stairs when the phone rang. "That'll be Cate," he said.

* * *

CATE AND LOUISE PULLED UP ten minutes later. Sitting on the porch where she and Brad had cuddled only twenty minutes earlier, Robin wasted no time grilling them about the visitation. Who was there? Did Lexi look like a grieving widow? How were the kids? Any friction between key players? Did they hear anything interesting?

Louise guffawed. "Oh, my gawd, you sound just like Cate."

Borrowing her line from earlier, Cate said, "Well, honey, you make that sound like a bad thing."

They began brainstorming. The No Ordinary Women had demonstrated over and over that their collective perspectives resulted in greater insight. Not that long ago their discussions about homicide had been purely academic, the thing of books. And then the book club had gone on that ill-fated trip to Spirit Falls, where they'd come upon a body and stepped precipitously into a murder scene. That discovery had forced them to see things differently. An item out of place, an overheard snippet of conversation, an offhand remark or a look passing between people could have great significance, or it could mean nothing at all. Now, processing all this together was as natural to them as discussing the books they read.

Three times before, their curiosity and concern had led them to believe a death had not been accidental, and three times they'd not only been vindicated, but had risked their own lives to prove it. Now, once again, they were faced with a possible murder. If Mr. Morgan had died at someone's hand, who was responsible? They zeroed in on the trio of women—Lexi, Zan, and Mallory.

"When a women dies under suspicious circumstances, they always start with the husband or boyfriend," Robin pointed out. "Did the couple argue, was there another woman, did he have a huge life insurance policy, that kind of thing."

Cate nodded. "So, when it's a man, do they suspect the wife of murder?"

"It would appear we're the only ones even considering murder." Louise kicked off her shoes and propped her bare feet on the ottoman. "But to answer your question, I think it's the same with either gender. So what do we think of Lexi Morgan?"

Cate said, "She didn't even shake my hand. Just took one look at me and got weak in the knees."

Robin grinned. "I've seen you have that effect on people—men, usually, but you never know."

"Cute."

Robin tried to piece together what she'd heard about Bryce's widow. "Didn't Lexi bolt when she saw you at the marina, too?"

"Yup." Cate leaned back, legs stretched out, hands behind her head. "And I've been breaking my brain trying to figure out why. Thinking logically, I can imagine reasons she'd want to murder her husband. Intuitively, I'm not so certain. The feeling I got from her on both occasions was discomfort more than fear."

"It wouldn't be the first time someone thought you were reading their minds," Robin said, squinting at her in the deepening shadows. She reached behind her and flipped the light switch.

"I don't know what to make of Lexi and Bryce's marriage," Louise said. "It was contentious, but also loving."

Cate yawned. "Well, that describes about a hundred percent of marriages, doesn't it? I love Erik to death, but it's not pretty when we argue. So far, no weapons have been involved, though."

"For us, words are our weapons," Louise said. "Mightier than the sword, they say. I cringe when I think about the night we watched the Morgans fight because I know if anyone saw us squabbling, it would be humiliating." She turned to Robin, expecting her to share.

Robin was reluctant to say what was on her mind, but honesty had always been the currency among her friends. She cleared her throat. "With us it's never risen to the level of all-out war—the opposite, really. We're on a much better track now, but for years, Brad and I could go for days talking about nothing more than the weather forecast or what's for dinner. I used to wish we'd have a knockdown, drag-out fight just to clear the air. Sometimes I thought if only we exerted ourselves enough to actually yell at each other, I'd know we still cared. Apathy's at least as damaging as anger."

"Damaging, maybe, but apathy probably wouldn't lead to murder," Louise pointed out. "I'm thinking about the times I really wanted to wring Dean's neck, and it's usually been over some stupid little thing. We're looking for some big awful reason to commit murder, but what if it's nothing that big? Maybe he wasn't having an affair, and maybe she didn't just take out a huge life insurance policy. Maybe she just got fed up with his condescending attitude and decided to silence him."

Cate said, "We don't know if Lexi was accounted for during the time he died. It wouldn't take long for the authorities to find out, but how would the three of us go about tracking that down? And do we know if Bryce spent the night on the boat or drove down on Friday?"

"Let's table all that for now and talk about how it might have gone down." Louise began to lay out a possible scenario. "Let's say Lexi gets the romantic notion to drive to Red Wing and surprise her husband on the boat, so she drops off the kids at daycare or with her mom or sister. She gets to the boat and the first thing he does is criticize her for wearing the wrong shoes or something equally picky and insulting. And let's say she just happens to have something in her hand, something innocuous looking but lethal, like . . . like . . ."

"A rolling pin," Cate said.

Louise took her suggestion seriously. "Nobody in that generation owns a rolling pin."

"Ah, killed by a cliché. The rolling pin–wielding wife took a serious toll on TV characters in the fifties," said Robin.

Suddenly Louise's sat up, her eyes focused on something outside. "Do you see that?"

It took a few beats for Robin to see what had caught her attention. Just beyond them in the dark, the air shimmered and twinkled. She laughed. "Fireflies. It's that time of year. What did you think it was?"

Louise's hand was still at her throat. She took a deep breath. "Even though it's probably a load of crap, I've been spooked ever since Simon talked to me about that dang presence. If it's not my father, maybe Bryce is trying to tell me something."

Cate walked to the porch railing to get a better look. "It's possible."

"I was hoping you wouldn't say that."

Robin prompted Louise to continue. "Let's play out your theory. Lexi and Bryce are on the boat, and he pushes all her buttons in the right order. What then?"

"She goes into a blind rage, picks up the, uh, thing and whacks him over the head with it." Louise rose to her feet gripping an imaginary weapon like a baseball bat and slashing the air with it. Then she jumped back, staring in mock horror at the hypothetical body at her feet. "It's possible she just wanted to get his attention, but doesn't know her own strength. If he's not dead yet, should she call for help?"

Cate tore herself away from the firefly show to say, "No, not if he's going to tell the police what she did."

Robin nodded vigorously. "And if he's already dead, nothing can change the outcome."

"Okay, let's go with that. He's beyond saving. What does she do now?" Louise said. "The dinghy's still tied to the sailboat so she didn't escape that way."

They volleyed ideas back and forth.

"She could've killed him before the boat ever left the harbor."

"And then what? Tie a second dinghy to the boat for escape, take the *Wayward Wind* out and sail to the place we found him?"

"That's premeditation. I thought we were talking about an impulsive act."

"Maybe the murder was an act of passion and the cover-up was more thought through."

"Maybe it was premeditated and she had an accomplice."

"Someone in a boat, waiting pick her up."

"How about her sister?"

"What's the motive?"

Louise picked up her story at that point. "I'm not saying Bryce was ever physically abusive, but what if he was? Maybe she was a battered wife who's always making excuses for his behavior. So what if he loses his temper now and then? She loves him, she wants to keep her family intact, he convinces her she brought it on herself. So she makes excuses, hides the bruises and tells herself she won't let it happen again. By the time it's obvious he's not going to change, she's too beaten down to leave. Deep down, she knows he'll get violent if she tries, so she tells her sister. Can you imagine what it would be like to stand by helplessly for years knowing your sister's being abused?"

"Zan was very protective of her," Cate admitted. "It would have taken some planning, but she could have gone out in a little power boat and waited for Lexi to give her some kind of signal."

Louise slapped her knee. "Like loosening the boom lines! Instead of the boom killing him, maybe it was just their signal. All she
had to do was release the boom and Zan would see the sail swinging
back and forth and know her sister had done the deed."

"Wait, does she kill him at the marina or when they're under
sail?

"I don't think that's the important question."

"I completely forgot," Robin exclaimed, jumping up and motioning for them to follow her to the living room, where she picked up a
large paper envelope and withdrew the contents. Then, clearing the
coffee table of books and candles, she spread out her photos. "I took
these just before I saw the sailboat with its sails—what was the word?"

"Luffing." Louise put on her reading glasses to examine the pictures. She shrugged and passed them to Cate, who looked at them
and shrugged back. "No little boats nearby."

"Look closer. What do you see?"

They didn't see it. Robin was afraid she'd tried too hard to see
something in the pixilated enlargements.

Louise held the photo closer to the light. "Are you talking about
this dark spot? What is it?"

"Could Lexi have been strong enough to swim to shore?" Cate
asked.

Louise frowned. "She'd have to be a damn good swimmer."

"Did you see her biceps?"

Louise pursed her lips. "I did. She's definitely toned."

Robin pointed out since they couldn't know when Bryce had
set sail in the *Wayward Wind,* or whether he'd even been alone,
they'd have to fast-forward to the moment the murder might have
occurred. "It's my feeling she'd have to take him by surprise. Setting
aside motive and whodunit, we're still back at figuring out the
weapon."

Cate asked Louise if there were wrenches on the boat that might be used as a weapon.

"A winch!" Louise said.

"Wench?" Robin and Cate said.

Looking at their blank stares, Louise explained, "Sailboats have winches to power-crank the sail lines, and winches have handles. They're about this long." Louise held her hands a foot apart. She described the handle as having a socket on one end and a big handgrip on the other. "If you swung one of those, it would definitely do damage." She demonstrated with a cranking motion, like a winding up for an overhand pitch. She described the molded plastic pocket where the handle would have been stored and asked Robin it she'd seen anything like it on the boat.

Robin's mouth went dry. "All I saw was . . . him sprawled out on the deck. I wanted to check for a pulse, but as soon as I saw the head wound my first thought was he'd been shot. Frankly, I didn't feel like sticking around."

Cate clapped a hand to her mouth. "What if the murderer was still on the boat!"

"Trust me, it crossed my mind," Robin said.

"Wouldn't the rescue crew have noticed blood on the winch handle? And if the murderer threw it overboard, wouldn't they notice it was missing?"

Louise looked crestfallen. "Okay, maybe it wasn't the winch handle."

They decided to think some more. Cate and Louise sat on the sofa and Robin perched on the edge of the coffee table facing them.

Cate sighed. "I'm still hung up on the murderer's identity. I don't think it was Lexi. Zan is even more unlikely."

Louise raised her eyebrows. "So if it's not them . . ."

"Mallory," said Cate. "My money's still on her."

Robin couldn't disagree.

"But listen." Cate picked up a throw pillow and hugged it. "I'm worried we're concentrating on those three based solely on my dream. What if it isn't a woman or someone with long, dark hair? Even if we limit ourselves to women with black hair, you might as well throw me in as a suspect."

Robin wanted to shake her. As long as they'd known each other, she'd observed that Cate was continuously at odds with herself regarding her intuition. She'd start out with a strong belief in her Sight, push people to see it her way, and then as soon as they did, she'd begin to doubt herself.

"Maybe we should consider the possibility he got into an argument with someone at the marina. Any one of the boaters could have killed him, well, except Louise." Cate looked unsure of her own words. "Maybe it happened on shore. In the dark of night, and then the killer dragged him onto the boat."

Robin waved her hands in front of her. "We're all over the place! Let's take a pause. Obviously we need more information."

25

The alarm went off, jarring her out of a dream in which she was standing over the corpse of her husband. Flinging her arms out, she knocked the alarm on the floor and it stopped. Her hand flew to her throat, feeling her heart beat wildly as she tried to sift through the images in her mind, searching for the part that was real.

Bryce was dead, that part really happened. Lexi groped on the nightstand until her fingers bumped into a box of saltines. She tore back the waxed-paper sleeve and chomped on one cracker after another until the nausea subsided.

From the kitchen, she heard BJ and Brian talking, their voices a little hoarse as if they'd just woken up. And then their grandfather's voice, assuring them they'd have their pancakes just as soon as he found where their mother kept the griddle. Pans clattered.

She tiptoed to the bathroom and then crawled back under the covers. She knew if she fell back to sleep, she'd still awaken to the same reality, but it was tempting to try. Her eyes closed and she was back in her dream. Bryce's not-quite-dead eyes followed her movements. His lifeless lips moved, beseeching her.

Her eyes flew open. She was fully awake.

As she banished the dream from her thoughts, fragments of her conversation with Delroy intruded. She'd met with Bryce's partner at a coffee shop yesterday. He brought a thick white envelope encasing a copy of Bryce's will, identical to the one she'd found in his desk at home. Together they reviewed the salient points. Bryce had left everything to her, except for small trusts for the boys, which were to be managed by her.

And then he'd gone in a whole different direction. According to Delroy—and she really had nothing else to go by, since her husband had not discussed it with her—he and Bryce had debated what to do about Courtney. Frustrated with his daughter's inability to save money, Bryce had confided in Delroy that although he intended to provide for her in his will, he wanted to stall a little longer in the hopes she'd grow up, settle down and learn to manage money and time better. "He loved her, and didn't want her to piss it away." That's how Delroy put it.

"What do you expect me to do about it now?" she'd asked Delroy point blank. A perfectly legitimate question, yet he'd looked at her oddly as if the answer were obvious. Well, what was obvious to her was that he'd left everything to her and her children. "Are you saying I should share the money Bryce left to me? Don't you think it's wrong to go against his wishes? If he didn't want to pay for her schooling, why should I? I barely know the girl!" She'd managed to keep her voice down.

Maddeningly, Delroy had given her a sad smile. "They may have been at a standoff, but it wouldn't have gone on forever. I know if she'd made the effort, Bryce would have met her halfway." He'd poured two packets of sugar in his coffee and said, "I want you to think about something."

She'd averted her gaze.

"Do you think it's possible you're misplacing your anger?"

"I'm not angry."

"I think you are, and you're making Courtney the scapegoat." He sipped his coffee and blotted his mustache with a hankie from his pocket.

"I'm not mad at the girl. I'm just saying she didn't live up to the bargain," she'd pointed out, and Delroy had pointed out that everybody deserved a second chance.

Three sharp raps on the bedroom door made her jump. "I'm up," she yelled to her mother, but instead of getting up, she put a pillow over her head and continued to replay the scene with Delroy.

She'd met his eyes and said, "But he left nothing to Courtney because he didn't trust her, right?"

"He loved his daughter and wanted to do right by her. He thought he had more time."

Feeling a little bit sick, she'd asked again what he expected her to do, but rather than answer her outright, he'd said, "You do realize she could contest the will, don't you? If she asked me as her attorney, I would inform her of that right."

She'd told him she needed time to think it over, to which he'd said, "He provided well for you, Alexis. The investments, the bank accounts, the house, the cars—all yours. You can do whatever you want with it. Keep it or share it, but think hard before you act. At the very least, Bryce would want you to look out for his daughter."

Another knock on the door told her she couldn't avoid facing yet another awful day.

As she had last night, Courtney stood apart from the others. Again Lexi's family and her father's mother and sister kept a respectful distance from each other. She wished she knew what that was all about. Lexi looked up from her conversation with a short, round-faced man and greeted Courtney with a thin smile. The man turned and looked her over, as if Lexi had been talking about her.

As soon as the two little boys caught sight of her, they broke from their mother and tackled Courtney around the knees, nearly knocking her down. BJ had teary smudges on his plump cheeks and she wiped them off. "It's a hard day, isn't it?" she said, tousling their hair. Brian jammed his thumb in his mouth, and his older brother told him he looked like a big baby. Courtney wondered if it was his mother or father who used that kind of shaming to affect his behavior. She was pretty sure she knew.

Taking them one by one in an embrace, she told them, "We have to be brave today. Can you do that?" After a few more words of encouragement, she sent them back to their mother. Watching them trudge across the room, she felt a moment of triumph, knowing her little half-brothers, at least at the moment, preferred her to their own mother. For one brief moment, she let her mind go down that road, imaging the boys being placed in her custody for some reason.

The round-faced man headed in her direction, and as he walked, he draped an embroidered scarf over his suit, the kind she'd seen priests and ministers wear on TV. Introducing himself as Pastor Norris, he took her hand and said he was sorry for her loss. She couldn't imagine that phrase ever being adequate under the circumstances, but she thanked him anyway. Then he said, "I know your name was overlooked in the obituary, but we rectified that in today's bulletin." Unaware of the omission, she was caught off guard and wondered aloud why she'd been excluded in the first place, and included in the second. "A simple oversight, I'm sure," the pastor said.

She wasn't so sure about that.

Before walking away he explained that the family would gather upstairs in the chapel prior to the church service.

Her brain seemed to malfunction, stalling on the word "family."

"We'll all meet up there and share a little remembrance and prayer, and then when it's time, the funeral director will come and bring you down to the sanctuary as a group. We've cordoned off the first three pews for family."

There was that word again. She wished for the first time that her mother were here. At least that way she'd be in the company of the family she'd always known, rather than this odd assortment. Her eyes reached across the room to the woman who was technically her grandmother, but was in reality a virtual stranger, despite the dutiful cards at Christmas and birthdays with a small check inside. Early in Courtney's memory, her Morgan grandparents had visited maybe a handful of times, but then something happened and the visits stopped. Her mother's attempts to explain their absence were feeble.

Over the years Courtney had imagined what it would be like to actually know her father's parents. Sometimes she'd picture a family—mother, father, grandma, and grandpa—gathered around a Christmas tree, opening brightly wrapped presents. When her friends came back from trips with their grandparents, she'd mentally inserted herself in the photos. Especially in her teen years she'd yearned for a grandmother she could confide in, someone who would keep her secrets and forgive her lapses of judgment. Someone who would take her side when her mother was being unreasonable. Looking at this dull and humorless woman, however, she may not have missed much.

She found her eyes searching the room for Devin, even though he'd told her flat out he didn't want to intrude on family time. When she'd said they weren't her family, he'd come back with the opinion that she'd never be part of their family if she didn't "grow a pair" and face them on her own. He'd tossed in a few platitudes about courage in his nonchalant way, as if he'd ever in his life been put in her position. His condo, his car, his education—they'd all been life rafts. Sink or swim, he'd said, as he threw her in the shark-infested water like a bucket of chum.

He'd invoked the work exemption, just in case she wasn't clear about his intentions. "Why should I take two days off and drive four hours each way to pay respects to that bastard?"

Maybe she'd overreacted, but for her that word was made of barbed wire. Even though he'd apologized when she'd tried to explain, he couldn't possibly understand. "If you're going to call anyone a bastard, it should be me," she'd said.

Once, she was playing with the neighbor kids and a couple of them were hurling the word "bastard" at each other. Suddenly her mother was rushing at them, her eyes all fierce and her mouth misshapen with anger. That night as she hugged her mother before bed, Courtney asked why she'd gotten so mad. "They said a very ugly word," she'd answered. Curious as always, Courtney had looked up the offending word in the dictionary. The "ugly word," as she discovered, meant someone whose parents were never married. That hadn't seemed so awful until she read on. In the next line was a word she didn't know—spurious—and another one she understood. She still got angry whenever she remembered reading the other meaning of bastard—it was inferior.

Someone pressed close to her. She looked up, but it wasn't Devin. Or her mother. She was all alone at her father's funeral.

She glanced over at the Family, clustered in two knots. Her grandmother looked her way and detached herself from the smaller knot. She wore a somber black suit that was too tight in the hips and creased in an unflattering way when she moved. Courtney saw the grim, determined line of her mouth. Nothing good would come out of that mouth. But instead of angry words, her grandmother beckoned with an open hand. "The family is gathering upstairs in the chapel now."

"But I . . . I," she stammered.

"That means you, too. Dear."

It struck Courtney that the last word, an obvious afterthought, had not come naturally to her.

Taking Courtney by the hand as if she were three years old, her grandmother led her up the half flight of stairs where the funeral director pointed them toward the chapel.

Her grandmother's stern features softened ever so slightly as they entered the small room. She inclined her head to where Lexi was bending down to talk to her sons. "Those boys have taken quite a shine to you."

Courtney's lips began to curl in a smile, but she caught herself. A somber occasion required somber expressions.

Her grandmother pointed to a spot next to her father's sister, Aunt Jean, who was a stone-faced clone of her grandmother. When they were all seated, she was effectively trapped between them. Aunt Jean primly dabbed at her eyes and nose and passed her the box of tissues, evidently the only acknowledgement she was going to get.

The small chapel easily held the family members. A row of vo-
tive candles and small droplights gave off a faint glow. A single
stained glass window depicted a very stylized Jesus, arms outstretched. Seeing his eyes focused on her made her squirm in her
seat.

Pastor Norris described Bryce as a brilliant lawyer, a community
activist, and most of all a loving husband, son and father. She held
her breath as he whipped off the relatives—Bryce's father, who'd
died only four years ago; his mother and sister; his wife, Lexi; and
their sons. Then he looked right at her and said, "and his first-born
daughter, Courtney Clark."

She was still basking in the fact she'd been acknowledged, pub-
licly, when he began to read from the Bible. His low voice rumbled.
"Do not let your hearts be troubled."

A troubled heart. Courtney sat up. The message was directed
at her.

"In my Father's house are many rooms."

She knew Pastor Norris was reading something Jesus said, that
he was going to "prepare a place for you," and even though she was
pretty sure Jesus was talking about heaven, she immediately thought
of her father's stucco house in Minneapolis, larger and more beautiful
than any place she'd lived with her mother. It was sure to have a lot
of rooms. She'd never been inside, but had driven past it often
enough. Sometimes she fantasized about sitting on the second-floor
balcony in that yellow Adirondack chair surrounded by ceramic pots
full of big, showy flowers.

The pastor's next words stopped her mid-fantasy. "I will come
back and take you to be with me." It took her a heart-stopping
minute to realize that those were the words of Jesus, not her father.
She really, really didn't want him to come and take her.

They sang a hymn called "This is My Father's World." She
wasn't the only one too choked up to sing, but as she thought about

those words, she saw no truth in them. Her father was gone. It was no longer his world. Although she had not been brought up in a church, she knew people went to one place or another, heaven or hell. She hoped he'd gone in the right direction.

It sounded like the pastor was wrapping things up. "Bryce Morgan—your husband, your son, your brother, your father—has gone to his reward, but the imprint he left will live on in all of you, and even though he's gone, you will always be able to hear his voice, telling you how much he loved you, and how proud he is of you."

Courtney swallowed hard. Proud of her? Maybe he loved her in his fashion, but proud of her? Not a chance. To him, she was a royal screw-up—even before the— . . . before he died.

"Ah," Pastor Norris's eyes lifted to the doorway. "He's here to take you down."

"What the—?" The words escaped her lips in a rush of exhaled air. Staring at the hands in her lap, she prayed when she turned around, she would not see her father at the rear of the chapel, waiting to drop her off at the gates of hell.

Was she the only one who heard? Nobody else reacted. Slowly her head turned and she saw that "he" was the funeral director ushering family members out and taking them down for the service. Sweaty palm to her throat, she tried to calm her pounding heart.

27

Last night when Louise and Cate proposed a mission, "should you choose to accept it," Robin accepted without hesitation. However, with Cate oversleeping and Louise getting tied up with her banker this morning, Robin was left with only descriptions of the subjects they wanted her to photograph. Sitting in the car by herself, camera in hand, she waited and hoped she'd be able to recognize them.

She and her friends had conjectured at length about Bryce Morgan's killer, or whether in fact it had been murder at all. Sometime after midnight, they'd concluded they knew even less than before. Her mind followed wisps of ideas until sometime after two o'clock, when she'd finally succumbed to sleep. She'd slept through the alarm. Luckily, her cats hadn't. Samson and Delilah leapt onto her pillow and wandered the length of her, from shoulder to hip to ankle, making piteous appeals for food. As obnoxious as the little beasts could be, they managed to get her to her stakeout before the suspects showed up.

She didn't wait long. It wasn't difficult to identify the first contingent to arrive at the church. The widow and her sons came in the same car as an older couple she assumed to be Lexi's parents. Shortly after that, someone who could only be her sister came with a man who had two little girls in tow. Just as Louise and Cate had described,

Lexi and Zan looked alike, but Zan, the shorter of the two, came across as softer, calmer, less edgy than her sister. Hidden in plain sight in her parked car with the window down, Robin got good, clear shots of the subjects. Normally digital was not her camera of choice, but in this instance, having instantaneous photos was a huge advantage.

A bit later a pretty blonde, whose description fit that of Bryce's twenty-something daughter, arrived. Pausing at the corner, she looked up and down one street and then the intersecting street. Robin guessed she was looking for her mother, Mallory, the one person still missing. Seeing the dejected daughter's shoulders sag as she trudged up the walkway and through the double doors, Robin snapped a picture. While she waited, she typed a message to Louise and Cate. "Mrs. White and Mrs. Peacock here. Still waiting for Miss Scarlett." Closer to eleven o'clock, more people showed up, including the mayor, the governor, and the Minneapolis police chief. But still no Mallory.

The sun, higher in the sky now, left the side door and sidewalk in shadow. Robin tucked the camera in the pocket of her slacks and left the safety of the car to wander along the north side of the church. Finding a good spot across the street, she leaned with her back against a tree where she was in a better position to see people entering either door.

From the church came sounds of organ music. She checked the time, reluctantly gave up her sentry post and wandered around the building. No hearse waited, since the deceased had been cremated. Two men in black suits stood stiffly at the side door, near the parking lot.

She felt let down. She really needed to catch all three on camera. Given the strained family dynamics, she might have anticipated Mallory wouldn't subject herself to further gossip by attending Bryce's service. But Robin wasn't quite ready to give up. To pass the time, she took some shots of the steeple from different angles, and a few of the magnificent oak tree shading a corner of the building. Through her lens, she followed the path of a squirrel as it scampered across the roof's peak, along a wire and down a tree trunk.

Through her lens, she saw a woman sitting on the bus bench. She wore sunglasses and a baseball hat over long dark hair, and appeared to be having a conversation with herself, gesturing and shaking her head. Robin zoomed in on the figure and began clicking. Maybe Mallory had shown up after all.

When voices joined the pipe organ in a hymn, she stood and began walking in Robin's direction. Robin slipped the camera back in her pocket and held her breath until the mystery woman veered to open the door of a silver sedan parked nearby. Once inside, she rested her forehead on the steering wheel for a moment and then drove off.

28

Stepping through the door at her father's house, Courtney noticed the mood had shifted dramatically. No more somber expressions and hushed tones. All that had been left at the church, as if they couldn't sustain grief of that magnitude and needed to return to a sense of normalcy.

The Morgans' house was as beautiful and as spacious as Courtney had imagined. Once when she and her mother had to move out of their rental house, a realtor had come and told them to strip it of anything personal. This house reminded her of that staged house, with its uncluttered counters, abstract art, and carefully placed throw pillows. If she owned this house, she would paint the walls bright colors, play music you could dance to and let the kids be loud and messy now and then.

Lexi's mother emerged from the kitchen carrying a deli tray, and in passing said she was glad Courtney decided to come. Last night when Alice had invited her and her mother for "a little lunch after the service," Mallory had declined. It was amazing how hostile the words, "No, thank you" could be. On their long drive back to her house, Mallory had tried to mitigate her rudeness by saying, "Look, you've been denied long enough, while everything has been lavished on those boys. I think it's time you claimed your rightful place in the family. I'd just be a hindrance."

Courtney knew that tone, knew there would be no further discussion, yet she couldn't help herself from saying, "Geez, Mom. For once, can you just let it go?" Her mother maintained a stony silence the rest of the drive.

Now, she was glad she didn't have to deal with her mother's reactions to everything. She saw her father's partner break away from the man he was talking to and motion to Lexi. Delroy and Lexi then sequestered themselves in the alcove of the dining room, talking earnestly. Something was definitely up, judging from his tight expression and the chopping motion of his hands as he spoke. Lexi looked flustered and angry in turns.

Desperately wishing she could hear what they were saying, Courtney inched closer. Delroy looked up, and even though she pretended to be looking at something on the bookshelf, she saw him alert Lexi to her presence. There was guilt in the way Lexi jerked her head up.

Having wanted for years to be in this home, Courtney now felt awkward and out-of-place. She wandered into the kitchen and sunroom looking for her half-brothers. They were the biggest reason she'd come. If she ever hoped to find a place in this family, it was going to be through them. She went back to the living room, where she saw Alice, Phil, and Zan talking to her Grandma Morgan and her aunt, who were actually smiling, in their reserved way. By all appearances they'd formed a truce.

"He outgrew it, but he really knew how to push my buttons," Aunt Jean said, and then she actually laughed.

Feeling conspicuous, Courtney looked for a place to hide. That business with Delroy and Lexi had put her on alert. She did not belong here. A small chair in the corner of the room was partly obscured by a large palm. She tucked herself into the corner and listened to the cacophony of conversation all around her. She longed to learn more about the man she'd only begun to know, and from the pieces of conversation, she gathered her father had been extremely smart and well liked, despite his arrogance. No surprises here.

She listened more intently to what Aunt Jean was saying, stories from their childhood. Nothing too exciting. He'd tormented his sister. Courtney's friends reported similar aggravations with their siblings. Her ears perked up when Jean started telling about the day when she and Bryce were teenagers and she couldn't find her diary. She was in the act of turning her dresser drawers upside down and pawing through them when her older brother walked in, holding it just out of her reach.

"I'm glad I didn't grow up with brothers," Zan said.

Jean raised her eyebrows. "Oh, but it gets worse. About a third of the pages were missing and what he did was more cruel than when he cut my dolls' hair or made me cocoa with Ex-lax. He said he'd sold those pages to the boy I had a huge crush on. I was mortified."

Grandma Morgan chuckled. "He always was mischievous."

"Is that what you call it? It was downright cruel. I could have strangled him."

There was a pause. Zan took her hand from her mouth. "How did you ever forgive him?"

Aunt Jean pursed her lips. "What makes you think I did?"

At that moment, Courtney was grateful to be an only child. She sat still as a manikin when Zan left that conversation to join Lexi, who hadn't noticed Courtney sitting four feet away.

Leaning close to her sister, Zan said, "How you holding up, Lex?"

"No morning sickness, if that's what you're asking."

"If you start bleeding again, promise me you'll lie down."

Whoa. Courtney held her breath. She could just imagine her mother's reaction to the news. Pregnant with two kids already, and no husband in sight. Mallory would miss no opportunity to point out the discrepancy between the way Bryce's legitimate children and Courtney were treated. And then she'd say something snarky, like she did when Brian was born. "Well, Courtney, it looks like you just dropped another pay grade."

"I was just spotting, and I haven't even done that in over a week."

"When are you going to tell Mom and Dad?" Zan asked.

Lexi surveyed the room. "Just let me get through today, okay?"

The sisters turned when the front door opened and two little girls in fancy sundresses spilled into the foyer, pushing each other in some kind of disagreement. She'd met Zan's daughters at the funeral, and compared to their boy cousins, they were well behaved. Zan sighed. "Do you have any idea what it'll be like when the twins come?"

Lexi closed her eyes and gave a theatric shudder.

Twins! Double whoa! With a lump in her throat, Courtney leaned forward and rested her head in her hands. This baby thing could be a game changer. She tried to think through what this would do to her plans. Her mother had been adamant that unless Lexi willingly shared the estate with Courtney, she should sue for her rightful inheritance. Now she figured the chances of negotiating with Lexi outside of a courtroom just dropped to zero. What single mom with four kids under five, two of them infants, would willingly part with a penny? Her mother never would have done it and neither would Lexi. No way in hell. Courtney had to figure out another way.

Just then she heard a whoop and saw Brian barreling toward her calling her name, and she knew her cover was about to be blown.

C ate got into the car slowly, as if she'd aged ten years overnight. She said her arthritic knees were hurting, but Robin sensed it was more than that. "Are you feeling okay?" she asked.

"I'm fine." Cate wasn't very convincing.

Robin and Louise let it go for a while. They had an hour-and-a-half drive to Lake City, and Robin knew Cate would get around to talking when she was ready.

"So, how did your morning as a paparazzi go?" Louise asked.

Robin response was automatic. "It's paparazzo. That's the singular form."

"Okay then, how was your morning as a pedantic grammarian with an English major and a camera?" Louise amended.

In the backseat, Cate exploded in laughter. "Thank you, Louise, I've been wanting to call her that for years."

"Oh, you've called me similar things." Robin passed the phone to the backseat. "Here are the shots I took. Please tell me I got the right women."

Cate swiped through the photos and grunted. "That's them, all right."

Robin started babbling about how she'd attracted no attention sitting in her car, the whole time taking pictures of people going into the church.

"Who's this?" Cate interrupted.

Robin looked at the last photo she'd taken, of the woman in a baseball cap sitting a the bus stop. "I was hoping you could tell me."

Louise tried to get a look, but her passengers thought it best to wait until the car was stopped.

Cate took the phone back and went through Robin's photos again. She was very quiet. "I had another of those dreams last night," she said with a heavy sigh. "It's getting ridiculous. Kind of like a mental strip tease that only reveals a little bit at a time. It was those same trees that turned into people. This time I noticed they were all women, and they all had long braids hanging down their backs. One of them put out a hand to me and I caught a glimpse of her face, or thought I did. It didn't look like any of these women, really, but for some reason I thought it might be Lexi's mother."

"You're right. It's getting weird," said Louise.

"When I didn't take her hand, something happened to her. I couldn't tell if she just melded with the others or went back to being a tree."

Robin had heard hundreds of Cate's dreams over the years, and she'd learned that the only interpretation that mattered was Cate's. "What do you make of it? To me, it sounds like Alice just eliminated herself as a suspect."

"That's not a bad theory." Cate rubbed her eyelids. A minute later she said, "I guess we'll just have to wait for the next installment."

By the time they got to Nosh, the lunch crowd had dwindled. This was the same restaurant where they'd eaten the night of Bryce Morgan's death, and overheard a waiter talking about picking up a girl and driving her to Red Wing.

The bar had a clean, citrusy smell. Approaching the bartender, Robin said they needed to talk to the man who'd served them last week. "We didn't catch his name, but—"

He concentrated on cutting up lemons and limes. "Not sure I can help you." It was not an unfriendly answer.

"He was tall with curly, light brown hair," Robin told him.

He dipped his head and started polishing the stainless steel bar. "Yeah? Listen, if you got a complaint, you can talk to the manager."

She hastened to say their service had been quite satisfactory.

Cate shouldered in. "We're really sorry to take up your time, but the thing is when we divvied up the bill, well, somehow we neglected to add the tip." She made a sheepish face and shrugged.

He glanced up, mildly curious.

Louise played along. "I guess we had a little too much wine that night. We weren't thinking too clearly."

He put down the bar rag. "I hope you weren't driving."

They assured him they were not.

When he still didn't offer up the information, Robin said, "There's no excuse for forgetting the tip. Is he here?"

The guy scratched his stubble. "You can leave it with me. I'll make sure he gets it."

"Or we could give it to him in person."

Reaching under the bar he pulled out a laminated sheet of paper and consulted it. "He's not here."

Robin leaned a hand on the rail. This twenty questions nonsense was getting old. "Not here as in not working here anymore, or not at this moment?"

He shrugged and gave a half smile. "You want to wait around, his shift starts at four."

That was over two hours away. They declined his offer of a drink while they waited.

In the parking lot, they faced the water. It was a perfect day for boating and several of the slips were empty. "I'll never look at this marina the same way again," said Louise.

Robin had been thinking the same thing. The memory of that day cast a pall over the harbor. After a moment of silence, they began discussing a new plan. Back in the car they headed north and a few minutes later, were turning down the tree-lined road to Hok-Si-La Park. On foot, they took the same path they'd walked the night of Simon's presentation, passing a playground where a handful of children climbed on the equipment, overseen by two adults. The smell of grilled meat drew their attention to a large group of people picnicking, their food and beer cans spread over several tables. They passed a couple of men in wheelchairs and an elderly couple who held hands and walked barefoot in the grassy area. Up ahead, the building where Simon had spoken about paranormal activity around Lake Pepin looked innocuous in the daylight.

A smaller path cut away toward the water. Even if the sign hadn't told them, the sounds of splashing water and laughter drew them to the swimming beach. Blankets and towels littered the tan stretch of sand, and although some people were sunning themselves or finding shelter from the sun under the trees, most of the four or five dozen people were in the water. Buoys defined a swimming area, occupied by frolicking children with their floating stock of inflatable rafts and inner tubes and water wings. Drag marks in the sand led to a row of kayaks close to the tree line, their bright colors looking like a child had dumped out a box of crayons.

The women had not come for the lovely panorama, though. Robin opened her envelope of photos she'd taken aboard the *Time Out*. Looking back and forth from photo to the real thing, the three of them tried to isolate where the mystery person had been swimming at the moment these pictures were snapped. Louise pointed out a tree, angled so its branches trailed in the water. "Do you think this is the same tree?" She poked a manicured nail at the shoreline on the photo. They estimated the swimmer had been thirty yards or so from that point.

They spread out then, looking at the scene from different vantage points. Climbing up the slope, Robin kept going until the brush made the going tougher. Behind her, the beach was still in easy sight.

"If y'all saw someone swimming beyond the roped-off area, wouldn't it attract your attention?" Louise asked when they converged at the beach. "Wouldn't you wonder about their safety?"

Robin wasn't so sure. "Look at them. Every one of them is wrapped up in what they're doing. I doubt they even noticed us." She took off her Birkenstocks and dumped the sand out.

Cate shook her head. "Not the parents. Look how they're keeping an eye out for their kids."

Robin saw she was right. Whether lounging on blankets, sitting in the sand or standing in the water, hands on hips, the adults had their eyes on the water, vigilant. "If a kid got past the ropes, I think someone would send up an alarm."

"Maybe they did. How would we know?"

Robin said, "We wouldn't. I can imagine if they saw someone swimming beyond the buoys, it might cause a moment of panic, but as soon as the parents counted noses and made sure all their little darlings were accounted for, they'd go right back to their sunny day at the beach. Even if they thought to look again, by then the swimmer would be long gone and they'd convince themselves they'd imagined it."

They were all barefoot now and wandering along the soft wet sand toward the slanted tree. Louise suggested their suspect might have swum under the ropes and come up on the beach.

Cate shook her head. "I think they'd have noticed that."

Robin stopped. The sun was hot on the top of her head and she wished she'd applied sunscreen. "The killer wouldn't swim to a public beach. Too many witnesses."

Cate's eyes were following the shoreline. "So we're looking for a more secluded place, but not too far away."

Robin winced when her instep landed on a golf ball–sized rock half submerged in the sand. "Adrenaline would get her to shore but she'd be exhausted. She'd find a place to rest." The soft sand gave way to pebbles and debris. "I'm ready to turn back."

"Wasn't there a road leading in that direction?" Cate jutted her chin out to indicate the direction they were headed.

Louise said she'd seen it too, and so they returned to the car. The road took them past tents and campsites on what turned out to be a loop through the woods. When they reached the far end of the loop, they got out and walked over a sandy patch with low vegetation until they had a clear view of the lake. It was shallow here, with visible sand bars. Farther to the right, perhaps a city block or two away, a building peeked out through the trees—a mobile home, perhaps, or a summer home. Without picking their way to the water, they examined their hypothesis and agreed it felt right. Swimming to shore here satisfied all the requirements. It was more secluded, not too far from the beach in one direction and within walking distance of civilization in the other.

Louise pointed out there must be a road leading to the houses and cabins, and so they returned to the car. Exiting the park she turned left, and left again at Central Point Road, where she parked at a resort. Stepping out, Louise lifted her sunglasses and stared up at the sign. "Skyline on Pepin," she read. "Isn't that where our waiter picked up the girl?"

"It all fits!" Robin was too excited to wait. Motioning to the others, she circled around the Skyline.

They could see how far the point of land stretched into the lake. A long row of buildings faced the lake. Louise said, "Way too visible. Let's walk on the road."

They followed the sidewalk as it wrapped back to the dirt road. They walked past the resort and condos. On their left, a creek paralleled the road for a bit before veering away. Cate stopped, staring into the woods and down at the creek, lined with tangled roots and ragged rocks.

Robin said, "It would be hard to climb the bank here. The trees are awfully tulgey."

Cate said, "That's not a word."

"Sure it is. It's from *Alice in Wonderland*. The Jabberwock came whiffling through the tulgey wood."

"You are so weird," said Cate, turning away.

"I'll take that as a compliment. C'mon, let's keep going."

Reluctantly, Cate went along. The resort could not be more than three blocks back, yet the landscape had changed. Manicured lawns gave way to rough-edged boulders, woodpiles, and boat trailers. When the road ended, they continued to where the land dropped down to the lake. Below them the creek emptied into the lake, forming a delta and cutting the sandbar in two.

Cate wandered a few paces, stopped, swung her head to the left, then pivoted right.

"Good grief, it's like watching a bloodhound," Louise said.

Cate rejoined them. "I saw this." She pointed to where the creek snaked close to the road.

Louise grinned. "Of course you did. We just came from that direction."

But Robin knew exactly what she meant. "You dreamt it." She tingled with excitement, knowing they were on the right track.

"The dream's gotten away from me, mostly, but I think maybe she followed the creek in."

"She? Who was she?"

She stared into the trees. "Well, that's the big question, isn't it?"

Louise said, "Come on. It's time to interrogate that waiter."

Courtney wasn't sure how long these things lasted. The only funeral she'd attended as an adult was for a university classmate and most of the younger people went directly from the funeral home to a club and got wasted. She wasn't a prude about drinking, but she hadn't thought it a fitting tribute to a guy who'd died of exposure after a night of partying. Maybe this was how grownups did it, with finger food and punch and quiet conversation, but as a way to mark her father's death, it felt too ordinary, too trivial.

While Zan's girls sat in the kitchen, one coloring and the other playing a game on her iPad, their little boy cousins wasted no opportunity to attract the wrong kind of attention. The more Lexi admonished for them for being too loud, too messy, too bratty, too obnoxious, too rambunctious, the more they acted up. Courtney watched it all with interest. Whether it was from embarrassment or exertion, Lexi's face became redder and sweatier, and when she could take no more, she banished her sons to their room.

Immediately, the younger one dropped to all fours and wiggled his way under the sofa.

"Brian!" Lexi said through clenched teeth. "Get out of there right now!"

Through his sobs, the younger boy yelled, "I hate you!"

"I don't care. You need to go to your room!"

Pointing at Courtney from the bottom of the stairs, the older boy said, "We'll go if she comes with us."

Lexi sized up the situation. Her mouth formed an O, but she faltered when she tried to speak.

Zan stepped in. "You boys go up and wait. If you do what your mom says and if we don't hear any noise from you, she'll be up in a few minutes."

As soon as they were gone, Zan turned to Courtney with an unreadable expression. Even though they'd talked for quite a while at the funeral home and a little more this morning, Courtney didn't really know her, and so when she asked Courtney to come with her, she was apprehensive. Zan drew her into an office just off the kitchen.

Lexi followed, shutting the French doors behind her. Facing her husband's daughter, Lexi said, "I know you heard us," she said.

She felt trapped. "What?"

"You heard us talking."

"When you were hiding behind the potted palm," Zan said. "So now you know my sister is pregnant."

With twins, Courtney added in her mind.

The office was decorated in deep tones of brown and burgundy. Little daylight came through the wooden blinds and little sound penetrated from the adjoining rooms. The hushed darkness felt like a secret. Lexi and Zan blocked the only exit. The sisters looked wary as well. Looking from one to the other, Courtney admitted overhearing their conversation.

Zan opened her hands in the way of appealing to Courtney. "Look, everybody's going to know soon enough, but my sister wants to tell it in her own way. I'm sure you understand."

Lexi, her hand over her minimal bulge, said, "I'm barely two months. I haven't told anybody, not even Bry—uh, your father—because until last week I thought I was having another miscarriage."

Why were they telling her this? Glancing again at the closed door, Courtney felt her throat begin to close up. "I won't say a word."

Zan's laugh almost put her at ease. "That's not really the point, but thank you for your discretion. What I . . .what we wanted to say is that with four little ones, Lexi's going to be stretched awfully thin. There's just not enough of her to go around, you know?"

Here comes the pitch, she thought. They were worried Courtney would fight for a share of her father's estate, and now they were going to threaten her with something horrible if she tried to get her fair share. She held her breath and waited.

Lexi pressed her lips together and shifted from one foot to the other. "This is all very awkward. I mean, we hardly know each other."

Courtney observed the way she held her hands just so as she enunciated each word. It struck her that Lexi looked like an actress playing the role of the bereaved wife. She wished she knew what the sisters were up to. She had to remind herself she had one advantage over Lexi. She and her father were related by blood. She tried to erase the word "blood" from her mind, and the image it evoked.

"This is new for all of us. I want you to know I appreciate how good you've been with Brian and BJ."

Okay, fine, Lexi had eased her guilt by thanking her. Now they were going to show her the door and tell her never to darken it again.

"Even Mom said you'd make a great babysitter, didn't she, Lexi?" Zan's smile was disarming. "She said you're a natural with kids."

Courtney didn't mind the direction this was taking.

Lexi shifted her weight. She sighed. "Bryce's mom said the same thing."

Not knowing what rules they were playing by, Courtney held her ground, the only ground that felt solid under her. "You mean my Grandma Morgan?"

Lexi blinked and cleared her throat. "Your grandmother, of course." Her eyes were shiny like she was about to cry. "Your father's partner even talked to me about you. He said you and my sons all got along splendidly."

Delroy had said those exact words to her.

The sisters reminded her of the popular girls at her high school, saying provocative things and judging her reactions. With that crowd, there was a right way and a wrong way to react, but they were the only ones who knew which was which. She wanted to like Lexi and her sister, she really did, but her mother had warned her not to be taken in by them.

Lexi was talking again, asking if she still lived in Wisconsin and what she was doing there. This new turn felt like a trap. She answered anyway. "I have an apartment in Madison for now. At the moment I'm between jobs." She couldn't interpret the look that passed between Zan and Lexi.

Lexi fondled her wedding ring. She bit her lip. "You know, if you ever thought about moving to the Cities—well, I know you're a lot older than they are, but BJ and Brian like you a lot. I hope you can have more of a relationship with—" She took a breath. "with your brothers."

Her brothers. Until now those words had been spoken as a foreign language. She didn't know what to make of it, but in the last two days, people had made a point of talking to her, with more kindness than she'd been shown in a long time. They'd referred to her as "the oldest child" or "the big sister." She couldn't deny it made her feel, well, fantastic.

31

They found him preparing tables in the inside dining room for the next meal. Louise, Cate, and Robin were the only ones in there, except for an older couple at the corner table. He looked up. Caution showed in his eyes for a fraction of a second and then his lips widened in a smile Louise found charming. "You must be the ladies who were looking for me earlier. What can I do for you?" The waiter ran a hand through his curly mop.

So much for the surprise factor. Louise was unruffled. "Sorry, but we're not here to eat. We have a little situation and we hope you can help us." She reached down to scratch an itchy spot on her ankle. When her fingernails came away with dried blood, she saw she'd scraped herself on the brambles. She also saw the hems of Cate's jeans were still wet and Robin had some kind of vine trailing from one of her sandals.

"You think I can help you," he parroted. A smile lingered, but it was no longer warm.

Louise sized him up. "Well yes, I hope so." She looked at the nametag on his chest and added the word "Chad." It occurred to her if she had a son, he'd be about Chad's age. She put herself in his place, being ambushed at his place of work, where he was already in trouble for coming in late last week. No wonder he was nervous. "I know we're blundering about, but we're trying to help someone and, well, it's kind of a delicate situation," she said.

His eyes slid from Louise to Cate to Robin. "I thought you wanted to tip me."

"That was a ruse. Sorry." Robin smiled at him and his gaze held. "We agreed to help my niece," she explained, as they'd rehearsed. "See, she's been getting death threats from somebody. She's ninety-nine percent sure they're from her boyfriend's former girlfriend, but she can't prove it."

He grunted.

"The trouble is, she's not sure which ex-girlfriend it is." Cate gave a little chuckle. "I guess he's attracted to jealous women."

He shifted from one foot to the other, looking more annoyed than anything else. "Yeah, and . . . ? I don't mean to be rude, but I'm on the clock here. Can you get to the point a little faster?"

Robin took her cue. "Of course. Short and sweet. How about if I show you pictures of three of his exes, and you tell us if you saw one of them here last weekend."

Beads of sweat popped out on his upper lip. "Why are you asking me?"

Cate flipped her hair over her shoulder and laughed. "We showed these pictures to a lot of people."

His eyes narrowed. Turning to Louise, he leaned in as if memorizing her features. "Look, I recognize you, okay? You and your friends were here. I don't know what you want, but you were here before eavesdropping on Jack and me."

Of course they'd considered he might remember them. She just hadn't expected the antagonism. Louise remained calm. "I assure you we did not want to overhear your conversation. We were waiting politely for you and—was his name Jack?—to step aside. However, we did hear something that piqued our curiosity."

He shifted his weight and crossed his arms. "Oh yeah?"

Louise knew she'd get nothing from him as long as he held that stance. Putting a hand to her chest she said, "Oh, I'm sorry, Chad. I'm really bungling this. Can we start over?"

He gave a grudging nod.

"See, we hope you're the key to all this, and we need your help before this crazy woman actually hurts someone."

He licked his lips. His breathing quickened as he looked around him. "You think I have something to do with her, the crazy ex-girlfriend?"

"Nooo." Robin drew the word out. "Not in a bad way. But we do think you ran into her in Lake City." Robin pulled her cell phone from her purse. "My niece sent me pictures of three of his exes. Don't ask me how she got them." She laughed and he began to relax. "She's sure one of these lovely ladies followed her and her boyfriend here a week ago on Friday and slashed her tires while they were staying over at the Skyline Motel."

"Ah," he said, not so much a word as an exhalation.

Louise said, "She found a threatening note on her windshield, the same kind she's found before, so she knows it was deliberate. She's very worried, and since the police aren't taking her seriously, we said we'd find out what we could."

He was digesting this when Robin said, "Overhearing you was just a fluke, but when my niece said she'd been at the Skyline, it rang a bell. It took me all week to remember where I heard it. You picked up a girl there last week, didn't you?"

He bowed his head and sighed. When he looked up again, he said, "She's really that crazy?"

"My niece is staying with me until we figure out who did it."

He threw up his hand in defeat. "Fine, sure. Bring it on."

Louise watched the transformation as he'd gone from friendly to suspicious to hostile to reconciled. Her college acting instructor would have used him as a stellar example to show range of emotion.

Phone in hand, Robin brought up the photos she'd taken outside the church earlier. The first one she queued up was Zan. She handed him the phone without comment.

He looked at it a while. "Ahhh . . ." He stretched out the vowel. I don't think so." He sounded tentative, though.

When she brought up Lexi's picture, he asked if it was the same person.

Robin told him no. He looked more closely and wrinkles appeared between his eyebrows. He shook his head, looked again and said, "Crap, I can't tell. I mean, the one I gave a ride to wasn't dressed up like this. She looked rough, and I think she'd been crying, so I . . . yeah, I just can't say." Finally he relinquished the phone. "Are they sisters or something?"

Louise shrugged noncommittally and held her breath while Robin swiped through her photos. She peered over Robin's shoulder until she came to the picture of Mallory, huddled on the bench across from the church. She held her breath, certain he was going to recognize Mallory. Their experience at the funeral home had convinced her that if provoked, Mallory could get nasty.

The photo wasn't clear. Much of her face wasn't showing. Chad stared at it a long time before he said, "I can't tell. I mean, she looks different. Older, maybe?"

"The one in the picture is older?"

"It's hard to say." As he spread his fingers on the screen to zoom in on her face, he squinted and said, "I just gave the girl a ride, y'know? She told me she'd had a fight with her jerk of a boyfriend and went on about how he left her there without wheels. I believed her, man." Using the same words he had with Jack, he said, "I mean, what'd you expect me to do? She couldn't exactly walk back to Red Wing."

This sudden protestation of innocence was a little over the top for someone who claimed not to recognize any of the women.

"Of course not. You were just being kind." Louise said, although she suspected his motive had been something other than charity.

"Take your time," she told him. She studied his face as he looked again.

His head snapped up when one of the other servers walked in and said the chef was ready to run through the daily specials with them.

"Crap, I don't know what to tell you. Listen, ladies, I know you're trying to do something nice, but I'm kinda freaked. I mean, this crazy girlfriend, you think she'd know how to find me?"

Robin said she didn't think that would be a problem. Using the language of her daughters, she added, "That wacko stalker chick is laser-focused on my niece and her boyfriend. She's not going to bother you, I'm sure."

His expression was dubious. "I feel bad about your niece. She was cute, but—" He stuck his hand out rocking it back and forth. "I mean she was so shaky I wondered if she was high or something, but I guess if all that went down . . . " He thrust the phone at Robin, but as soon as her fingers touched it, he increased his grip. "Agh, wait, where'd it go?" He swiped at the screen and brought the phone closer to his face. "Nope."

Taking the phone back, Robin looked at the picture on the screen. It was Courtney's. "Do you know her?"

He rubbed his eyes. "Nah, I thought for a minute I'd seen her before. Probably ate here. But as far as the others, hell, it could be any of 'em. Or none of the above."

Louise wondered what he wasn't telling them.

Brian and BJ were only too happy to show Courtney their room. They ran to meet her at the top of the stairs. With a boy hanging onto each hand, they passed a closed door. "That's where our mom and dad sleep. We're not s'posed to go in there," Brian said. But Courtney didn't care so much about that room.

Tugging her toward their own room, they were jumping with excitement, not the over-managed little guys she'd seen at the visitation and funeral. Their room was better than she'd imagined, with bright bedspreads and cartoonish decals of trains and trucks, airplanes and boats on all four yellow walls. Stuffed animals filled a skinny hammock over their beds. Brian struggled out of his shirt, bundled it up and tried to throw it through the low basketball hoop positioned above a plastic bucket. He missed and tried three times before he made a basket.

The hardwood floor was almost completely covered with a shiny mat depicting roads and parking lots and buildings. When BJ dumped a bucketful of tiny vehicles on the mat, she knelt on the floor with them. At first, she'd been surprised to find she actually liked these boys. Now, she couldn't shake the feeling of belonging.

The older boy crashed into his brother's truck once too often, and Brian withdrew to sit against the wall. BJ reached out and swatted Brian's hand away from his mouth. "Dad says you're too old to suck your thumb." Brian glared at him and rolled under one of the twin beds. He emerged wearing a Superman cape. Soon he was racing around and around the room, crowing, "I'm flying, I'm flying." Cars skittered across the mat as he flew. He jumped off the bed twice until BJ said, "No jumping. I'm telling."

Courtney thought it was time to shut it down before Lexi got involved. "I bet there's another room upstairs," she whispered. By their expressions, that room was off limits, too.

BJ scrunched down, pulling his head in like a turtle. His voice was low and scratchy. "Wanna see it?"

The third-floor room was almost bigger than her whole apartment. Ceilings sloped down at the sides like a giant tent. It was stuffy like a tent, too. Courtney sat on the edge of the double bed and bounced a little. The blue-and-white comforter was puffy and felt like down. The shag rug at her feet was off-white and looked like a giant sheepskin. Kicking off her flats, she ran her bare toes through the soft fibers.

Labels on the boxes atop the window seats said they contained Christmas decorations and baby toys. A small door in the center of the long wall was flanked on either side by a skinny row of windows. In her mind she sat in the yellow wooden chair and put her feet up. She imagined relaxing out there on the deck when the sun went down and the stars came out.

Brian, still wearing his cape, tugged open the bottom drawer of a dresser, with its stacks of carefully folded clothes. "They're too little for me. They're for babies," he told her. She was delighted to realize she was in the position of knowing what perhaps only two other people knew. There were going to be new babies in this house. For the first time she dared to think of them as her half-brothers or sisters.

Suddenly nervous about being discovered, Courtney quietly nudged the drawer shut with her foot. Raising her voice just enough to be heard, should anyone be aware of her ranging around where she didn't belong, she said, "Okay, guys, I don't think we're supposed to be up here. Let's go back to your room."

Before shutting the door, she cast a longing glance at the comfy bed and the little balcony with its yellow chair.

Leaving them in their room with instructions to take a little nap until she returned, Courtney stepped down the stairs without attracting notice from anyone except her grandmother, whose smile matched a kind expression in her eyes. It was crazy how everything had changed. Suddenly people were looking at her differently. She floated across the floor, feeling she had almost magical powers to will things into existence. There would be no need to connive to find a place in this family. She had allies—BJ, Brian, her grandmother, Alice and Zan, maybe even Lexi.

She did not find Lexi among the guests. Wandering through the kitchen, she ran into a woman in a floral dress wiping trays and another woman with spiky red hair loading the dishwasher. Neither noticed her as she slipped into the darkened office.

At first she thought it was empty, but then she saw Lexi, camouflaged with her black dress and black hair against the mahogany blinds. Her back was to the room. Her movements struck Courtney as furtive as she lifted a glass to her lips and drank its contents. Her head dropped to her chest and a tiny moan escaped.

Courtney didn't make a sound as she took a step backward into the doorway.

After a few seconds, Lexi sniffled and made a quarter turn. Her hand was almost on a crystal decanter on the sideboard when she realized she was not alone. She jumped a little and let her hand slip to the tabletop as if to steady herself. Despite her attempt to mask it, the look on her face told a whole story.

Pretending she was just walking in, Courtney said, "Sorry to bother you. I just wanted to let you know the boys are taking a nap."

Still clutching the highball glass in her other hand, Lexi drew it close to her ribs, sliding it around her as she turned to face the intruder. When she moved away from the window, the glass, with a trace of amber liquid at the bottom, sat with the other highball glasses, as if it had been there all along. "Oh, hi, Courtney," she said. Her voice was breathy and her eyes shiny. "Oh, thank you! It was so nice of you to . . ." She seemed to search for words.

"They're really sweet," Courtney told her. "Is it okay if I give them a cookie or something for when they wake up?"

Lexi tilted her head back and chuckled. "Those little con artists! Well, I can see why they like you." Her words held a hint of bitterness. Then her shoulders sagged. "Sorry, I forget it's hard for them, too, even if they don't understand what's happening. " She pressed her lips together and gazed over Courtney's head.

Courtney nodded. "I know." Having worked in a bar, she recognized the unmistakable smell of bourbon on Lexi's exhalations. She'd drunk more than a little of it, too. Drinking and pregnant. A most interesting development. Why was it some of the most incompetent mothers got to have children? She'd seen too many women come into her bar, thinking their designer clothes and refined language kept them from being what they were. Once she pointed out to Devin that those people thought money or class made them exempt from alcoholism or negligence in parenting. He said his mother referred to it as the pink elephant in the room. They'd laughed about it, but she found it disturbing. Parents needed to protect their kids. It was their job—their only job, really.

She and Lexi stood for an uncomfortable moment, neither acknowledging Lexi's current state, which verged on inebriation. Too bad her mother wasn't here to witness it. That thought was immediately replaced by thanking a god she wasn't sure she believed in for keeping her mother away. Mallory would surely turn it into a grief competition, pointing out that Lexi's children came into the world knowing they had two parents who loved them.

"Let's see if we can rustle up some cookies." Lexi's words were getting a little slurred. She motioned for Courtney to follow. Passing a kitchen counter littered with mostly empty food trays, she snatched a mint from a crystal dish and popped it into her mouth.

The spiky-haired woman dropped a platter she'd just washed. The clatter startled them both. Everyone laughed. The woman picked it up, then crossed the floor to put a hand on Lexi's shoulder.

Courtney took it as a cue to leave. She found some frosted brownies, wrapped three in a napkin and turned to grab a couple of juice boxes from the refrigerator. From behind the refrigerator door she saw the woman put an arm around Lexi's waist.

Her touch was intimate, concerned. Recoiling ever so slightly, the corners of her mouth pulled tight, she said, "Oh, Lexi." Courtney had to strain to hear her next words. "Oh, sugar," she crooned. "You can't backslide. Not now. I know you think it'll take away the pain, but you know it won't." She took both of Lexi's hands and said something Courtney couldn't make out.

Lexi's face crumpled and she began to sob.

The spiky-haired woman looked directly at Courtney, who quickly slipped around the corner. There, she lingered long enough to confirm her suspicions about their relationship.

"There's a meeting tomorrow morning," the other woman said. "I'll pick you up at a quarter to."

Lexi said, "You don't have to."

"Nonsense. That's what sponsors do."

The thought came to Courtney, unbidden. What if something were to happen to Lexi? She could get in a car accident or get cancer or maybe even die in childbrith. Those things happened. Her father's death proved you didn't have to be old to die. If that happened, who would take care of Brian and BJ? Zan already had kids. Four more would be total overload. Lexi's parents and Grandma Morgan were too old to raise them.

With Lexi gone, she could make them see she was the perfect one to take over. It could work. Especially if she didn't have to get a job other than raising four little kids. Better yet, if she got to raise them right here in this house.

She thought about it all the way back to her apartment.

Rendered uncharacteristically speechless, Alice stared at her daughter. Lexi could see her trying to restrain herself from bombarding her with a million questions. Had they planned to get pregnant? Did Bryce know? Had Lexi known on that trip to Red Wing? Did Zan know? With all Lexi was going through, was it safe for the babies? Babies. Twins! How, in the name of God, was she going to handle them all?

Instead, Alice's look was one of wonder. "Oh, Lexi, twins. Two more babies." She pulled her daughter to her and held on.

The place had cleared out. Lexi had tucked the boys in for the night an hour earlier than usual. The poor little guys were awfully smart, but they couldn't comprehend what had happened to their father. This afternoon she'd heard Brian ask why their daddy couldn't come to the party. His older brother told him, "Dad can't be here. He's dead."

An hour ago Lexi checked on her sons and thought they were asleep. As she turned to leave their room, Brian sat up and said, "Is Daddy going to be dead tomorrow, too?" It had nearly broken her heart and she'd been weeping off and on ever since.

"Let me fix you some tea. You just sit on the couch and put your feet up." Alice rummaged around in the pantry. "Would you rather have a hot toddy?" she called out.

Lexi's answer was muffled so she asked again.

"Mom, I just told you I was pregnant. I can't drink!"

"I drank wine now and then through both my pregnancies, and it certainly didn't harm you or your sister."

She pulled the cashmere throw from the couch and wrapped herself in it. She was about to snap back that her mother had done her a great harm by passing on her genetic inclination to drink. But the words of her sponsor still rang in her ears. Shelly hadn't merely left it at a plea for abstinence, she'd called Lexi out on her perfectionism. "We deal with temptation ever day, sometimes many times a day, but if you slip, you just can't look around for someone or something to blame. There will always be things to drive you to drink, if you're looking for an excuse."

Wasn't her husband's death enough of an excuse? To be perfectly honest, being caught sneaking a drink in her own home made her want a drink. Shelly had reminded her now was going to be her biggest trial yet, with Bryce's death, not to mention the pregnancy hormones coursing through her body. During her first pregnancy, she'd been edgy and quick to take offense. A year later, pregnant with Brian, her moods had been volatile. Did twins mean the emotional swings would be doubled? Dear God, she hoped not.

She had to stay strong. That's what Shelly said. And she had to look at this time as both a trial and an opportunity. "Your life is going to change in ways you can't imagine. Why not make a good change and enjoy sobriety," she'd said. Shelly had pushed her hard to tell her family she was an alcoholic. How could she? She could barely say the word at meetings, and those were people who understood.

Alice handed her a cup of tea with a slice of lemon. "You're not alone, honey," she said, taking a place on the couch next to her daughter.

"Are you kidding me?" Lexi patted her belly. "I'm three people now." The irony made her laugh. She laughed too long, she could tell by her mother's expression.

Patting Lexi's knee, she said, "What I mean is you have people to help when the babies come. I know you and Zan already swap off a couple of days with the kids. Maybe she can take the older ones so you can bond with the babies. Your father and I can take them overnight on the weekend."

"All four of them?"

"We'll see."

Lexi caught her glancing at the mantel clock. "Mom, you're already looking at the time and wondering how soon you can get out of here."

She sighed. "I'm tired. You're right about that, but you, my dear, are exhausted. You can barely keep your eyes open."

"Seriously, Mom, you work full time. You're not going to have the energy to take care of four little hellions on weekends?"

"I worked and raised you girls."

"Boys are different."

Alice laughed. "Thank you for that insight."

Lexi sipped her tea, thinking if her mother weren't here, she'd just curl up on the sofa and sleep.

Alice sucked in her breath for her next round of suggestions. "Your mother-in-law and I were watching Courtney with your little hellions, as you put it. She's good with them."

Lexi rolled her eyes. "Yes, I know you think she's perfect."

She laughed again. "Not perfect and not their own mother, but good enough. Better than good enough. When I talked to Courtney for a few minutes I thought she was bright and showed initiative. Your mother-in-law thinks so, too. Courtney has goals. She told us she wants to go into social work, maybe work with battered women and children."

"Saint Courtney," she muttered.

"Don't be unkind. Don't you think Bryce would be thrilled to see how they get along?"

Setting her cup on the coffee table, Lexi drew her feet under her and rested her head on her mother's shoulder. "That's what Delroy said. He said Bryce would have wanted me to look out for her. I don't even understand what that means."

She seemed to be weighing her words. "I think it means he'd like you to take her under your wing."

"I already have two kids with two more on the way. You really think he'd expect me to take on a fifth?"

"Except that fifth child is actually an adult, Lexi. Please hear me out, honey. I'm only looking out for you. Look at it this way. If you draw Courtney closer, you can kill two or three birds with one stone. At least think about it."

She sat up. "Think about what? That Courtney would be a better mother to my children?"

Alice shook her head. "That's ridiculous. I'm saying she can't afford to finish school right now and you need an extra pair of hands . . . and eyes and ears. What if you offered her room and board in exchange for babysitting?"

"A live-in nanny?" Staring into the distance, Lexi took several deep breaths while all sorts of emotions collided.

"Well, okay, let's call it that. You and Zan kept me busy. I can't imagine handling twins on top of it."

Lexi reached out for her teacup but it was empty. She thought about the remainder of the sherry Shelly had coerced her to pour down the sink.

"How many hours a week would keep you from being overwhelmed? Think what you could do with help four hours a day, for instance."

The wheels were turning.

"Even if you threw in part-time tuition, it would be far less than you'd pay a babysitter or a nanny. She wouldn't have to pay rent. I don't know what she's paying now, but I know it would save her several thousand dollars." She paused. "You have that lovely dormer room you don't even use. Think about it."

"You're forgetting one little detail. She has a boyfriend in Madison."

"Well, honey, it wouldn't hurt to ask. You don't know how serious she and this boy are. Maybe at the same time she's helping you, you'd be able to get her to finish her schooling, like Bryce wanted. It would be good for everyone."

"Mom, give me a chance to think about it, for God's sake!"

"You know I'm right, Lexi. Call her. What do you have to lose?"

34

Courtney was about to tell him she'd already eaten. The truth was, she was too nervous to eat. Devin was cooking one of her all-time favorite meals, shrimp scampi and risotto, and as soon as she caught the aroma of garlic and butter, she was suddenly ravenous. He poured a crisp Italian white in her glass and turned back to the stove. She watched him from a relatively safe distance on the high kitchen stool as he created chaos in his kitchen. In no time the stove and counters were a mess. When the rice boiled over, he switched burners, sloshing more water on the stovetop. When he bumped the wooden spoon he'd propped precariously on the pan, she was in the splatter zone. Snatching the towel from his shoulder, she wiped hot olive oil and butter from her bare leg. There was no point in making a fuss. He might be a little klutzy in the kitchen, but he was a good cook.

Tonight he wasn't his usual talkative self. He barely hugged her when she showed up at his condo, and instead of his usual warm greeting, he'd asked how the traffic was. Their meager conversation had been inane. Now he was talking about the pleasant weather, telling her the price of fresh raspberries, and asking if she needed to fill up her tank since gas prices had dropped over ten cents. All perfectly acceptable topics of conversation—if you were talking to someone in line at Wal-Mart.

"I feel bad about not going to the funeral," he said over his shoulder. "I hope it wasn't too horrible."

Horrible? Swimming among the sharks? That's what she thought it would be like, but it hadn't turned out like that at all. She didn't doubt her father's family could be disapproving by nature, but they'd been decent to her.

Devin looked over his shoulder again, waiting for an answer, but she just shrugged noncommittally. He wasn't the only one who could speak more eloquently with awkward silences than with words, she decided. Besides, he deserved to feel bad. What kind of boyfriend would refuse to hold her hand at such a crucial time?

By the time they sat to eat, the tension had evaporated. They lingered over the meal, which was delicious. During dessert, panna cotta with perfectly ripe berries, he changed the mood again by asking what was on her mind.

She couldn't delay forever. She'd rehearsed what she wanted to say but still had trouble meeting his eyes, afraid he might interpret her words as a power play, and maybe he'd be right about that. She gazed into the flame of the soy candle on the table and told him about her discussion with Lexi and her sister.

When she got to the part about Lexi's offer, he raised his eyebrows, just a little. Tilting his head, he listened to the whole plan without interrupting. She couldn't read his face.

"I'm excited about it but conflicted," she said, her voice cracking. "I'd have to give up my apartment."

He drummed his fingers on the tabletop and nodded. "Giving up your apartment was a foregone conclusion when you didn't come up with the rent."

Those words may have angered or shamed her a week ago. Today, they fell on her as a bald attempt to keep his superior role in their relationship intact. Why had she never seen before how important it was for him to be smarter, earn more money and, frankly, have a better pedigree? "You have to admit it would solve my housing problem. Anyway, it's more than just a place to stay."

He took a deep breath and pushed his chair back. Pacing to the window, he stood there with his hands in his pockets.

She couldn't stand the silence. "What are you thinking?"

Swiveling his head to look at her, he said, "I think you should do it."

He certainly got over that fast! And here she'd been so worried about breaking his heart. Her own heart beat so loudly she wondered if he could hear it across the room. "So we're done, then? Just like that?"

The muscles of his jaw tightened and then he gave her a thin smile. "I didn't say that, honey badger. You're not exactly trekking off to Tibet now, are you? You'll be four hours away. Anyway, I wasn't planning on hanging around here after my internship ends. God knows where I'll be six months from now."

She avoided looking at him.

"What?" he demanded when he saw her expression.

"Never mind."

Arms folded across his chest, he followed her into the kitchen and watched her stack their dirty dishes and put them in the dishwasher.

She gave a derisive laugh. "You know what, Devin? I don't think you meant to tip your hand." She looked at him sideways and saw his incomprehension. "You may think you're being subtle, but I know what you're up to, even if you haven't figured it out yourself. This is how it's going to go. You'll hang out with me for now, as long as it's convenient, but as soon as your career takes off, when you're no longer dependent on your father or when a prettier girl comes along, I'm history."

He recoiled and shoved his fingers through his thick hair. "I didn't say that! Jeez, you can be such a prickly porcupine." It was so like him to provoke her into a fight, and then jump back as soon as she reacted, treating her like a grenade whose pin he'd pulled by mistake.

"No, of course you didn't say it. You didn't *not* say it, either. And for once, would you just stop with the effin animal names?"

He stroked her bare arm. "Not even panda bear?"

She slapped his hand away.

"How about polliwog?" He kissed her shoulder. "Listen, there's a lot at play here. We need to give it time to sort itself out."

Surprised she wasn't melting at his touch, she took a moment to realize a new calm had settled on her. "No commitments? No problem, Devin." She picked up her shoulder bag. "I gotta be on my way, but thanks for the dinner. It was lovely." Cool, aloof. That's how she was going to play this. Tossing her head back, she turned toward the door.

"Don't be that way," he called after her. "You just dropped this on me."

"Yeah, well I'd have given you more notice if I'd had any myself." Maybe she had caught him off guard, but his first reaction told her precisely what she needed to know about him. Her talk of leaving had not tripped his emotions at all.

"I'm just being practical, Court. I mean, somebody has to think about these things. How soon does she want you to move in, anyway?"

She gave him a backward glance. "No reason to stick around here. I'll post pictures of my furniture on the board in my building, and it'll be gone in a day. By then I'll be done packing and ready to drop off a few things at my mom's."

"Your mom's? How's that going to go over with her?"

"What do you mean?"

"How do you think she'll react when you tell her you're moving in with her rival, and oh, by the way, could you clutter her house with more of your junk?"

Junk. She guessed that's exactly how he thought of her possessions. "As long we're being practical, would you mind helping me haul my boxes of junk to my new home?"

A t the Minneapolis-St. Paul airport, Louise found a sympathetic agent at the Delta counter who walked her through
the TSA checkpoint. After he left her at the gate, she
watched with trepidation as the plane disgorged its passengers. Finally, Colonel Trenton shuffled along the jetway. He looked disoriented. Louise was startled at how much he'd changed in the half year
since she'd last seen him. He'd always been a substantial man, wide
shoulders, erect posture. Now, his stooped shoulders and wisps of
white hair framing a gaunt face made him appear small and frail.
When his eyes, hooded under heavy brows, landed on her, his expression didn't change.

"Dad! Dad, it's me, Louise."

Then his mouth spread and he bared his teeth in some version
of a smile.

For years she'd been intimidated by him, yet now she wondered
if he'd grown larger and more menacing in her imagination. She took
his hands and kissed his cheek. "It's so good to see you! How are you
feeling? How was the flight?"

He drew his hands back. "You're late," he snarled. "I had to
wait for all those goddamn people to get off ahead of me. Where
were you?"

Ah, there it was. The father she remembered.

He refused the use of a wheelchair, and by the time they reached baggage claim, he was leaning heavily on her arm and his breathing was labored.

His was the only luggage on the carousel. As tired as he was, he insisted on taking the larger, hard-sided suitcase. Dean waited for them at the curb and the two men shared a cordial greeting. Soon they were talking like old friends. *Or,* Louise thought with annoyance, *like good ol' boys.*

Sitting in the backseat, she thought back on her last maddening attempt to get answers from the bureaucracy about her father's arrangements. Neither she nor Dean had been successful in pinning down the people at the Veteran's Home about how long it would take to get him into memory care there. "The requirements for state residency are murky," someone at the home had explained. Veteran's Affairs referred them to the county, who referred them to the Veteran's Home in Minneapolis. Each time she asked a question, she got more questions thrown back at her. Did he enter service in Minnesota? Is he paying state taxes? Does he have a valid Minnesota driving license? Does he currently have a permanent residence in Minnesota? What benefits is he already receiving and from which agencies?

Twice she heard her father call Dean "son." The second time, Dean turned to her, sitting like the family dog in the backseat, and winked. By the time they were home and her father was ensconced in the family room, remote control in hand, Louise was too weary to cope. She loved her father and had even looked forward to spending time with him, really getting to know him in a new way. Unfortunately, he'd utilized their brief time together finding fault with her. Either she mumbled or yelled at him. The way she buckled him into the car seat made him feel like a damn fool. Her furniture was too low. She hadn't prepared his dinner properly and he couldn't understand why she wore her hair like that.

She left the colonel and Dean and ducked into the bedroom to call Robin. Speaking quietly into the phone, even though her father's hearing had not improved with age, she said, "The albatross has landed."

Robin broke into giggles.

Then she got into the reason for the call. "Just a couple of hours with my dad and I'm thinking a nasty temper like his could drive anyone to drink. Or worse. I'm thinking maybe Lexi killed him, or Mallory. I swear, if Bryce Morgan was as hard on the mothers of his children as my father is on me, I'd have to say it was justifiable homicide." She was only half kidding.

Robin said, "What if it wasn't one of them? What if it was like *Murder on the Orient Express*?"

Louise immediately grasped the literary reference. "Are you thinking all three of them did it?"

"Lexi, Mallory, and Zan. It's not as far-fetched as it sounds. People do things together they'd never have the guts to do alone."

36

They filled her car with a few items to take to her father's house in Minneapolis, then Courtney and Devin loaded his father's SUV with boxes to store at her mother's house. She was glad she'd given her mother a couple days to calm down about the new arrangement before they showed up with boxes. Mallory's first reaction hadn't been the freak-out Courtney had anticipated.

Today, Mallory's face broke into a tired smile when they showed up at the back door. The air smelled of stale cigarette smoke. Papers scattered on the kitchen table and the surrounding floor told Courtney her mother was going through bills, putting them in two piles—one which she would pay immediately and the other she would delay for another month or two. As long as Courtney could remember, they'd been on a strict budget, and she'd learned to step lightly on bill-paying day. She'd never understand why money was so tight. In the last couple of years, it had gotten worse, though, with Mallory amassing exorbitant interest on her credit cards. It was the very thing she'd cautioned her daughter against.

While Devin stacked larger boxes in the garage, Courtney hauled bins down the steep stairs to the basement. More bags of clothing had accumulated in the north corner since she was here last. Opening a Nordstrom bag and seeing four cashmere sweaters with their original tags, she sighed heavily. Tucking the bag under her arm, she fumed. As long as she could remember, she'd believed it was her fault her mother was always scrimping to get by. She trudged up the stairs, determined never again to take the blame for existing.

Upstairs, she found Devin wiping dusty hands on his cargo shorts. "I guess I'll take off, then," he said. Her mother raised an eyebrow, but didn't counter with an invitation to dinner. Mallory had always liked him, or perhaps it was merely the idea of him. He was smart and educated and might someday make a good husband and father.

He kissed Courtney hard before he left, and as soon as the door shut behind him, Courtney lowered herself to the chair, her eyes stinging with tears.

"Oh, baby, don't be sad." Her mother reached a hand across the table. Her fingers twined with her daughter's. "They come, they go."

"It's not like that. We're not breaking up. I'll see him in a few days. Anyway, this move might be good in the long run, give us time to sort out a few things. Maybe he'll even realize he can't take me for granted."

Her mother was instantly on board. "That's right. Don't ever let him think your mission on earth is to take care of his needs. You're a person in your own right. I'd hate to see you settle down before you figure out what you want to do with your life, because you'll regret it."

Courtney had heard the litany. The point was always the same. Her mother had passed up career opportunities with the belief it made her a better mother. She'd been made for better things, and if only Bryce Morgan had manned up and provided for the two of them, Mallory would have had the chance to pursue her ambitions. Her intelligence alone qualified her to go into any field, and she'd gotten a smattering of education in everything from law to chemistry to psychology. Over Courtney's lifetime, her mother's goals had changed, each iteration firmly grounded in "if only." If only Bryce had been there she might have been a defense attorney, a lobbyist, an environmental engineer, a professor of women's and gender studies, even a stay-at-home mom who had the time and means to travel.

It's time to get over it, Courtney wanted to say. *Quit blaming and guilting everyone around you and get on with your life.* But the words never escaped her lips. Heads bowed, they held hands across the table until her arm ached almost as much as her heart. And then, just as she was about to withdraw her hand, her mother addressed the question Courtney knew she would have to answer some day. "You never did tell me whether or not you saw your father the other day—the day he died."

She felt her mother's eyes on her, trying to divine the truth. Her tongue stuck to the roof of her mouth. Her voice wavered. "Mom, is it important?"

Mallory's stare intensified.

She searched for a way to divert the conversation. "Mom, if I tell you something, promise me you won't freak out."

Mallory narrowed her eyes. "I think I can handle it."

"Lexi's pregnant. She's having twins."

With a sharp intake of air, Mallory withdrew her hands.

"That's why she needs me there, to help with the boys for now, and the babies when they're born." She rolled her eyes up to meet her mother's.

Predictably, Mallory started down the Road of Resentment. "Twins! That's just great. Your competition just doubled. How do you feel about that?"

Courtney threw her head back and groaned. "Go ahead and think of them as competition. That's what you do. I think of them as family."

"I'm your family!" The retort was quick and angry. "You're my only family, and no matter how many kids she pops out, you're still his firstborn. Don't forget that." She paused. "And what, pray tell, is she going to do with four little ones? I know firsthand how tough it is to raise one child, much less four."

Courtney swallowed hard. *Which is it Mom?* she wanted to say. *Was I your biggest joy or your biggest burden? Make up your mind.* She'd thrown that line at her mother often enough in her teen years, but the message had never sunk in. She said nothing. She'd hurt her mother enough.

Mallory's tone was snide. "Do you think she's up to being a single mother?"

"She has her family to help. Plus me."

"There's something you're not telling me."

She hated how well her mother could read her face. Before she knew it, she'd told her all about Lexi's drinking problem. "I'm worried, but I think I can help her with her sobriety, and as long as she sticks with her recovery, she'll be okay."

Mallory sniffed. "Alcoholics don't ever quit on the first try, you know."

"Some do," she said, as if trying to convince herself. "At least she's doing something about it." She decided not to tell about seeing Lexi with a drink in her hand the day of the funeral. No point in fanning the flames. Instead she told a funny story she'd heard after the funeral. Zan was teasing her sister about locking herself out of the car. Apparently they'd met for a glass of wine a few months back that turned into three glasses apiece. After that incident, she'd bought Lexi a magnetic key holder so she'd always have a spare key stuck to the outside of the car. In the retelling, Courtney told her mother, "Everyone was laughing about it, so obviously they're not worried about her drinking."

Courtney wished she'd never brought up the subject. They fell into an uneasy silence, during which she thought about her conflicting feelings toward Lexi. Although she'd defended her to her mother, she really didn't like dealing with addiction, even though she knew it was an illness. She'd served enough alcoholics in her time at the bar to know how it affected families. There were the women who left their kids at home, or even worse, in the car, while they went clubbing. There were the obviously pregnant ones with a cigarette in one hand and a drink in the other, and mothers who became obnoxious and combative when they drank, who would undoubtedly go home to abuse their children.

Her mother's mouth formed a hard line. "Why do you feel the need to stick up for those kids? If their mother can't care for them, let Protective Services haul them off."

Courtney slammed her hands on the table, scattering papers as she stood. "They're just little kids, Mom! Their life is changing in a big way and their mother is preoccupied with her own grief. I just want them to have a chance to grow up without a hateful, vengeful mother." She shook with the power of her emotions.

"You're saying that's who I am?"

"I'm saying if enough people help out, those kids might get through childhood without being too warped."

They gazed past each other for a long time, both blinking back tears. When Mallory spoke, her voice quavered. "I can't help but feel anger that she gets an army to help her out. Don't you think I wanted that for you?"

Courtney sank back into the kitchen chair and reached out her hands. "I know you love me. I know you did the best you could. I just want you to be happy."

Her mother stroked her hands. "I know. I know."

When Courtney thought there was nothing to be gained by staying any longer, her mother squeezed her hands harder. "You never did answer my question. Did you see your father that day? You said you wanted to make him understand how it hurt your heart to see him with his real family. You said you wanted to persuade him to help you finish your degree," her mother coaxed. "He owed you that much after skating on child support all those years."

Courtney's throat closed up, so when the words came, it was as if she were choking them out. "I . . . I called his office on Tuesday to set up a meeting. I didn't identify myself. They said he'd be out of the office Thursday and Friday. I was pretty sure he was on the boat. After work that night, I got the idea that if I went home and changed and got on the road, I'd get to the marina early and catch him off guard, you know, so he wouldn't have a chance to plan a defense."

37

Her mother pressed the back of her fingers to her lips as she listened. Her eyes glistened and the furrow between her brows deepened.

"I got there before sunrise and took a little nap in my car." As she told about that morning, she could picture it as if it were happening right now.

Already apprehensive as she walks down the dock, she halts, almost turning around when she sees him. A little thrill overtakes her then, when she realizes he hasn't noticed her. She takes her time, wanting to observe him before she announces herself.

He's sitting in the cockpit, hunched over so his elbows rest on his knees. He's holding a mug of coffee in both hands. His hair sticks up on one side and is flat to his head on the other. His posture and his sleepy expression makes her think of all those mornings when she's not totally awake and she sits on the edge of the bed just like that, all groggy and disheveled.

She takes a step closer. He turns toward the sound of her feet on the dock boards, more curious than surprised. He motions for her to come aboard.

Wordlessly he stands, once more motioning to her as he goes below. He returns with another mug of coffee and hands it to her.

Mallory's eyes had been boring into her as she talked, but now she sat back and chuckled. "He was a horrible morning person. Kind of like you, actually. I couldn't talk to him until he had at least two cups of strong coffee."

Picturing this little domestic detail made everything that happened feel more tragic. Courtney had heard so many disparaging remarks about her father, it was hard to reconcile the few good things about him. This little glimpse into their life showed a different side, both casual and intimate.

"He was so bleary sometimes, I'd tease him by asking if he was smoking weed, even though we'd given it up by then. He told me I should never be a pothead because it made me so paranoid." Mallory's laugh was dry and tinged with sadness. She swiveled in her chair to open the kitchen drawer and pulled out a pack of American Spirit cigarettes.

"I thought you quit." Courtney rubbed the spot on her forehead where a headache was starting.

Mallory lit one and took a drag. She rummaged under her papers for the ashtray. "Want one?" She tilted the box to Courtney.

Courtney blinked back more tears. "They're nasty."

Mallory shrugged and returned the pack to the drawer. "Suit yourself." When she finished the cigarette, she stubbed in out in the copper bowl and turned back to her daughter. "You were saying?"

Courtney took up the narrative.

It's so peaceful sitting on the boat, drinking coffee and not talking a lot. When the coffee pot is empty, she helps him tidy up the galley and then he asks if she has enough time to take the boat out. She tells him she's working a short shift tonight, filling in for someone, so she has plenty of time. So they leave the harbor and set sail. It all feels very natural, a father and daughter out for a little day sail. The wind is perfect, just enough to get some speed and still be easy to tack.

They're on a nice smooth course when she broaches the subject. She tells him she's totally serious about going back to school and explains how hard it is to hold down a job, especially the shift she usually has to work, and still maintain her grades.

Because his expression doesn't change, she's lulled into thinking it might go well, but then he balks. Tuition only. Maybe book money, too, but he's not going to pay for her to live off campus. "Have you thought about moving in with your mother?" he asks. "Hastings to the University of Minnesota is an easy commute. Your credits should transfer."

She counters with the problem of still having to come up with general living expenses, gas money, car insurance, etc. His face softens and she's sure he's going to give in. But then she says, "And entertainment. You can't expect me to live in a convent."

There's a slight curl to his lip when he tells her he doesn't appreciate her sarcasm. He says she needs to find a more suitable job than bartending, something with better hours and better values, whatever that means to him. He says he worked in the mailroom on campus one year and in food service another. The implication is if he could do it, so could she. Could and should because his way is not just the right way, it's the only way. Of course everything he says can be construed as helpful. He never once comes right out and tells her she's a failure or that she'll never measure up, but he might as well.

As she talked, she saw the shift in her mother. Her mouth became a straight line and she pulled away, arms wrapped around herself. Courtney withered under her gaze. It was impossible to tell whether her mother's vitriol was directed at her or at her father. "Go on," she directed.

But Courtney's vocal chords were paralyzed. She and her mother had had their conflicts over the years, but she'd never had to confess anything of this magnitude. What was the point of going on, anyway? Forgiveness wasn't her mother's to grant. What was very clear to her was that once her mother knew the whole story, she could never unknow it. And that did not bode well for either of them.

So many times since that awful day, she'd pictured different points in the narrative she might have acted differently. If she'd called ahead instead of ambushing him. If she'd asked him about money in an e-mail or gone with her mother. If she'd asked Devin to come with her, he'd have been a good buffer between her and her dad. If she hadn't given in to sarcasm. There were at least a dozen ways it could have ended better. She closed her eyes, unable to go on.

38

sn't it kind of a cliché?" Cate asked. "A ghost hunter and a psychic meeting at the most famous haunted spot in Saint Paul?" The Wabasha Street Caves, dug into the sandstone cliffs near the Mississippi, had once boasted a nightclub—a speakeasy, actually—where some of the most infamous gangsters were said to hang out. This was not Cate's first time at the caves, but she'd never been to the adjacent coffee shop, Grumpy Steve's.

Simon chuckled. "I come here all the time, partly because of the history, but mostly because it's in my neighborhood. In fact, it's my favorite haunt."

She knew he was waiting for a laugh but all she could muster was a half-hearted smile. After a restless night, she wondered why she chose to sit here and listen to his corny jokes when she should be working on her jewelry for the Uptown Art Fair in August. "You said you wanted to pick my brain. The way mine is functioning, you'd be better off if you picked someone else's."

"Sorry, but your friend said she'd be tied up all morning at the VA."

"I meant pick, as in choose . . . never mind. Trying to be funny. What's up?"

He told her his frustration in gathering data in Lake City. "If I relied on supposed eyewitness accounts, I'd be chasing my tail all over the place, but I'm intrigued about your E.S.P. and whether you might shed new light on what I'm hoping to find." He peeked into his empty cup. "Refill?"

By the second cup she started to come alive. She told him about her dreams that began the night they discovered Bryce's body. "Who knows whether it relates to his death or the ferry disaster or something else entirely. I don't expect others to take it seriously, but once I think I'm receiving important information, I can't get it out of my head. The only thing I can do is pick through the clues and wait for the fog to clear. Sometimes it never does."

He asked intelligent questions that helped her distill her belief, bolstered by yet another dream last night. This dream began as the first had, with a woman who was and wasn't Cate swimming and coming ashore amid sand and trees. The trees took on human shape as they had before, until they were a handful of nude women dancing in a circle. This time she really wanted to see what they were circling. Either they'd cornered and killed whatever or whoever lay hidden inside the circle, or they were protecting it.

She'd woken with the knowledge that she would keep having this same dream until she figured out the answer.

Simon jotted something in his notebook. "Did you get the impression they were living, or could they be the women who died on the *Sea Wing*, dancing to let us know they're at peace?"

Cate said she didn't know.

"I'm going back to Red Wing tomorrow. I got a guy who's going to take me out on the water. Who knows if I'll get any readings, but it's worth a try, right?"

She leaned forward and told him she'd be very curious to hear if he was successful.

"Hey, maybe you and Louise want to come along," he said as if he'd just thought of it.

She left Simon in the coffee shop without having made a commitment one way or another. Stepping into the sunshine, she headed toward her car, passing a low stone wall, on which sat a man in baggy pants and camo tee-shirt. He held in his hand a thick paperback. "What're you looking at, you crazy old lady?" he called out to her. "Go home and leave us alone!" There was no one with him.

She had to pass him to get to her car, and as she got closer, he held up his book, as one might hold up a cross in the face of a vampire. She saw the word "Werewolf" in the title, and a laugh erupted from her before she could stop it.

"You laughin' at me?" he challenged, rising to his feet.

"Not yet." She couldn't believe she'd said it aloud.

His laugh was like the braying of a donkey. "Good one. 'Not yet.' Good one. Not bad for a witch." He slapped his book against the palm of his hand and walked past her into the street.

Crazy old lady. Witch. They were only words, and yet he'd spoken them at the exact moment she was thinking how crazy she must sound to people who'd had no experience with premonitions or answers given in dreams.

He stumbled into the street, stopping in his tracks when a car horn sounded. Shaking his book at the driver like an evangelist with a Bible, he yelled, "Shut up, you crazy old bitch! Leave us alone!"

Cate shook her head, surprised how quickly she'd gone down the rabbit hole of psychic paranoia. The man, she could see, was as harmless as his equal opportunity insults.

Before pulling out of the lot, she dialed Louise and told her briefly about her meeting with Simon and his invitation.

Louise hesitated. "I've never been ghost hunting before." She lowered her voice and said, "I'd love to go, I really would, but until we work through this ridiculous convoluted system of government, my time is not my own. The colonel's in the bathroom right now, and I'm on call to grant his next wish. I've been trying to convince myself things between us were never that bad, but he's even more demanding than I remember. You'd think I had nothing better to do than—"

Cate heard a gruff male voice in the background. "Get off the damn phone."

"Sorry. Gotta go." Louise disconnected.

When she got home, she texted Simon to let him know they would not be joining him. She retreated to her jewelry workshop on the second floor. In no time, she'd used her aviator snips to cut wide bands of copper for cuff bracelets and used her blowtorch to anneal them before hammering them into different textures and shapes. As she worked, she thought about poor Louise, whose life had been suspended until further notice by a thankless parent. It could happen to any of them.

She sat back to look over her inspiration wall above the workbench, with sketches of her own jewelry and photos of designs, hers and other artists'. In the center was an art calendar, showing a geometric Kandinsky painting in vivid colors. The calendar was still open to June, which ended days ago. Flipping the page, she found herself staring at the familiar Matisse painting titled *Dance*. Five female figures, each with black hair, held hands as they danced in a circle. It was uncannily like the image that had been haunting her dreams.

Leaning back in her chair, she shook her head and laughed at the crazy connections her mind made. Her dream had been nothing more than an animated version of this light-hearted painting.

S he doesn't have a plan. Her arms and legs know what to do. Kick, stroke, breathe. Repeat. When she isn't sure she can keep going, she rolls onto her back. The Wayward Wind is smaller now. But she can't outswim the image that's seared her brain forever.

Kick, stroke, breathe. Gasp.

This time when she pauses, the reality of what she did—what she's doing—begins to sink in. It doesn't matter that she never meant for it to happen, that if she could do it all over again, she'd stay calm, not react. But the truth is undeniable. She did something in anger—something stupid, immature, thoughtless—and because of it, he's dead.

The wake of another boat washes over her and she gulps river water. When she's done gagging, she turns so she can see her father's boat—so far away now. It's too late to go back, too late to call for help. Too late.

How can she expect anyone to understand why she didn't stay, when she herself can't comprehend it?

Each time she closes her eyes, the image of him appears—arms flung wide, head misshapen, mouth half open in a scream that never leaves his lips.

Paddling toward the shore, her lungs are on fire, but she doesn't stop. Can't stop.

Collapsing on the sandbar, she thinks she might die as she vomits water and sobs until her heart breaks in two, though it's still beating. Sitting up when she can cry no more, she brushes caked mud from her face. She hardly dares to look out on the lake. Two boats are converging on the Wayward Wind, a houseboat and a cabin cruiser. Soon her father will be discovered and it will be completely out of her hands.

She rubs her aching shoulders, stretches her legs until the muscle cramps subside, and tries to think beyond the next minute. Exhausted and wildly thirsty, she has to do something. From the water, she saw a busy public beach on her right. She could make her way there, grab the first adult and tell them everything. But as she pictures what would happen next, she knows in her heart she'll never follow through. By fleeing the scene, she can't claim innocence. She couldn't bear people thinking she murdered her father. For all her mixed emotions about him, she never, ever wanted him dead.

For the first time, she sees what she must do. She surveys the area around her.

The sandbar where she sits is at the mouth of a creek. She finds her keys, still in her pocket, and her phone still secured around her neck, but when she pulls the phone out, she sees water has seeped into the waterproof case. Standing, she waits for the vertigo to pass. She slogs across the squishy sand and through shallow water. For a while she can actually swim up the creek. When it gets too shallow, she wades, grateful for her rugged sandals. It's slow going. The creek twists through a heavily wooded area. Before she reaches a low bridge over the creek, she swishes her hair in the water and does her best to wipe the mud and leafy debris from her exposed skin before scrambling up the slippery bank by grabbing onto low branches and tree roots.

The bridge turns out to be an extension of a wide path that leads her past homes. Sitting on a fallen tree, hidden from the houses by a large woodpile, she assesses her situation. She thinks she was at the marina early enough that nobody else was out and about. In all probability, nobody noticed her on the Wayward Wind, and even if they did, they'd remember someone with long, dark hair. By now, her father's body must have been discovered. She pictures his wound. There's no reason to think he was killed by anything other than the boom.

All she has to do is get home. If she can hitch a ride, she'll tell the driver her boyfriend took off and left her with no way home. She'll say she lives in Red Wing and ask him to drop her off near the hotel. From there she'll walk to the car and maybe even be back in Madison in time for her evening shift.

It'll probably be a guy who picks her up. She doesn't want to hop in any old wheels. No creepy dudes. But her instincts about men are pretty good. She'll be able to sort out the psychopath from the eager young man who hopes to get lucky.

She shouldn't look too scraggly. It would attract attention and besides, nobody wants to pick up a hitchhiker who looks like a vagrant. Her shorts and swimsuit are already beginning to dry in the warm air, but her hair will take longer. She gathers up several twigs, bundling them to assemble a makeshift brush. She can't get all the tangles out, but it will have to do. Twisting her damp hair, she secures it by running fresh twigs through the knot like a pair of chopsticks.

The path becomes a road that runs past a resort. That's a lucky break. People wouldn't be surprised to see someone in a bathing suit and cutoffs here. Still, she skulks along at the tree line, watching for signs of activity.

Up ahead, just off the main road, is a parking lot where her prospective driver can pull over. She's almost there when she's overtaken by vertigo again, as the enormity of her father's death hits her with no less force than a swinging boom. She stumbles toward the freshly mown grass. Her legs buckle and she goes down.

She doesn't slip completely into unconsciousness, though. That would be too merciful. Lying on her side in the grass, she pulls her knees to her chest, trembling. Rolling to her back, she watches a single cloud float away, *leaving a perfectly clear sky. She's a survivor, she's always been a survivor, she tells herself. She gets up and trudges toward the road.*

"Hey!" someone calls, and she looks up to see a guy hanging out the window of his Saturn. "You okay?" He has a nice smile, good hair.

"I'm, I'm good, I guess. You're not going to Red Wing, by any chance?"

The rest of it goes almost too smoothly.

By the time she gets to Madison, she's ready for the forgetting to begin. Showered, hair and makeup done, dressed for work, she arrives half an hour late. At the end of her shift, her boss tells her not to bother coming back.

40

Y ou're hollering loud enough to wake the dead," Louise said to her father through the closed door. "Are you okay?"

"No, I'm not okay, you fool. I'm lying here in my own blood."

Dean swiped the top of the doorframe, found the hex key and poked it into the lock. A trickle of blood from the corner of her father's mouth was all the blood Louise saw. She asked if he could sit up and he waved her away. "Goddamn it, girl, you know better." She left Dean with him while she called 911.

The colonel couldn't explain how it happened. One minute he was standing at the sink brushing his teeth and the next he was lying on the bathroom floor with the taste of blood in his mouth. That's all they got out of him before the ambulance came. As the EMTs examined him, she told them about his dementia.

"Goddamn you! I'm fine. Just ask Bobby," the colonel growled, his speech slurred.

Tears sprang to her eyes. She backed away.

He jerked his arm away from one of his rescuers and then grimaced at the pain. They probed his side and said he'd probably broken a rib. They did not find other fractures, although they were concerned about his hip. They asked him several times if he'd hit his head on the floor or the counter or the wall. He said he couldn't remember.

At the ER, X-rays and an EKG showed nothing other than two broken ribs. He already had a nasty hematoma on his hip, but no other bone breaks. He'd bitten his tongue. They said the deep laceration would heal by itself. The doctor told Louise and Dean his confusion could be entirely due to Alzheimer's, but they wanted to keep him under observation for a couple of days to make sure he hadn't suffered a concussion or stroke.

When her father was settled in his room, they conferred with the house doctor. Louise had papers giving her power of attorney in case her father was unable to make health decisions, but the doctor said they would need to further evaluate his capabilities before enacting it. He asked if they'd talked over what to do after his hospital stay. "We'd like to keep him seventy-two hours," he said. "In the meantime, our social worker will look into availability at the VA Hospital or the Veterans' Home for convalescent or long-term care."

Before they left, Louise bent to kiss her father's forehead. The colonel batted her away. "He can stay," he said, pointing to Dean.

Dean said, "You need to sleep and we need to go home and get some sleep, too. We'll be back tomorrow."

"Just you. Annabelle can go to hell."

"Dad, it's me, Louise. Annabelle's your wife."

He squinted at her. "Not anymore!"

"C'mon, Colonel. Louise is your daughter. You know that." Dean patted his hand.

"I know that," he growled.

Louise held back her tears until they were out of the building. Halfway home, she threw her head back and laughed like a lunatic. "All the aggravation with government rules, all the back and forth with different administrations, and Daddy found the only solution! Can it really be as simple as this?"

Dean roared with laughter. "Don't tell anyone. There'll be an epidemic of old people mysteriously falling down stairs, maybe with a little help from their kids."

That's when the tears chose to come. "Don't even joke about that."

Dean put his arm over her shoulder and drove with one hand, like he did when they were dating. "Listen, hon, I'll mind the store. You've got three days to spend however you want."

She thought half a second before pulling out her phone and sending Cate a message.

41

It was hot that Sunday afternoon in Red Wing, and without a breeze, the humidity was suffocating. Louise and Cate arrived at the marina with nothing more than a change of clothes and a few groceries.

Louise pointed out the man ambling along the grass between the parking lot and docks. He looked up and waved. As soon as she recognized Simon, Cate waved back.

Despite the fact they were there to go ghost hunting with him, Louise was visibly upset on seeing him. "This is uncomfortable. I can't imagine why I told him so much about my messy family dynamics. I was like those people you get stuck next to on a plane. Sometimes they come to the shop, too, and they think it's okay to spill their guts to a total stranger. Besides, I don't particularly want to hear about another spirit hovering over me. You're the intuitive. It should have landed on you."

"There's no explaining taste." They both laughed at that.

Spying the pile of equipment two docks over, next to the *Wayward Wind*, Louise said, "I think I know how to connect those dots."

Simon scurried to catch up with them, saying, "Let me help you with that," and snatched the grocery bag from Louise's hand.

She said, "Let me guess. You're trying to summon Bryce Morgan's ghost."

He scuffed along at her side. "Not . . . well, yes, I guess I did set up the EVP meter, but that's just because I was killing time until the guy gets here."

"The guy with the boat?"

He nodded. "He's running late and I was bored just standing around with nothing to do."

Louise checked her watch. "He still has another hour to get here."

He ran a hand through his hair and explained he'd hoped to get his equipment in place and do a run-through with the boat captain before leaving the marina. He followed them to the *Time Out*, checking his watch compulsively. The three of them sat below, guzzling cold water.

Cate told them about her strange encounter with the man in a camo shirt outside of Grumpy Steve's. "Did you see him?" she asked Simon. "Is he a regular there?"

He shook his head.

Louise sighed. "I'm sure he didn't mean anything by it."

"Well, that's comforting." When she was done laughing, Cate told them both about finding out the dancers of her dreams were inspired by a real work of art.

"So it was just your own dark and twisted interpretation of Matisse's masterpiece." Louise sighed.

"Pretty funny, huh?"

"Why that particular painting?" asked Simon.

Cate swallowed hard. He was right to ask, of course.

Louise's eyes widened. "I know that painting. We just saw a sculpture in Key West in January." She pulled out her phone and flicked through her photos. She held her phone for both of them to see. "The statues are right by that place everyone gathers to watch the sunset. Keep going, I took a few shots."

Staring at this reproduction, Cate started laughing. The sculptures were certainly based on the painting, but with a whimsical twist. The same five ladies, now three-dimensional, held hands to dance in a circle. But there was one more figure, lying on the ground gazing up at all their lovely nakedness. Cate swallowed hard. It was a man, also a statue, wearing shorts, striped tee-shirt, and a single boat shoe. "Bizarre," she said when she handed the phone back.

Simon looked at his watch again. Concern crossed his features. "I'd better go back. Don't want someone stealing my equipment."

Cate watched the dejected curve of his shoulders as he shambled up the dock. "I think he's been stood up."

"Simon, wait." Louise called after him. She and Cate hopped onto the dock. When they caught up to him, they mopped sweat off their faces in the stifling air. Together, they shambled over to the *Wayward Wind*. He squatted to turn a dial on the single meter he'd set inside the rail of the sailboat.

"Did you pick up anything on your . . . thingy?" Louise asked.

"My thingies didn't detect a thing." He sighed.

"Maybe it will tonight," Cate said.

"I'm beginning to think it won't happen. We made plans almost a month ago. It was still a go when I talked to him yesterday. If he doesn't get here pretty soon, it'll be too late."

Cate's eyebrow went up a notch. "Why is it too late? If he can't make it today, can't you try again tomorrow?"

He jammed his hands in his pockets and shuffled his feet. "You'll think I'm being silly. Thing is, I doubt ghosts actually care about calendars. I always thought their world was timeless, y'know, but a lot of people think the best time to break through the veil is on anniversaries."

Cate and Louise exchanged a glance.

"Today is the anniversary of the *Sea Wing* disaster. You may not remember, but I mentioned that in my talk the other night. That's what I've been preparing for. The *Sea Wing* sank sometime after seven on the night of the thirteenth, not too long after it left Lake City. My plan was to go out on a boat today and hang around the spot in the river where it went down." He looked at his watch again. "We really should be on our way by now, so I can get everything set up before the, uh . . ."

"Witching hour?" Cate suggested.

He pressed a button on the meter before snapping it into a metal case. "Yeah, something like that." He pulled a phone from his pocket and his lips tightened. He scratched his head and swore. "Now he's stuck in traffic the other side of Mendota Heights. He says it's pouring rain in the Cities." He looked up at the clear sky and scowled. "Highly unlikely." His jaw was clenched as he tapped in a response.

Cate thought he might cry. "So now what?"

"I told him to go the hell home. We're gonna have to scrub it." In the spirit of killing the messenger, he glowered at the phone before stuffing it back in his pocket.

Louise looked at Cate and Cate wiggled her eyebrows and grinned. Louise turned to Simon. "Well, come on, then." She hefted his duffle bag before slinging it over her shoulder. "The quicker we get this stuff on my boat, the sooner we'll be on our way."

His eyes lit up. "Really? You'd do that?"

* * *

THEY WERE MAKING GOOD TIME. Louise said she loved those evening hours on the water when most of the boats were docked for the night. "It's almost magical. The noises die down and you can just see the water settling and becoming more peaceful."

Cate could see what she meant. An egret flew low at the shoreline and made a graceful landing. Simon set one and then another of his gizmos next to her, securing both of them with bungee cords from his duffle. Below, he mounted a third, clamping it to the table's edge. Obviously he'd thought this through. When he was sure it was all in order, he came topside, where he told Louise how he wanted her to proceed.

She nodded. As soon as they were lined up with the Lake City marina, she slowed the engine at Simon's request and steered the boat in a loop, a little unnerved by the knowledge they were on a similar path not only of the *Sea Wing*, but that of the *Wayward Wind*'s last voyage. The phrase that popped into her mind was "voyage of the damned." She imagined how Dean would react if she was dumb enough to tell him about this latest escapade. He'd be within his rights to question whether she might have inherited her father's predisposition to Alzheimer's.

Simon was bending over one of the meters when an eerie sound brought them all to attention. They gaped, not at the ghost hunter's monitors, but toward the Minnesota shoreline. Once more they heard the mournful wail.

Cate gave a nervous laugh. "It sounds like Jacob Marley's ghost."

Simon nervously licked his lips.

Holding fast to the wheel, Louise said, "Well, what did y'all expect? I thought we were looking for ghosts, so what's everyone so riled up about?"

"It's too high-pitched to be a loon call," Cate said. "But it's familiar."

Suddenly Simon whooped and pointed. Through the trees they saw a railroad track, and on it, a locomotive chugging toward them.

A train whistle! Louise let out her breath and they all had a good laugh at themselves.

Simon said there was nothing to do now but wait for the instruments to go crazy. He filled the time by playing travel guide. "Lake

City goes all the way back to the time of the Civil War. It was a resort town even then." He talked about the sawmills and flourmills and apple orchards. He talked about birdwatchers coming from far and wide during the big migrations. Louise kept the boat cruising along and Simon kept talking.

"It's this stretch, right here between Frontenac and Lake City, that the steamboat skippers feared most. It's hard to tell, but look up ahead. See where the channel narrows?"

Louise said, "That's Point No Point." It was her turn to explain, and she told them it was so named because boaters coming from the northwest thought they were seeing a distinct point jutting into the lake, but as they approached, the sharp outline of the headland softened until it disappeared into the shoreline.

"Hmm, a point of land that never materializes," Cate mused.

"It's an optical illusion."

"Interesting. It sounds a lot like my work." Simon grinned. When he spoke again, he switched from travel guide to weatherman. "You know about Bernoulli's principle, don't you—the lower the pressure, the higher the speed?"

Cate had a vague memory of her college engineering class. "It's the reason airplanes can fly, right?"

"Yes, indeed." He beamed. "The principle works for water as well as air. Now, take a river where the channel narrows. On a calm day, you don't notice the difference, but throw in a strong wind and all of a sudden it's a big deal. The wind hits that narrow spot and picks up speed, maybe a lot of speed. The water's speeding up, too, so you get the wind pushing the water ahead of it, too. It can catch boaters unawares and cause one helluva problem."

"You're describing what happened to the *Sea Wing*," said Louise.

Simon's head jerked up as one of his instruments crackled. As he bent to check the reading, lights danced across his handheld meter. "Here we go," he said. He popped down below to check the other instrument and came up shaking his head. "It definitely picked up something, but it stopped. Calm as can be."

"What does that mean?" Louise asked.

"I'm not sure," he answered.

42

In Minneapolis, Dean set the phone down, wondering if he should call Louise.

The television was on the Weather Channel. The first squall had passed the Cities, with another, weaker one on its way, but that wasn't what concerned Dean. The radar now showed a small cell on top of Red Wing, heading southeast. Winds were strong. He reminded himself Louise had taken to boating as if she'd been born to it. She was as competent a boater as any. She knew the proper way to tie up the boat in a storm—two bow lines, crossed stern lines and two spring lines. The *Time Out* would be fine unless another boat in the marina pulled away from its mooring. A loose boat could do a lot of damage to neighboring boats. He poured himself two fingers of scotch and relaxed. He was damned glad Louise told him they were just hanging out in the marina tonight.

* * *

WALKING INTO THE KITCHEN from the bathroom, Robin was dismayed to see Samson and Delilah sashaying across the kitchen counter where she'd been poring over her most recent photos only minutes ago. Of course, knowing they weren't allowed on counters didn't stop them. In fact, they flaunted it. They knew enough, however, to leap down when Robin got close. In their scramble to get away, they kicked up her photos, sending them flying in all directions.

"Bad cats!" She picked up the pictures and placed them on the counter as they'd been earlier. Seeing them again, she was discouraged. There was no way to further manipulate, enlarge or enhance them enough to prove there'd been an actual person out there in the lake. And yet this thing, this blob in the water, was roughly the size and shape of a human head.

"Look at this." Brad called to her from his leather recliner. "Aren't you glad you're not still on that boat?" He was pointing to the television. "See that? I bet they're really catching it on the lake."

She'd been so relieved earlier when the heat broke with a drenching rain, she'd given little thought to what it would be like on the *Time Out* in a storm. Standing in the doorway, she studied the radar map and said, "The red area's pretty small. Maybe it'll miss Red Wing altogether."

* * *

GRACE HAD SPENT the last hour picking through items people had donated for the church rummage sale. Those sales never made a lot of money for the church. Last year's proceeds paid for new sheet music for the choir. This year the money would go toward a youth mission trip. Half of her dining room table was covered by stacks of books and videos, grouped by subject matter.

Her husband, Fred, walked through on his way to the kitchen. "I didn't even hear the bomb go off," he said, looking around at the mess. "Is all that garbage?" He pointed to boxes and bags crammed against one wall.

"The stuff on the right is garbage. We're not selling clothing this year, so I'll take those to Salvation Army when I get a chance."

"Ah. Would it help if I dropped them off for you?"

"Absolutely. Let me find out what their hours are." She opened her laptop. A map to Red Wing popped up on the screen. She typed in her search. The screen froze. She tried refreshing the screen, but the map stayed. "I'll let you know after I reboot," she said, but he was already in the kitchen getting his evening bowl of ice cream. She pressed the button to shut it down. Instead of shutting down, a new tab opened, and although she didn't remember searching for movies, the cover of a DVD filled half her screen. It depicted fifteen or so faces in a rectangle around the title, *Voyage of the Damned*. She did a double-take. She'd just put that movie in a box for the rummage sale.

* * *

FROM HER SECOND-FLOOR apartment in St. Paul, Foxy sat in her favorite chair, immersed in a book. The rainsquall had come and gone, leaving the grass brighter green, the air sweeter, and her mood lighter. A single candle on the coffee table burned, giving off the scent of orange blossoms, and soft jazz played on her radio.

All was well. And then suddenly it was not. Molly Pat, her canine detective and honorary member of the No Ordinary Women, leapt up from a sound sleep and began barking. She was a dog of few words but many intonations, and Foxy recognized this was not her bark of greeting, nor was it the one to say she needed to be let out.

"What's going on, Mol? You're worrying me." Foxy patted her lap and the terrier jumped up and flattened herself on her owner's legs. Her ears flicked back and forth.

"You aren't still afraid from the storm, are you?"

Molly Pat's eyes rolled up to meet Foxy's and she gave one sharp bark.

"Are you trying to warn me about something?" Foxy's thoughts darted, just for a second, to Cate and Louise, and she wondered how they were faring on the boat. Just then, the candle's flame burned higher, then flickered and went out. The dog hunched into a smaller silhouette and whined.

Foxy reflected on what the paranormal investigator had talked about. At the time, she'd been amused and skeptical. However, she had to admit, if ever she were to believe in ghosts, it was now. She stroked Molly Pat's head even after the dog's eyes closed in sleep.

43

With the next turn of the boat they had a good view of the narrowing of the channel. The first clouds rolled in, and within minutes the sky began to darken, though it was well over an hour before sunset. In the lake's chop, whitecaps began to form.

Louise's breathing quickened. Simon's boater friend had said it was pouring rain in the Cities. Why hadn't they considered the possibility the storm would move southeast toward Red Wing? It was standard operating procedure to check the weather before setting out. Why hadn't she done it?

Simon's eyes darted from the towering clouds to Louise, his question unspoken.

Below them, the water churned and heaved. The situation had the potential of a disaster, and she, as captain of the ship, had to assess the situation and make the right decisions. Breathing deeply to calm herself, she gauged how long it would take to motor to the marina. If only they could get safely inside and tie off in time, they'd be okay, but this storm was building too fast.

Cate, she saw, was wearing her life jacket. She sat in the corner biting her lip, her eyes scanning the lake.

"Simon, get your life jacket on. There's raingear in that locker."

Cate threw open the lid and pulled out a yellow slicker and two khaki ponchos. Louise grabbed the slicker, jammed her arms into the sleeves and cinched the hood around her head. Cate threw one of the ponchos over her head, saying, "I thought there was only a chance of showers."

"Yup," said Louise. "A good chance, like about a hundred percent."

Simon donned his poncho. He looked grim. "It's just like the night the *Sea Wing* went down," he muttered to himself, looking at the veins of lightning sparkle and crackle in the ever-darkening mass of clouds.

Louise stopped, chilled by a thought. "Simon!"

His head jerked up.

"Please tell me you didn't drag us out here in this weather on purpose."

He struggled to keep his balance as the boat rocked. One of his gadgets sprang from its constraints and slammed onto the deck. Lunging to catch a dial that had broken off, he stumbled. The broken meter slid to the corner where Cate sat shivering.

"You chose tonight, the anniversary, to recreate the scene of the ferry sinking. Did you know a storm was coming?"

His mouth fell open. "No! How can you even think that?" he protested, just as big drops of rain began to fall. Cate handed him his glasses, which had fallen when he stumbled.

Louise took one look at her woefully unqualified crew and knew their fate was in her hands, just as it had been their last trip. Now, she knew, was the time she would have to put all her book learning to the test. "Go below and stay there. Both of you!"

She didn't have to tell them twice. As darkness closed in, they huddled in the corner of the U-shaped banquette that wrapped around the table. Their eyes were wide. Louise pulled the hatch cover shut, leaving only a three-foot-square opening through which to see them.

She kept the motor running, intending to keep the boat at roughly the same bearing until the storm passed. Pointing the *Time Out* into the wind, she braced herself.

The storm moved fast. Rain came in horizontal gray sheets, driven by the wind. Only the lightning strikes illuminated their surroundings long enough and often enough so that Louise was fairly sure they weren't being blown to shore. The noise was deafening with the wind, the pounding rain, and the splashing of waves against the boat.

She held the wheel fast as they rocked and bobbed. Every few seconds a wave would crash hard into them and she'd feel the wheel trying to twist out of her hands. She could not allow that. If she let the wind and waves take them broadside, they could wind up on the bottom of the lake.

Drenched and blinded by the driving rain, she hung on. Through the howling of the wind, she heard locker doors slam and wondered what other things were banging around below.

Then she heard it. A different howl, like someone wailing for help. It was soon joined by a second. Her heart went out to Cate and Simon, stuck below, wailing in terror. Then, in a bright flash of lightning, she saw them. Cate was gripping the tabletop with both hands and bracing her feet against the table base. Wedged in the corner of the bench, Simon had one arm around her and the other pressed on the seat for balance. Their lips were pressed tight in fright.

And yet the eerie chorus continued. Louise couldn't say how many voices joined in the lament, or even whether they were human. The storm raged on. Louise held the wheel in a death grip.

At some point she realized the wailing had ceased.

And then, as quickly as it had blown in, the storm passed. Miraculously, the boat was still in the middle of the channel and not much farther downstream than when the squall had begun.

Turning to stern, she was amazed to see the storm had already lost its intensity, and now looked little more threatening than a typical summer rain. She gave a huge whoop of triumph.

Two faces appeared in the opening and hands clawed at the hatch to slide it back. Below them, Simon's instruments were strewn about the sole of the boat. Way up ahead as far as they could see, the clouds cracked to reveal a sliver of dark blue sky. It was just about time for the sun to set.

Louise pushed the throttle forward and headed for safe harbor.

* * *

AT THE MARINA, A BEDRAGGLED and shivering Simon gathered up his damaged equipment, apologizing over and over for his recklessness.

"You didn't hold us at gunpoint," Cate said, handing him a towel. "If you remember, we offered."

He rubbed the towel over his hair and face before pulling his glasses from his pocket and trying to put them on. They hung on his nose at a goofy angle. He removed them again and stuck his finger through the hole where the left lens should be. "I swear I didn't know a storm was coming. I never would've . . ."

"It's okay," Louise said. "Everything's okay."

Slinging the full duffle over his shoulder, he cast a backward glance at the now placid lake before trudging up the dock to spend the night at the St. James. "I hope their resident ghosts are asleep, too. I'm not interested in any hauntings tonight. What about you girls?"

Much as they wanted to go home, Louise and Cate were simply too exhausted to drive. "We're sleeping on the boat tonight," Louise told him.

They watched him go. Cate went below and came up with a bottle of wine and plastic tumblers. She pulled the cork and poured two generous glasses.

After taking a large gulp, Cate set her wine down. "Did you hear them?" Her eyes held fear.

"You heard it, too?"

"What the hell was that? I was scared to death."

"Me too." She could still hear it, but this time she knew the wails and cries were in her memory only. "How would you describe it?" She didn't want to influence Cate's interpretation.

"Voices. Terrified voices screaming for help."

Louise's skin prickled. "That's exactly what I heard." Neither of them spoke for a long time. "Want to talk about it?" she asked.

"Nope."

Finally, they got up and took turns showering in the tiny enclosure. As soon as she'd dried herself off, Louise crawled under the blanket in the forward berth. In a few minutes Cate appeared beside her bed, wearing pajama pants and a tee-shirt. Sliding her necklace over her head, she handed it to Louise. "Look." There was a tremor in her voice.

Louise held the turquoise under the reading lamp and tilted it back and forth in her hand. A shiver ran from her fingertips up her arms and the back of her neck. "It's cracked."

Cate took the necklace back, and as soon as the cord was around her neck again, she clung to the amulet, her eyes wide.

Louise flipped the blanket back and edged to one side. "Want to sleep here tonight?"

"Oh, God, yes."

She moved over and soon she heard light snoring.

During the night, Louise woke with a start.

Cate was sitting up in bed. "Where are you?" she moaned.

"Honey, I'm right here," Louise said in the dark.

"Oh!" Cate gave herself a shake and said, "I was having that dream again."

"Well, did you learn anything new?"

Slowly, she shook her head. "I was there again in the woods. I wanted to see the dancers. I expected to see them, but they were just trees again. I want to know where the women went."

"We already know that. They went to Key West."

Cate's laugh was half-hearted. "I guess everyone needs a vacation now and then."

Just the thought of Courtney coming to live with them had been emotionally draining, but Lexi had to admit the actual process went smoothly. Bryce's daughter arrived just as the summer squall ended. She'd brought so little with her—three armloads of clothes on hangers, two laundry baskets full of miscellaneous stuff, and a few boxes. She hauled it all up two flights of stairs without scuffing the paint or tracking in anything on her feet, and Lexi felt no compulsion to supervise.

The boys' excitement reached a fever pitch as they hauled her through the house, competing with each other in an over-the-top version of show and tell. Their excitement made bedtime a disaster. Half their bath water, it seemed, ended up on the floor, and while Courtney mopped it up, Brian threw himself, naked, on the bedroom floor and rolled under the bed. Courtney knelt down, tickled his flailing feet and slid him out before he knew what was happening. Once they were in their pajamas, BJ was bouncy and silly, but Brian sobbed and sucked his thumb.

For Lexi, the whole situation had a surreal quality to it. She hadn't yet grasped the idea that Bryce was gone, and now here she was, making another huge adjustment by taking in his daughter. She knew so little about the girl. Lexi could honestly say she'd never felt hostility toward her. Taking a stance of neutrality, she neither encouraged or discouraged contact between father and daughter. In fact, she'd gone through life pretty much oblivious to Courtney's existence.

That had all changed since Bryce's death, with Delroy practically shaming her for allowing Bryce to shirk his fatherly duties, and then pointing out that Courtney was within her rights to sue her. From all indications, Delroy would side with Courtney. When her mother and sister hammered her about the practical advantages of having live-in help, she'd given in, and now Courtney was here. In her home. Taking care of her boys. What had she done?

The boys were asleep and Courtney was upstairs, making herself at home. Lexi lay in bed and let her mind go to dark places. How many scary books and movies and plays had to do with taking in a relative stranger who proves to be a deadly threat? An estranged son with a hidden drug problem returns home and puts his family in grave danger; a woman gives refuge to her long-lost sister, only to discover she's plotting to steal her husband; a nanny increasingly takes over the mother's duties, all the time scheming to take the children away.

Rolling on her side, she clutched Bryce's pillow, still bearing his scent, and buried her face in it, trying to curb her crazy thoughts. Wearing Bryce's soft chambray shirt over her panties, Lexi curled up, still holding the pillow, and rocked herself until she was calmer. She stopped crying when she heard the faint ring of Courtney's cell phone. For a few minutes she'd forgotten Courtney was even there. She couldn't hear her talking. Lexi had almost drifted off when she thought she heard the creaking of stairs. She felt her heart race.

She jumped up and tiptoed down the hall to the boys' room. They were sound asleep. Creeping down the stairs, she saw the living room lay in darkness. Circling through the main floor, she assured herself there were no intruders, either from the outside or from inside her own house.

She parted the blinds and looked onto the patio. Moonlight shone in patches. One of the path lights had burned out, she saw, and she wondered where Bryce kept the spare bulbs. It was just one more thing to put on her list. Just this morning the oil warning had come on in her car. Yesterday she'd pulled off a knob wrestling with a stuck dresser drawer. Her father had said to call him if she needed anything, but she couldn't be calling him or anyone else for things she could learn to do herself. Maybe there was a class in simple household repairs. House Maintenance for Widows.

Padding across the limestone pavers, she settled on the chaise longue. How long had it been since she and Bryce had sat out here together, just the two of them? The last time she could remember had to be two years ago, when he'd successfully negotiated a case involving a school administration that looked the other way when bullying was reported. With the boys down for the night, she and Bryce had snuggled up together on this very chair. Halfway through the bottle of Grand Cru, they'd made love under the stars. She tried to remember the feel of those citrusy champagne bubbles on her tongue, and Bryce's lips on hers. It had been a magical night, followed by a killer hangover. As soon as Bryce had left for work, she'd called her mother to give her a hand with the kids so she could sleep. Alice never questioned how she'd been the only family member to come down with the flu.

At first the idea of going to AA had filled her with shame, but the morning after celebrating a little too much at Zan's last birthday party, she'd known she needed help. At the first meeting, Shelly, the woman with crazy spiky hair, had offered to be her sponsor, but Lexi hadn't taken her up on it. Not then, anyway. She made it to eight or nine meetings, and then, like everyone else in the room, she'd convinced herself she had this little drinking problem licked. So when Zan had made a pitcher of apple martinis, she'd tried one. And another. The next day, while she still felt like hell, she'd found the spiky-haired woman's phone number and called.

Since she'd successfully hidden her drinking from Bryce, there was no reason to tell him she'd quit. Shelly said not telling him was playing with fire. She tried to convince her being totally honest with her husband was essential to her recovery, but Lexi didn't buy it. She had her own way of doing things, which meant she had a nonalcoholic wine with dinner whenever he had the real thing. However, once in a while, when he asked her to fix him a Manhattan, she'd take a little taste before handing it to him. He liked scotch, too, but the smell of it, especially now, made her feel ill.

Buying the sherry for a seafood pasta recipe—after pouring the rest of the previous bottle down the sink—had created this new dilemma, but thanks to morning sickness, she wasn't too tempted by it. In fact, she realized, this would be an ideal time to get rid of it all, when it didn't take much to make her queasy. Padding into the kitchen, she opened the top cupboard and withdrew the half-empty bottle of sherry from its hiding place behind the cereal boxes. Suddenly, she felt the presence of someone else in the kitchen. It took her half a second to realize it wasn't Bryce.

Courtney stood only an arm's length away. Her pale hair looked ghostly in the semi-darkness.

Lexi let out a little yip. Suddenly she heard a crashing sound and felt sticky liquid spatter on her feet and shins, accompanied by a quick, sharp pain. For a fraction of a second, she wondered if her water had broken, and then she realized she'd let the bottle slip from her fingers.

"Don't move." Courtney ran to the sink, wetting the dish towel to help mop up the mess, starting with Lexi's bare feet. "No, stay there 'til I get you some shoes."

"In the mudroom." Lexi grabbed the towel and wiped her shins before sliding her feet into the rubber gardening shoes Courtney fetched. Together they wiped the floor with fresh, soapy water. Lexi said, "I was just seeing how much sherry I have left for a recipe." She didn't look Courtney in the face.

"Oh." Her tone was flat, noncommittal.

She felt fury and humiliation rising in her throat. How had she allowed herself to open her house to this person? Because of that blind act of kindness, she was now under scrutiny in her own home. She thought about the bottles in Bryce's office. She also had a vodka bottle in the laundry room and one of bourbon hidden in a large vase. How long would it take this girl to find them all? Who was she, a homeless bartender and college dropout, to judge her, anyway?

"Oh, you're bleeding." Courtney tore a paper towel off the roll and ran it under the faucet.

Sure enough, a red trickle came from a small cut on her shin. "I must have caught a shard when the bottle broke." She took the wet towel and wiped the blood away.

"Listen, I really appreciate what you're doing for me," Courtney said.

Lexi felt the dynamics shift. She looked into the girl's face and saw none of the judgment she expected to see. The girl actually looked tentative and awkward. "C'mon, let's sit on the patio," Lexi said. "Can I offer you a glass of sherry?"

It took a beat for Courtney to realize she was making fun of herself. Suddenly, they were both laughing. Sitting outside together, Lexi wondered what it would take for them to totally trust each other. She knew she had her secrets. Maybe Courtney had her own, too. "Is this situation too weird for you?" she asked.

Courtney took her time. She bowed her head and her chest rose and fell with her breath. "I don't know how to answer." She looked up. The patio light illumined her on one side, giving the impression she had only half a face. "I don't know what you've been told about me. Or my mom."

There was a fine but important distinction between cautious and cagey, Lexi thought. She wanted to put the girl at ease. "Your father loved you," she said truthfully. "I think he may have loved your mother, too. It was a sticky subject with us. He told me he would've married her, but she didn't want him." Just saying the words, she started to picture the two of them together. That never came to a good end.

Courtney swiveled her head to face Lexi. Both sides of her face were lit. "Is that what he told you?"

She was surprised to hear the shakiness of the girl's voice. "You have a different version?" Why had she opened that can of worms?

"My mom said when she got pregnant, he offered to marry her out of pity. If you knew my mom, you'd know how much she hates being pitied. She said no and he never asked again because she'd released him from doing the right thing."

Lexi crossed her legs, bouncing her foot as she thought. "But she turned him down."

"How would you feel? What if you got pregnant and you tested him like that and he failed."

"I did. I was." She wrapped her arms around her waist. "I got pregnant and we got married." Why was she telling her this? She'd never even told her sister. "As soon as I told him, he asked if I was sure. The next day he said he'd marry me and I was thrilled. I miscarried ten days before the wedding and didn't tell him for two months."

"You tricked him."

She saw Courtney's eyes on her and felt hot with shame. It wasn't the first time she'd wondered if he married her out of duty or love.

It was a long time before Courtney said, "For my mom, she had all that doubt, but none of the support you got. The harder life got, the more she resented the way he handled it. Yeah, she can talk all she wants about being independent, but she saw how all that hurt me when other kids had dads. Even the divorced dads came and took their kids out to do fun things."

Lexi's cheeks burned. Courtney had uncovered a truth about Bryce and, by extension, Lexi. Even when she and Bryce were dating, she could see he was neglecting his daughter. For Bryce, his daughter was, more often than not, an afterthought. And Lexi never pushed it, because, to be honest, it was more convenient to think of family as the four of them. If Bryce was unkind to Courtney, then Lexi was complicit. And Courtney knew it.

"Mom was always looking out for me, and she hated to see your sons getting all his attention."

Lexi was instantly on guard. "Do you resent them? My children?" She couldn't read the look on Courtney's face.

Upstairs, one of the boys yelled out.

"That's BJ," said Lexi as she jumped up. "He's been having nightmares." She rushed up the stairs.

Sitting straight up in bed, her older son continued to yell even after his mother came in. His face was florid and she tried to pull him to her. He wriggled in her arms as she tried to rock him back to sleep. On the other bed, Brian had his knees to his chest and his thumb in his mouth.

"I'm here. BJ, you were just having a bad dream."

He pulled away. "No, it wasn't a dream," he said adamantly. "Daddy came. He was sitting right there." He pointed to the foot of his bed.

Her eyes stung with tears. "Dreams can seem very real," she said as she stroked his silky hair. "It's a nice way to talk to him, though, isn't it?" When Brian crept across the space between the two beds, she gathered him into the hug. His thumb never left his mouth.

"He's here!" BJ suddenly sprang from her grasp. Rushing to the door, he stopped, his shoulders sagging. "Oh, it's just my sister."

Courtney picked him up and snuggled him. "Hey, big boy, I believe you. You saw your dad." He nodded his head vigorously and pointed again to the spot on the bed.

"I believe you," she repeated. "Even if you're the only one who saw him. He just wants you to know he's very proud of you and loves you even when he's not here. Both of you." She smiled at Brian.

Long after the boys were asleep, Lexi pondered what had happened. Courtney hadn't needed words to tell her how she felt about the boys. Not only was there no resentment, but she'd come to protect them and share their grief. Delroy and her mother and sister had been right. She'd been right to open her home to this young woman, whose loss of a father was no less than that of her half-brothers.

After what she'd seen tonight, she might even be able to open her heart.

45

What's the rush?" Alice stood with her hands on her hips. "Can't you wait for Zan to go with you?"

Lexi looked at her feet and shook her head. "I've been steeling myself and the boys for it."

"Do you think you can handle it? The boys are too young to understand, anyway. You could wait 'til next weekend. Then your father and I can go with you."

Three objections in three seconds. Impressive. "Mom, stop. I wasn't asking your permission. I know I can't pilot the *Wayward Wind* by myself. I know my limitations. Courtney is coming, too."

Alice tilted her head. The worry lines on her face smoothed. "Well, that's something, I guess."

Brian flapped his way through the living room in his cape and undershorts.

"What do you have on your head?"

He answered on his second pass, telling her it was a crown.

Recognizing the terry sweatband from her jazzercise class, she told him to stay out of her gym bag. She didn't bother to tell him Superman didn't wear a crown.

Alice slowly shook her head. "Listen, Lexi, you can see what you're dealing with. They're a handful in their own house. Just imagine them on the boat."

"Well, you know what? I have that covered. I just talked to Louise, the boater who found Bryce—you met her at the visitation—and it turns out she's in Red Wing this weekend. She offered to help and I took her up on it. She's going with us."

"Why would you call her when you have family?"

"She's offering to pilot the boat, not auditioning to be part of our family. Anyway, she's the one who called me. When I told her about scattering the ashes, she came up with the solution. It was like an answer to prayer. She's really a very nice person, Mom."

Lexi was confident she'd made the right decision. This morning Courtney had said something about how her mother, Mallory, was both her biggest cheerleader and the voice of self-doubt. Lexi had been caught off guard by her own tears. "That's exactly how it is with me and my mom," she'd said. In that moment, she'd gotten a glimpse into what it must have been like to be raised by Mallory. Lexi had never quite trusted the woman, and could well imagine how she'd poisoned Courtney's mind against Bryce and Lexi and her half-brothers. Maybe it was just her pregnancy hormones giving her such strong maternal feelings for Bryce's daughter.

Alice looked displeased with her. "Mom, I don't get you," Lexi said. "You've been bugging me to take Courtney in to help with the kids. I thought you'd be happy."

Alice turned her head to look at the latest family photo on the mantle. She sighed.

"Bryce would have wanted all his children there." Yesterday, that statement may have sounded silly, based on the fact he'd never troubled himself to get them all together. But as soon as she said it, she knew it was true.

46

This was the worst time for her, lying in bed, unable to sleep because of the Memory. Courtney tried in vain to convince herself what she'd done had been justified, that any normal person might act the same way. She even tried to pretend it hadn't happened at all. As soon as she thought she'd shoved away the memory, her imagination reclaimed it in an attempt to alter the reality so that in the end, her father was still alive.

Deep down she knew she'd crossed a line and her eternal punishment was the insistent memory that could hijack her thoughts at odd moments throughout the day, and burst inside her eyelids in Technicolor when she tried to sleep.

It always began with this image.

The sun is high in the sky and wind gusts make it increasingly harder to keep the boat on course. There's tension between them. One moment they're father and daughter, captain and mate, and then a critical word or expression would tap into her reservoir of resentment and she'd react with defensiveness. He'd treat her reaction as insubordination and react accordingly. Then they'd both stand down, lapsing back into something that resembles kinship.

They don't talk for a while and it feels good to just be on the water with him. After a while he starts lecturing about how pulleys work and explaining the mechanics of airflow across sails. She can only listen so long to that know-it-all mindset of his. "I'm not five years old," she tells him, and points out his habit of over-explaining. He reacts by giving her the silent treatment, and when conversation resumes, his sentences are clipped.

"You need to tie that off so the tail isn't dangling," he says, pointing to a hank of rope hanging on a mast cleat.

"Which rope do you mean?" she asks without thinking.

"Not a rope! Call it a line, for God's sake!" His lips curl ever so slightly, just enough to reveal an attitude of contempt before masking it again.

"My boyfriend calls it a rope." She doesn't actually think that's true, but she wants to deprive him of any more ammunition. "Devin's been teaching me to sail on Lake Michigan."

He stops and gives her a look, his eyes widening theatrically. "That's exactly the crap you'll have to cut out if you want to prove to me you're serious about your education. You don't have time for sailing lessons."

She's instantly reduced to a child.

"You need to be single-minded." There's something so arrogant the way his eyebrows arch. "No fun and games. How do you think I managed to graduate with honors?"

She looks over the top of her sunglasses at him. "Uh, yeah, except for that little walk on the wild side that ended with you getting Mom pregnant." The dark look that comes over his face gives her a brief moment of triumph.

He glowers without looking directly at her and tells her to take the wheel. He checks the tautness of the line she just secured, and unable to find fault with her work, takes back his post at the wheel and falls silent again.

It would be hard, but she could let it go. Instead she stretches out on the starboard deck cushion, thinking up dialogue to put him in his place. She imagines after his initial response, he'll break down and beg forgiveness for being a shitty father. But what if he really doesn't care about her? What *if he says he doesn't need the aggravation of having a mouthy, ungrateful daughter like her? What if he goes back to his real family and never even misses her in his life?*

Knowing she's working herself into a red heat, she forces herself to rein in her thoughts. Taking deep breaths, she stares at the water. Her heart rate begins to slow. Just off the shore, a great blue heron wades, stabbing the water with its long beak and coming up with a fish it dispatches before stabbing again.

Call in morn." Cate's abbreviated text didn't specify who was supposed to call whom, and judging by the time stamp, she'd sent the message and then turned off her phone to get uninterrupted sleep. Knowing Cate, she'd seized on some new theory.

Robin tried to discern the tone, whether casual or urgent, from those ten letters. Her mind started whirring away on the possibilities until she was wide awake. It looked like her streak of insomnia was going to continue. The more she thought about it, the more she came to see their intense interest in Bryce's death as lunacy. What did they have to go on, really? A death that was in all probability an accident, a flawed memory about the gate, which may or may not have been unlatched when she and Louise checked on the boat, and an unidentifiable blob in the water that sort of resembled a human head.

Then there were Cate's dreams. For every dream or hunch that later proved to be true, there were dozens that led nowhere. On the other hand, the fact that the dream recurred, with added details each time, weighed in favor of it being significant. If it hadn't been for those dreams, Cate and Louise wouldn't have gone to the visitation on reconnaissance, she wouldn't have photographed the trio of dark-haired suspects, and they wouldn't have interrogated the waiter at Nosh. If his description of the girl hadn't dovetailed with their wild theory and Cate's dreams, they would have all breathed a sigh of relief and let the whole matter drop.

Robin was left with her thoughts as she sat in the dark, her two cats sprawled across her thighs. When she finally went to bed, sleep was elusive, as she knew it would be, and as it usually happened on such nights, she drifted off to sleep at just before dawn and woke to the alarm a couple of hours later.

Before rolling out of bed, Brad commented on her restless night. As an obstetrician he knew her hot flashes and night sweats were common to women her age. He also knew they'd perversely gotten worse since her oncologist put her on hormone therapy.

"You should try having a hot flash sometime. It's like panic attacks with heat."

"A small price to pay to keep you alive," he said. His tousled hair made him look boyish. "I woke up feeling like I was sleeping with three little furnaces. Maybe we should try keeping the cats out of the bedroom."

As if they understood him, Samson and Delilah set up a yowling that almost drowned out her response. "Do you really think they'd allow that? This is exactly what we'd be listening to all night." She bolted out of bed and asked Brad to feed them.

Showered and dressed, she and her husband sat at the kitchen table and talked over freshly brewed coffee. Through the open windows came the rich earthy smell from last night's rain. The grass and trees had greened up since yesterday. From her windowsill perch, Delilah lashed her tail.

When the coffee urn was empty, Brad went to the garage, giving her a chance to call Cate, who said she and Louise had survived the storm and were having coffee on the boat.

Samson jumped up next to Delilah, and soon their tails twitched in unison. Robin went to the window to see what had caught their attention, but didn't see a thing. "Did Simon conjure up any phantoms yesterday?"

"As a matter of fact, he did. Turns out yesterday was the anniversary of the *Sea Wing*'s demise."

She paused. "I never made the connection."

"Neither did I."

"So what happened? What did you see? I'm all ears."

Cate said only that they'd been caught out on the lake during the storm and Simon's instruments had gone berserk. "We got more than we bargained for, but I'll have to fill you in later. I need to tell you about something else."

What could trump a ghost sighting, she wondered, annoyed at the abrupt change of topic. Cate launched into telling her about Lexi's invitation to go out on the *Wayward Wind*. When she paused for a breath, Robin jumped in. "Wait! You're going out on the boat with Lexi. Are you out of your mind?"

"Louise is going. I wasn't invited."

"Invited?" Robin groaned. "Are you kidding?"

"The two boys and Courtney are going, too. Even if Lexi's the bad guy, she's not going to pull anything with her kids on board. Louise thinks it's an ideal opportunity."

"For what? What does she think is going to happen? A confession? A reenactment of the crime?"

Cate laughed and relayed her words to Louise, who laughed even louder. "She says she'll be able to get a read on their dynamics and maybe pick up some clues. Honestly, I think the request is legit. It makes total sense for those four to dispose of Bryce's ashes, and for them to scatter the ashes from the boat he loved."

"She hardly knows Louise. Why wouldn't she ask her sister, for instance?"

"They're not boaters, Robin. Certainly not for a boat that size."

Something didn't feel right. "But why Louise?"

"Because Louise said to call her if she needed anything. Lexi knows Louise is a boater and asked her to take them out for a private ceremony. Listen, Robin, I don't think we need to worry about Lexi. Louise will be in control of the boat. What could go wrong?"

"Did you really just say those words?"

"Yeah, I see your point."

"Let me talk to her." As soon as Louise got on, Robin said, "Are you nuts? You're voluntarily getting on the boat with one of our prime suspects? Do I need to remind you the *Wayward Wind* has already claimed one life?"

Louise's chuckle infuriated her. This must be how Brad felt each time she made a rash decision that put her in danger.

"We're just going to motor out. No sails. No chance of the boom swinging."

Just then Brad poked his head in the door to announce he was about to take off. Early in their marriage Robin had wished he'd spend more time with family, but she'd grown to appreciate her own friends, especially the No Ordinary Women, and was glad he had a regular tee time for eighteen holes of golf with his buddies, including Cate's husband, Erik.

"Everything okay with Cate?" he asked from the open door.

"She said there'd been no storm damage and all was well. I may pop down there for the day." She tried to sound casual.

He leaned his head against the doorframe, his hand on the handle and his mouth open—a bit of theater to make the point. "Damn it, Robin, I know that look. If you're thinking of doing something stupid, I'm going to put my foot down."

She giggled. "Your feet are down."

"Very funny."

"Furthermore, I never actually plan to do anything stupid."

"That's so comforting." His words were full of sarcasm. "What's going on?"

She smiled. "You're going to hang out with your friends and I'm going to hang out with mine. Honestly, I don't know what you're worried about."

"Fine. Whatever." He scowled, backed down the steps and pulled the door shut with more force than necessary.

She watched his car pass the window and breathed a sigh of relief. The conversation continued in her head as a monologue—*Make one little error in judgment and you treat me like a child/Give me credit for learning from my mistakes/You're concerned about me but I'm worried about my friends and there's safety in numbers.* She wouldn't have had to tell him anything. She'd be there and back in time to make dinner.

By the time she turned onto Highway 50, she'd convinced herself there truly was nothing to worry about. Not when she was surrounded by her intrepid friends. Just as she pulled into the marina parking lot, the loud ring of her cell phone startled her. The caller spoke in a hoarse whisper. "Don't get out of the car."

The sinister command made her skin crawl. "Who is this?"

"Robin, it's me. You just passed me."

"Cate! Why are you whispering?" She peered into the trees.

"Because I don't want anyone to see me."

What the hell? She searched the parked cars. "Cate, what—?"

"Don't sit there spinning your head around trying to find me. You look like Linda Blair."

"Who?"

"In *The Exorcist.*"

Clearly Cate had lost her mind. "What's going on? Where are you?"

"Behind a tree. Louise went into town. Just after she left, Mallory showed up and went on the boat."

"She was on our boat?"

"No, the *Wayward Wind*. Then Courtney came. It must've been her boyfriend who dropped her off."

"What's with all the secrecy?"

"There's something weird going on. Courtney and her mother are in the tepee now, and it looks like they're arguing."

Robin remembered Louise showing them the tented poles toward the end of the park.

"You have to go in there."

Robin understood immediately. As the only one Courtney and Mallory hadn't met, she was in the best position to eavesdrop. She got out and walked toward the metal structure—three slanting white poles crossing near the apex to resemble a tepee. As she sauntered to the near side of the circle, the mother and daughter stopped talking and were looking at her. Turning her back to them, she pretended to read the historic information set into the low stone wall. All was quiet. She moved to read the next plaque.

"Don't be a fool."

Robin jumped. The clarity of those words gave the impression the two were standing inches away. Then she remembered Louise telling them about the tepee's unusual acoustics, and her breathing returned to normal.

"She'll go right to the police."

Robin stopped breathing. When the other responded, the words were muffled but the tone was undeniably contentious, and then the first speaker said, "Do not get on that boat." There was a pause. "Just say you changed your mind." She didn't pick up on all the words that followed, but one of them was "secret" and the other was "snoop."

"She's not paying any attention to us. You're being paranoid."

They were talking about her! Aiming for nonchalance, she wandered back the way she came, looking sideways to see if she could spot Cate. She followed the edge of the parking lot, past the docks leading to the Louise's boat and Bryce's, resisting the urge to look back. Up ahead, partially hidden by trees, was the public bathroom. Walking around it, she stood under the overhang and pulled out her phone, about to hit the "Call Back" button when she realized if Cate's phone rang, it would give away her hiding place. It would be safer to send a text. "Mother worried about police finding out," she wrote.

"I knew it!" Cate texted back immediately. "Yikes, I think they're headed toward you."

Ducking into the bathroom, she stepped into the last stall. When she heard them come in, she peeked through the crack in the door to see Courtney going into the next stall. Although she couldn't see Mallory's face, she saw long fingers gripping the sink. Robin waited. Soon Courtney exited the stall, and as she washed her hands, her mother touched her cheek and said, "What good purpose could it possibly serve? What's done is done."

Cate saw Courtney's reflection. Tears rolled down both cheeks.

"I'll take the blame myself if I have to," said Mallory.

As soon as mother and daughter were gone, Robin wanted to tell Cate. Pulling the phone out of her pocket, she heard a splash. Her reading glasses had fallen into the toilet. There was no way she was sticking her hand in a public toilet for a pair of cheap drug store glasses. In the dim light, she texted Cate about her new theory.

C ate stared at Robin's message on her screen. "Now I hinky it scooter," it said. She read the autocorrected message again, and despite the potentially serious situation, she giggled.

"Huh?" she texted back.

The voices came from her left. She checked to make sure her phone was muted.

Courtney and Mallory passed no more than twenty feet from where she stood, so absorbed in conversation that they didn't notice her.

"We'll lose everything," the older woman said.

"We? This is not about you, Mom. Besides, I've already lost everything, anyway."

"You have me. All I've ever done is try to protect you. I'm begging you not to do it." Mallory's body language was eloquent as she jerked away from her daughter's outstretched hand. "Maybe Lexi can give you a ride. Oh, wait, you live with her now. How convenient." Striding to the parking lot, she got into a car. Her squealing tires announced her departure.

Cate observed how Courtney's posture changed. Shoulders squared, the young woman proceeded to the dock, following it down to the *Wayward Wind*. She stood there for several minutes. It seemed she might turn and run, but instead she hopped aboard and stood, statue-still. A minute later, she moved forward in the cockpit, stretching her arm out to touch something, jerking it back before her hand made contact with the boom.

Cate shrieked when a hand encircled her arm. She whipped her head around to see the heart-shaped face and short blondish hair of her friend. "Look at Courtney. She's freaking out," Robin said. "You got my text. What do you think?"

"It was very interesting," Cate said.

"I don't think Louise should go out with them, do you?" They both had their eyes on Courtney, who was scrambling off the boat like she'd seen a ghost.

"I don't know. I depends on what you mean by 'I hinky it scooter.'"

Robin looked at her as if she were an alien. "What?" She looked at her phone, squinting to see the message she'd sent. "My glasses fell in the toilet."

They both jumped when a horn honked.

Louise leaned out the window and called out to them. "You two look like trouble on a stick. What are you up to?" She stepped out. "I had this harebrained thought that we should make an occasion of this, something festive. I mean, the boys can scarcely understand their father is not coming back, and they certainly can't equate him with a box of dust." She showed them a paper sleeve holding yellow and red roses. "Maybe this way they'll have positive memories."

Cate asked for an explanation.

"I read up on it. Cremains aren't just powder, they're more like coarse sand with recognizable bone fragments. I already talked to Lexi and she liked the idea of divvying up the ashes into four portions and mixing them with flower petals. That way they'll remember scattering rose petals rather than a handful of fillings and chunks of bone."

"It sounds lovely." Cate stuck her nose in the bouquet and inhaled.

Yes, lovely," Robin said, not concealing her impatience. "But we need to talk. I think we've got it all wrong about Lexi. I was in the bathroom and I overheard Courtney and her mother talking."

"Oh, here they are!" Louise turned away. "Over here!" she said, waving to Lexi as she drove up in her SUV.

Courtney materialized, opening the back door and freeing the boys from their car seats.

Robin elbowed Louise. "She's the one to watch out for." She gave a nod in Courtney's direction.

49

Abandoning her car near the other end of Bay Point Drive, Mallory wandered through the park, working her way to the docks, oblivious to the beauty of the town across the bay, the puffy clouds in a blue sky, and the boats cutting through the water. Instead, her mind was traveling along the familiar, well-worn path of her past.

Long ago she'd reconciled herself to Bryce's absence from their lives. He'd been astonishingly compliant in letting her raise their baby alone. There had been one brief and dismal attempt at reconciliation, which ended when his car was broadsided by a tractor on a country road—on the passenger side, naturally. Bryce had walked away unscathed, while Mallory had suffered a concussion and Courtney, a toddler at the time, had begun having night terrors. Even then she knew it was a metaphor for their lives.

He moved on, and by the time he chose someone else to share his life, Mallory no longer wanted to marry him, but seeing Lexi, a younger version of herself, made her feel discarded like yesterday's fish. She'd been reasonable, though. For Courtney's sake, she allowed father and daughter to create their tenuous bond.

And now her beautiful Courtney, a child who'd always been softhearted, was devastated to think she'd smashed that bond to smithereens. She claimed she'd never get over her part in his death, but she was young. People got over things. It would have been un-derstandable if, in the heat of the moment, she'd lashed out impul-sively, but his death had been no more than an accident. In Mallory's experience, Bryce had been easy to love but hard to like. So the fact he'd accidentally died in the very act of making disparaging com-ments . . . well, it was downright poetic.

Courtney would come to see it that way, too, if she could resist long enough the urge to unburden herself to someone else. What possible good could come of that? Who would show leniency if she admitted leaving the scene of an accident? She, Mallory, was the only one who needed to know. In time, Courtney would forgive her-self and get on with her life.

Grass gave way to paved playground. A young woman clapped as her son came down the slide. A little girl in polka-dot overalls hung from the monkey bars, her father at her side to catch her when her arms grew tired. Mallory watched them until her eyes stung with angry tears.

Past this tableau, a line of trees blocked her view, and beyond that, another row. When she could get a good view of the parking lot where she'd left her daughter, she saw Lexi and the boys had ar-rived and were surrounded by Courtney and three others. Mallory recognized the poufy platinum hair, partially concealed by a fishing hat with a chinstrap. She couldn't remember her name—Lou or Lou Ann, something like that—and she was talking to Courtney and Lexi as if they were old friends, and showing them a bouquet of flowers. She'd been at the funeral home, as had the tall, slender one who wore her hair in a long braid that made Mallory think she might be part Indian. Just as she had at the visitation, Mallory was unnerved by a sense of déjà vu, as if she'd already dreamt this day.

With a jolt, she realized the third woman was the same one eavesdropping on them in the tepee. The big fancy camera hanging around her neck made her look like a newspaper photographer. An investigator, maybe. She didn't want to think what that might mean.

Bryce's sons, the heirs apparent, were squirmy bundles of energy. One jumped on the pavement like a crazed kangaroo, then stuck his arms out and airplaned in ever widening circles. His older brother bolted in the direction of the boats, but Courtney caught him up with one arm and brought him back to the fold. How natural her daughter was with them, she thought. Not like Mallory had been as a mother—self-conscious and uneasy.

The group started moving toward the dock. When they arrived at the *Wayward Wind,* she held her breath. She willed her daughter to stay on dry land, but Courtney hopped aboard with no hesitation. Platinum Pouf stood behind the wheel and began checking out the instrumentation. Courtney and Lexi slipped small lifevests on the boys and then donned their own.

Black Braid and Camera hung back on the dock, untying the lines and tossing them to Courtney's waiting hands. It took a while for them to actually leave, and then the *Wayward Wind* slowly backed away from the dock, and with a little rudder and shot of gas, turned, bending around the point and into the river. The two women scurried over to watch the sailboat's progress, walking dangerously close to her. Mallory melted into the shade of the trees, from where she could observe them observing, one through her camera and the other through binoculars.

50

Louise navigated past a string of shoals on either side, conscious of the deeper draft of the sailboat. She'd been distracted just before they left, but now Cate's words came back to her. She'd said Courtney was the one to look out for. Only now Louise understood what she'd meant by it. Cate wanted Louise to look out for Courtney's safety, because the person who wished to do her harm was on this boat. What had she gotten herself into?

To make matters worse, Dean had informed her this morning that scattering cremains on the river might be in violation of state law and the Federal Clean Water Act. She hadn't bothered asking Lexi if she'd gotten permission. A bit late for that now. Overriding caution and lawfulness, she decided as long as they didn't do it in plain view, it would be okay.

Despite all their theories of a dark-haired murderess, Louise felt remarkably comfortable with Lexi on board, that is, until Lexi started talking about how she hadn't been much older than BJ when she'd begun acting in community theater. They had that in common, and for just a second she thought she'd found a kindred spirit, but then it occurred to her that a good actor was capable of great deception. Her eyes flicked from Lexi to Courtney to the boys and back again. The two woman appeared to be polite, respectful, even warm with each other, but was it a façade?

She groaned inwardly. Why, in the name of Common Sense, had she agreed to this? It was her nature to help, but surely by this age she should be able to say no to a badly conceived plan. And yet here she was, steering an unfamiliar boat full of people she scarcely knew, one of whom might be a murderer. And on top of all that, they were all about to commit a potentially illegal act.

They motored past the populated areas of Red Wing. The boats in their vicinity weren't terribly close. "Let me know when you want me to stop," she said.

BJ sat sideways on the bench, legs bent, forehead resting on folded arms. Courtney ran her fingertips across his shoulders. "Doin' okay, buddy?" she asked. He threw his head back, bucking against her touch. "I counted two eagles already," she said as if they were having a normal conversation. Sticking his lower lip out, he gave her a fishy stare. Courtney smiled when he tilted his head to look up. Without saying a word, he lifted a stubby finger to point at a treetop where a hawk was landing. "You're a great birdwatcher," his sister said.

On the other side of the cockpit, Brian let his legs dangle so he could bang his heels against the vertical wall of the bench. Lexi put an arm around him, pulling him closer, but his feet continued to beat a tattoo against the fiberglass molding. Looking around, she chewed on the corner of her lip. "You said it's too far to the spot where . . . where you found him, right?"

Louise nodded. "Right." She and Lexi had gone over this. Yes, it was much too far, especially considering her unfamiliarity with the boat, and the energy it would take to ride herd on the boys. But even if it were close by, she had no desire to return to the place she and Cate and Simon had run into that freak storm. Just thinking about the unearthly keening, she felt her skin prickle and looked down to see goosebumps.

"I think anywhere is good, as long as it's on the lake," Courtney said.

Lexi agreed. "Yes, anywhere on the lake. It's the place he loved most."

Louise picked up on the bitter undertones of that statement. She had to strain to hear Courtney's reply. "Don't let it make you resentful," the girl said. "I've seen what that does to a person."

Louise slowed the engine. "How about here?"

Courtney nodded and picked up her plastic bag. Lexi looked nauseated. She swiped a hand across her mouth and said, "Let's do this."

Louise checked the wind and directed them to the port side so the ashes wouldn't blow back on them. The family leaned over the side and tossed the contents of their bags into the wind. They were able to track the flow of ashes in the water by watching the flower petals dancing on the surface.

Whatever apprehensions she'd had, Louise was pleased at the resulting catharsis. She tried to fix this image in her mind, the trail of red and yellow petals, the family—three with shiny black hair, one whose hair was white-blonde, all of them relaxing, smiling, bonding at the end of this important rite, forming a new kind of family. She noticed the wind riffling through Courtney's short hair, with its dark roots and white tips. How odd hair trends could be, she thought. For years she and her friends who colored their hair had spent a lot of money keeping their roots from showing, and now the younger generation spent even more money doing this bi-color thing.

She's the one to look out for. Look out for Courtney! She looked again at Courtney's cute, short, mostly white hair. With dark roots. Louise's breathing quickened. Why had it never occurred to them to include Courtney among the suspects? Had they all been so easily fooled by a bottle of bleach and a pair of scissors?

247

"Where did the flowers go?" BJ asked, trying to peek over the side with Courtney hanging onto him by his lifevest.

The petals were no longer visible.

Lexi cupped her hand on the back of his head. "They're on their way to the ocean."

"Why?" he asked.

"Because that's where rivers go."

"You mean on vacation?" Brian asked.

The adults stifled their laughter. Lexi said, "In a way, yes. The ocean is all the way down by Florida. Remember when we went on vacation to Florida?"

Florida, Key West. Vacation. Dancing women. Earlier, Louise couldn't recall the name of the place people gathered to watch sunsets. She remembered now. She'd just shown her friends pictures she'd taken there. The nude Matisse dancers were in Mallory Square!

She grabbed her phone. She had to tell Cate.

51

For a few minutes, Mallory lost sight of the women who stayed behind, and then she saw them circling back. She saw their feet, anyway, one pair clad in wedge sandals, hot pink and turquoise, and the other in well-worn Birkenstocks, the old style, with two brown straps. The two walked down one of the docks and boarded a cabin cruiser.

Returning to her car, Mallory opened the trunk and pulled out her gym bag. In the bathroom, she changed into tight jogging capris and long tee-shirt, and exchanged sandals for tennis shoes. She glanced behind her to make sure no one was in the stall, and in that instant, she recalled that just before she and Courtney left the bathroom, she'd noticed a pair of shoes in the stall. They were Birkenstocks with two brown straps.

It was no coincidence. She was one of them and they were suspicious. She could see it so clearly now. How long had they been watching the boat? What else had they seen? Did they know about Courtney? She replayed her conversation with Courtney in the tepee. The photographer couldn't have heard that. Not like in the bathroom, when she was trying to convince Courtney not to tell Lexi how her father died. But what had they said, exactly? She closed her eyes and put a hand over her heart. She'd told her daughter she'd take the fall for her? Not in those exact words, but whatever she'd said, it was incriminating.

The crones definitely suspected, otherwise they wouldn't be following her and Courtney around, showing up at the funeral home, at the tepee, the bathroom. That wasn't the end of their meddling, either. Platinum Pouf was even intruding on scattering Bryce's ashes, something that should've been a private family affair.

She leaned against the wall and hung her head, which was whirling with desperate thoughts. She breathed deeply, as her therapist had taught her, and tried to focus on one thing at a time. "Quit worrying and make a plan," she was fond of saying. Mallory had spent several hours doing just that. Courtney must never take the blame for her father's death.

She'd woken yesterday thinking about Bryce's promise to provide for Courtney in his will. Maybe he'd meant to, but in fact, he hadn't. Maybe Lexi talked him out of it. She seemed like the type to be ashamed of her husband's love child. Pampered and self-absorbed, she'd acted as if Courtney didn't exist at all. And then, suddenly, she invited Courtney to live with her. There was only one reason and that was to keep Courtney from contesting the will. She'd magnanimously give her a place to live, flatter her and make her feel like part of the family, hoping she wouldn't sue for her share. There was nothing altruistic about it. She wouldn't be Family, she'd be the Help, nothing more than a cheap, live-in nanny.

Mallory leaned against the sink, almost dizzy with outrage. Don't get mad, get even—isn't that what they said? Well, as it turned out, Lexi had a little secret, and secrets could be exploited. She'd stayed up half the night until the wild thoughts coalesced. She had a plan, and she wasn't going to let a bunch of middle-aged snoops distract her from it. She wrapped a terry band around her hair and jammed a baseball cap over that before continuing with her plan.

She knew what she was doing wasn't totally above-board, but Lexi did make it all too easy. Besides, it was for her daughter's sake.

Courtney had given her useful information about Lexi's drinking without even realizing it. At the time, Mallory had known the little tidbits were significant, but was not yet aware what she was supposed to do with them.

While the Snoop Sisters were on the river side of the park, Mallory looked for Lexi's car. There were plenty of cars in the lot, yet she'd seen only a handful of people. Seeing all the empty slips, she understood. On a summer day like this, boaters went out early and returned to the marina late.

She saw a red SUV. As she got closer she saw two car seats in the back. Bingo. According to her daughter, Lexi was always guzzling iced tea or juice or energy drinks, and there, wedged into the holder in the console, was a giant plastic cup.

Crouching at the back bumper, she felt around underneath it and came up empty-handed, except for smudges of road dust. She found the magnetic key case in the second place she looked, in the right rear wheel well. Pulling on a pair of latex gloves, she opened the door, pulled the liter bottle of vodka from her gym bag and cracked the seal. Prying open the oversized car mug, she added a couple inches or so to the fruit punch and stirred the mixture with the straw. She took a sip and though she could detect the alcohol, the taste wasn't overpowering. Distracted by her kids, Lexi would automatically pick up the cup as she was driving, and drink it without noticing.

Slipping the bottle back into its brown paper bag, she jammed it under the front seat and relocked the door. After replacing the key in the wheel well, she paused behind the car long enough to memorize the license plate. It had all taken less than ten minutes. Returning to her own car, she flung her gym bag in the trunk and decided to wait near the docks for Courtney to return.

As she cut across the lot where Lexi's SUV was parked, she heard voices and recognized the two women coming toward her.

They were strolling at a leisurely pace, unaware of her presence. Ducking behind a conversion van, she bent and retied her shoe in case anyone should look her way.

The women paused very near to the van. One of them spoke her daughter's name.

"If it was an accident, why didn't she call for help? And why go to such lengths to conceal the fact she was there?" the other said.

How did they know? She started shaking.

"Wait, Louise just sent a text. Damn! It came a while ago. Why didn't it ring?"

"What is it?"

"Guess where the nude statues were. Mallory Square!"

The other one gasped. "It was Mallory! That's what she's telling us. I knew Courtney's mother had something to do with it. That woman gives me the creeps!"

"Oh, yeah, she looks like she eats her young."

One of the wretched women giggled and they started walking again.

Mallory slipped to the van's other side as they passed, getting a head rush when she stood up. The blood rushed back to her face, and she gripped the bracket of the sideview mirror to steady herself. The anger came in waves, throbbing hot in her throat, turning the sounds around her to white noise. Those bitches knew nothing about her. *She eats her young.* Other spiteful words out of other cruel mouths slithered into her mind. *Shriveled heart, unstable, irrational, calculating. Professional victim*—Bryce had called her that one the last time she tried to reason with him. Each remembered insult fueled her outrage.

The smug bitches continued walking, following the dock past the empty slip of the *Wayward Wind*, and to the end. Heedless, she followed them across the weathered boards. Ahead of her a long wooden oar leaned against a post. That kind of sloppiness would have sent Bryce into a ten-minute lecture, but to her it was providence. She picked it up.

She slowed down, stepping more carefully. The black-haired one she'd met at the funeral home pointed to something far away. The other one raised her camera. They didn't even look up. Raising the oar, she sliced it through the air like a baseball bat. She felt the wood shiver in her hands twice as she made contact with them both in one motion. Her yell, more like a war cry, blocked out any sounds they may have made. One slammed into the other and together they torpedoed into the water. She dropped the oar into the same vortex where they sank. They didn't come up.

She staggered backwards, for the first time taking in her surroundings. She stood in the open, surrounded by boats, yet nobody rushed to their aid. No one had seen it happen, a miracle that proved she'd done the right thing. The necessary thing. Shaking uncontrollably, she became aware of the sound of a motor, very close on her right. She stumbled toward the nearest boat, unsnapped a corner of its waterproof cover and clambered inside.

52

Cate knew she was in trouble, but she endured the shooting pain in her shoulder and clawed her way up. An instinctive gasp brought air to her burning lungs. Wiping her eyes, she looked for signs of Robin, not wanting to think what would happen to her if she'd lost consciousness. Her foot bumped into something. She plunged her face into the murky water, groping with one hand until she felt the object, seizing it and kicking to the top to see she'd found nothing more than an oar. Frantically, she continued to search for her friend.

Suddenly something seized her ankle and she shot up, spluttering, trying to rid her airway of lake water. Something bobbed to the surface next to her. Flailing her arms, Robin threw her head back, gasping like a fish on land. Cate reached out to her. Her fingers wrapped around something ropey and she pulled. Robin's face came closer, eyes wild as she tried to stay afloat.

Cate struggled. When they both went under, it was Robin who pushed Cate to the surface before she came up again, gagging and vomiting water. Cate watched helplessly and then suddenly everything started to go dark. *This is what people meant when they talked about blacking out*, Cate thought.

"Behind you," Robin croaked.

Alarmed, she turned and saw what had darkened her vision. They'd come up in deep shadow under the dock, protected on both sides by boats. Cate almost screamed out in pain when she slammed into a wooden post. Robin had latched onto a cross brace, still coughing to empty her lungs. Shoving off the post, Cate came to her side, hands touching as they held on. "What happened?" she said as soon as she caught her breath.

Robin shook her head and spluttered some more. "It just hit us," she managed to croak.

They both felt the vibrations of a boat's motor at the same time. Staring at each other in the gloom, they carried on a whispered conversation. Robin's first assumption was that something had fallen on them, but neither of them remembered any structure over their heads at the end of the dock. It took a minute for Cate to figure out the oar she'd discarded must have been the weapon. Robin remembered having a flash of realization that someone was behind them on the dock just before the attack.

The vibration became almost deafening in this closed space. Cate saw Robin's teeth were chattering. She mouthed words Cate couldn't make out. "Friend or foe?" Robin hollered into her ear.

Cate winced when she tried to shrug. The noise abated as the engine slowed and then shut off altogether. "Think that's the *Wayward Wind*?"

"It's the right direction," Robin answered, still shivering. She let go and paddled a few feet, and then a few more until she was in open water again. She turned to Cate, pointed to indicate she was going to investigate. Cate shook her head violently.

"Until everyone is accounted for, I'm not going anywhere," she said when Robin came back. "For all we know, Courtney's the one who tried to kill us."

Sounds drifted from the other dock, clunking and clattering, but human voices, too. The first she recognized belonged to the boys, and then they heard Louise's laugh. "Oh, thank God," Cate breathed. Until that moment she'd feared the worst, that their assailant may have failed to kill her and Robin, but had succeeded in murdering Louise.

Robin cut loose and swam toward the sailboat. Cate waited for a second, then gritted her teeth and kicked off.

53

Harsh, but necessary. Those stupid women couldn't see they'd put themselves in this mess. It wasn't a conscious decision. In fact, until she almost tripped over that oar, she hadn't known what would happen next. She thought she heard gasping and coughing in the water, but it couldn't have been the Snoop Sisters, not after she saw them practically fly through the air with the force of her blow and then get sucked into the vortex.

"Sometimes shit just happens," Mallory said in a low whisper. Often it soothed her and helped her organize her thoughts to say them out loud. Lying perfectly still under the stifling waterproof cover, she heard them get off the sailboat. She heard Courtney's voice.

It was so hot. She turned her face to the open corner of the boat cover. As long as she heard voices, she was trapped.

The sound was faint at first, more like a ringing in her ears that grew louder. When it became an unholy shriek, she couldn't mute it even when she pressed her hands over her ears. Sweat trickled from her forehead and stung her eyes. The shrieking swelled and then suddenly died down until it cut out altogether. A siren. So the police had come.

Don't panic, she told herself. *Think it through. What's your main objective?*

Lying flat on the padded bench, she reached up and closed the last snaps of the boat cover from the inside. She got the last snap just as footsteps thundered down the dock toward her. Two sets of footsteps. A man's voice spoke only feet from where she lay. "Okay, show me exactly where you were standing."

"I was here. Cate was on my right."

It wasn't possible! Her heart squeezed like a fist.

He kept asking questions, and she kept telling him by the time she was aware of someone else on the dock, it was too late.

They'd seen nothing at all. They were on the dock and in the water, and in between those two things there was pain. They couldn't identify her. Mallory relaxed, but just a little.

The man wanted her to be checked out by a doctor. She refused. "Can I go check on my friend now?" she asked. He must have allowed that because she went away. He stayed, and paced, and then he went away, too.

Voices on shore faded. Car engines started. The heat was oppressive. When she could wait no longer, she undid the snaps, eased back the heavy-duty fabric and cautiously stepped into the sunlight.

54

C ourtney gaped at them, unable to make sense of what she was witnessing. When two drenched women bobbed up between the two docks, yelling at Louise, she strained to hear their story. What she heard made her wonder if they were insane.

Someone had knocked these two in the water and one of them said her shoulder hurt. Courtney had been at enough parties where people got shoved into pools or lakes. Nobody actually got hurt. These were grown women making all this fuss. They didn't know who knocked them into the water. So what? She didn't always know who'd shoved her in. But then looking at Louise talking to these soggy, shivering, obviously frightened ladies, she knew there had to be more to the story. The three older women huddled on shore, talking to the policeman. They were totally wrapped up in their own drama.

Courtney was on one knee helping BJ take off his lifevest when Brian leapt on her back, bouncing as he demanded ice cream. "I am not a horse and I do not take orders from short people." She rolled to one side, catching him as he lost balance. "And you need to have better manners." She tried to look fierce.

Lexi said they should wait on shore. They found a shady spot in the grass where BJ and Brian could cavort. Lexi said they couldn't simply leave Louise and her friends, not after how much they'd helped. The shorthaired one was named was Robin. She still had a camera hanging from a strap. They'd met the taller one at the funeral home. Her name was Cate. When Louise helped her to her car, Cate held her arm close to her ribs with her other hand, and even though she laughed at something Louise said, Courtney could tell she was in a lot of pain. They left.

As soon as the sheriff's car pulled away, Robin left, too.

While Lexi and the boys played tag, Courtney walked back to the dock. This place held so much power for her, for good or for bad. She wanted to see the *Wayward Wind* one last time, alone. Without boarding the sailboat, she stared into the cockpit, imagining him at the helm. "I'd take it all back if I could," she said. She forced herself to remember this part.

The heron flaps its wings and sets down again a little farther down the shore. It peers into the water. Suddenly, with lightning speed, its neck snakes out, and its powerful beak spears another fish. The fish never saw it coming.

Turning against the wind, she feels one wisp of hair and then another escape the twisted knot on the crown of her head. She tries to reposition the large hair clip but even more black strands of hair whip across her vision. She probes the pockets of her cutoffs to see if she's been smart enough to bring an elastic band, but all she feels is her key ring. No need to check the waterproof case on a lanyard around her neck, either. All she has in there is her cell phone.

She can see he's still brooding. On any given day she can look in the mirror and see the same expression. If he's anything like her, right now he's humiliated by the way she's pointed out the flaw in his narrative and is searching for a way to even the score. His eyes settle on her sandals. She looks down, assuring herself the soles of her Keens haven't left dark marks on the deck. She's wearing the close-toed style for safety, so that can't be the problem.

But then his features relax and things seem okay again. For a time they sail in companionable silence. When she again caches him staring at her, his look is not unkind. "Just now you look so like your mother," he says. The corner of his mouth twitches.

"What happened?" she asks.

His head jerks up. "What do you mean?"

"With you and Mom?"

He shrugs. "I offered to marry her, you know. Did she tell you that?"

"You mean when she got pregnant." She presses a fist against her mouth, afraid she might say more.

"Up 'til then, we were kind of off again, on again. She was a free spirit that way. When she told me about the baby, we hadn't been together in, I guess it was a month or so. I wanted to do the right thing, but . . ." He rolls his lips inward and bites down.

"So what happened?" She watches his face for signs of deceit.

"She turned me down. She was so damn independent back then. She and her friends were all into that, you know. They were fierce and told each other they didn't need men to make them happy. She stood her ground, saying she didn't want anything from me. She wanted me to know she was perfectly capable of raising a child on her own. After a while I moved on."

She wracks her memory. "Bryce never loved me." She's heard that often enough, but she can't remember her mom ever saying she'd loved him.

"She even hinted I might not be the father, but we both knew I was. I am."

His account was similar to her mother's, and yet it sounded so different, almost reasonable, coming from him.

"As you know, her parents helped for the first year after you were born. But her damn feminist friends stayed true to form, independent. Not one of them stuck around to help her."

She has no memory of her grandparents' involvement in her upbringing. They were both sick for years. She has a picture in her head of her grandfather dragging around an oxygen tank. She remembers both her grandparents dying from lung cancer when she was in junior high.

It was about that time, she started noticing how different her life was from that of her friends, who had big family get-togethers and whose parents had social lives. Between her mother's jobs and studying to get her master's degree—which she never actually finished—she devoted most of her spare time to her daughter, who at some point wanted a life of her own. She couldn't say when Mallory went into her funk that lasted, oh, a few years.

She has to ask one more question. "Do you ever wonder what it would've been like if you and Mom had gotten married? Did you ever wish you'd raised me together?"

He takes a long time to answer, and when he does, the answer leaves her far from satisfied. "I was selfish, I guess. I could see my future being stolen from me, but I still tried to do the right thing."

How magnanimous of you, she almost says.

He says, "Did she tell you where we met? We were at the same rally to protest the Gulf War. Everyone was chanting 'No blood for oil,' and I looked over and saw this raven-haired beauty. She looked right at me and started yelling, 'Make love, not war!' I was hooked." He grins.

She gets the feeling he's wanted to tell his side of the story for years.

"We were both young. I thought for a while I loved her, but it was probably just lust. She was beautiful and impulsive, which made her wildly interesting." His expression darkens. "But then she became more, I guess you'd say, erratic."

She can attest to that. She remembers shortly after her grandparents died, Mallory took her on a surprise road trip, packing for an overnight or two. But on day four, when they arrived at the Grand Canyon, they both had to buy clothes for their three-day stay. Then, instead of going home, she pointed the car west. It was fun driving past all the mansions in Hollywood, talking about how they'd live if she ever won the lottery, but by the time they got to Disneyland, Mallory's credit card was declined. They barely had enough money for gas to get home again.

"It's hard to maintain a relationship with someone that unpredictable. I admit, she scared me a little."

"Yes, I'm well aware."

He doesn't miss her sarcasm.

They're quiet for five minutes or so, then he turns to her and asks, "Do you know how to come about?"

She guesses it's his way of distracting her from pointing out any more flaws, but it feels like a test. "Come about?"

"Yes, it's a sailing term."

Now she remembers. Like a petulant child, she says, "Uh, duh, I dunno, Dad. Is that where you, like, make the boat go in, like, a different direction?"

His mouth purses in disgust. "I thought you said you knew how to sail."

"I said Devin is teaching me how to sail."

"Really, I have to say he's pretty much worthless if he didn't teach you a basic maneuver like coming about."

Her eyes sting, and not just from her hair lashing in the wind.

He looks up at the sail and scans the area again for other boats. "We're going to come about. I'll have to talk you through it." He tells her which is the jib line and tells her to unwrap it from the cleat. She does. "Now keep holding on and start unwrapping it from the winch. Make sure you leave two turns on the winch and then hold onto the line until I tell you what to do."

"Like this?"

"Good, now keep holding on 'til I give you the word." Standing, with his left hand on the wheel, he gropes with his right. "Where's the winch handle that was in this pocket?"

She can't believe she screwed up again. Pointing to a nearby cushion, she says, "I think I left it right there."

"If you put things in the proper place, this wouldn't happen."

The sail starts to flap. It's really loud. "Keep holding on and take the wheel with your other hand. Don't do another thing until I give you the word." He turns his back and slides a hand between the cushions. "I hope your boyfriend isn't charging for these sailing lessons."

She shakes her head.

He flips the cushion up and bends down to pick up the handle, she assumes. "The guy sounds like a real bastard!"

Her anger rises to a new level. That must be the word. Looking at her white-knuckled hands gripping the line, she opens them. Immediately the line slashes through the air like a giant cobra. She ducks. The line whips by her face, missing her by a hair. At the same time, her father stands up. The boom swings. She hears the crack and from the corner of her eye she sees him lurch, his head snapping to the side, his body twisting, his legs buckling beneath him. He falls hard.

Ducking under the swinging boom, she catches her first sight of the damage. Red spatters like butterfly wings form on either side of a large gash on his head, at his temple. A pale mass bulges from the opening. When she's a couple of feet away, she stops. Her whole body shakes. Her teeth chatter. She screams, "Dad! Oh, God, no!" as if she can shock him back to life. "No, no, no, no," she moans. Reflexively, she lurches back, losing her balance and falling with her legs splayed in front of her. Her toe is touching his outflung arm.

Her body is not in her control. In fact, it hasn't yet registered she's in motion. Crablike, she scrambles to get away from the horror. Her back slams into the seat molding. There's no thought, just a primal need to put distance between herself and the blood. She looks at him again. Nothing has changed. He's still just as dead as the last time she looked. Before she knows it, the gate is open and she's backing down the ladder. She hesitates only a split second before plunging into the water.

55

Mallory watched Lexi and sons take off on foot, headed, she assumed, for the playground. Courtney, on the other dock, had her back to her. She seemed to be almost catatonic. Mallory wasted no time getting away. She made it as far as the tepee when her daughter turned around and came toward her. She waited.

Courtney was only a few yards away when she looked up, surprised to see her mother hadn't left her there after all. Just surprise. Not delight, or even relief that she'd returned to take her home.

"Why are you here?" She had that guarded expression Mallory hated, as if she didn't always have her best interests at heart.

"I wasn't going to leave you here."

Courtney crossed her arms and jutted out one hip. "You're beet red. You need to get out of the sun."

"I was jogging, blowing off steam. So, did you spill your guts?"

Courtney hung her head. "I couldn't."

Mallory nodded. "Good." Pulling her into a sweaty embrace, she pointed out a bench. "We can wait for Lexi."

"How do you know they didn't leave already?"

"Because I've been waiting for you, watching all of you sitting there like one big happy family."

"Yeah, that's not stalkerish at all." Her half-grin told Mallory she'd already forgiven her. They reached the bench and sat facing the boats.

"So how'd it go, your burial at sea?" she asked.

Courtney rested her forearms on her thighs, her hands interlaced. She took a couple of breaths before answering. "It was nice, actually. We put rose petals in with the ashes and . . ." She looked like she was going to cry, but then she sat up, that same half-grin returning. "The thing is, you can throw the ashes into the wind, but there's still blowback, so if I ever do it again, I won't wear lip gloss."

They shared a laugh and Mallory knew it would all be okay between them. That's how it was with families. You could say and do hurtful things, but in the end you always forgave. Someday she might even confess to her daughter how she'd lost her cool and pushed the Snoop Sisters off the dock. Since they'd survived, she could make a funny story out of it.

"He frew dirt at me." Brian's voice cut through their happy moment. Both boys stopped beside the bench.

"Did not, you big baby."

Lexi struggled to catch up with them. One hand was pressed to her belly. "Knock it off or no ice cream." She stopped when she saw Mallory there. "I thought Courtney said you left."

"No, I just took a run. How did it go?" She smiled. She couldn't have been more pleasant.

Lexi responded in a light tone. The weather was beautiful, the boys were well behaved, Courtney was helpful and Louise was a skilled boater.

Mallory thought Lexi might say something about Louise's friends who showed up looking like a couple of drowned rats, but she didn't. Instead, she asked if there were public restrooms nearby. Courtney said she needed to use the bathroom, too.

Mallory found it amusing that when Lexi tried to get the boys to come with her, they acted up, pushing each other and yelling. One wanted to go back to the jungle gym and the other wanted to go out on the boat again. "Go ahead. I'll keep an eye on them," she offered.

Lexi hesitated. Courtney gave her an odd look.

"What? You'd think I hadn't raised a child all by myself," she said. She watched them walk away together, and when she turned around, the boys were racing to the dock. She watched them go, amazed how fast they could run on their short legs. They ran along the water's edge. The older one was faster. Mallory was glad she hadn't had boys. They could be so competitive. When they headed down the dock, she reluctantly got up.

As she watched them run up and back, up and back, she experienced the same adrenaline rush she had when the oar had materialized. This time, though, she wasn't fueled by anger, but by a conviction that things would take their course. She didn't have to do a thing.

56

What am I going to do with four kids when I have to go to the bathroom?" Lexi said from inside the stall.

"I know. I was thinking the same thing." Courtney wondered what was taking her so long. She couldn't shake the feeling that something bad was going to happen. "I'll go check on the boys, okay?"

Her mother wasn't on the bench. She looked around for BJ and Brian, listening for their voices. Her skin prickled when she felt a hand on her back. She jerked her head around, but no one was there. Something made her look at the *Wayward Wind* and then beyond to the dock's end, where her mother craned her neck to see something in the water.

Run! She couldn't see who had spoken the word, but she ran. "Mom!" she screamed.

Mallory turned slowly, robotically.

"Mom! Have you completely lost your mind?" She hit the end of the dock at a run, her feet still pedaling when she hit the water. She sank and kicked her way up, searching frantically for a sign of them. She heard a cough and turned toward the sound. BJ clung to the metal rung of the swim ladder. Somehow he'd managed to find refuge on the *Wayward Wind*. "Hang on, buddy."

He nodded and coughed again.

"Where's Brian?"

And then she saw a something in the water about ten yards away. Taking a big breath, she swam toward the dark shape. Brian was totally submerged now, but just below the surface. His arms flailed, reaching, reaching. She caught him on the third try. With one hand under his armpit, she tugged. He started to slip away and she went down with him, still holding on. Pulling him to her chest with one arm, she kicked and pulled with her free arm until they broke the surface. Immediately, he wrapped his limbs around her, and the weight pulled them back down, only a few inches this time. A few flutter kicks and she was able to take another breath. She flipped onto her back, holding his head against her chest, frog-kicking toward the boat where BJ was still holding on, sobbing.

She felt Brian's body relax. "No! Stay with me!" she screamed, and then suddenly he started flailing his arms.

"Climb up," she yelled to his brother. "You can do it, buddy."

Still sobbing, BJ tried, and slipped and tried again. Courtney saw a blur just before water splashed over them. Lexi's head popped up inches from her elder son. "You can do it," she echoed Courtney's words as she pushed him up the ladder. As soon as BJ was on board, Lexi turned.

Holding onto the ladder with one hand, she reached down to Brian. Together she and Courtney maneuvered him up and laid him on the boat cushion. Brian squirmed when they rolled him on his side. His skin was pale, but not blue. A little water trickled from his mouth and nose and then he struggled to get up.

Lexi said, "They're on their way. I dialed 911 just before I jumped in." She wanted to know if either of them had lost consciousness and Courtney said they hadn't. Tears coursed down their cheeks as they knelt side by side in the cockpit. While his mother examined Brian, BJ clung to Courtney's arm.

At one point Lexi turned to her, angry in a way Courtney had never seen her. "Where is she, your mother?" she said through clenched teeth.

"Gone." She rocked herself. They both scanned to dock, but Mallory was nowhere to be seen. "I never should've trusted her. I knew there was something wrong."

Lexi pulled both of her sons to her. "How could she do this?"

Courtney said she was sorry. She said it again and again. "I didn't know she was . . . so broken," she sobbed.

When help arrived, Lexi insisted on driving them to the clinic to get everyone checked over. The paramedic walked with them to the parking lot, where they found a man in uniform bending into Lexi's car. "This your vehicle?" he asked.

Lexi nodded. He pointed to the mug she always had in the console. She confirmed that belonged to her as well. He nodded to his partner, who held up a brown paper bag in a gloved hand. "And the vodka bottle?" the first officer asked.

"What? No!"

"We got a call about an open bottle." He nodded to the boys. "Reckless endangerment. It's a serious charge. Where were you when your sons went swimming?"

* * *

LEXI MORGAN WALKED INTO the clinic, accompanied by an officer of the law. Louise and Robin jumped up to talk to her but before they could get to her, Lexi and her sons were whisked away. Courtney collapsed onto a bench, hugged her knees to her chest and rocked herself as she cried.

57

Louise and her friends could never have predicted the speed with which it unfolded. To begin with, Cate's broken shoulder was a simple, albeit painful, break, requiring no surgery. She and Robin had other minor injuries that would heal in time.

Several days after all the craziness, they got an invitation from two women who'd once been their prime suspects. They all met at the Morgan house, where Courtney apparently was living now.

The story Courtney told was both more and less than they'd imaged.

Her emotional retelling was remarkable in its restraint and honesty. In detail, she took them through the day of her father's death. Not a murder, as they'd surmised, but a horrible accident. And yes, she had left the scene, pretty much according to their deductions, and consistent with Cate's dreams. She was the ringer, the woman with long dark hair they hadn't figured on.

She'd already confessed to Lexi in the presence of her father's partner, and Delroy had promised to make sure she was treated fairly—actually, "kindly" was the word Lexi used. He believed it could be handled without publicity, and in the confines of the judge's chambers. He hoped for nothing more than psychological counseling and community service.

The second part of Courtney's story was more horrifying. Mallory had, for years, been suffering from an undiagnosed personality disorder. Even though Courtney insisted she'd been a loving mother, it was hard to reconcile that with the routine poisoning of her daughter's mind. Lexi called it a persistent pattern of holding onto resentment, building on it and passing it on to the next generation.

"It ends here." Courtney said the words with utter conviction.

The resentment had erupted in violence, unplanned, yet executed in total accordance with Mallory's warped worldview. Like so many caring mothers, she wanted her daughter to lack for nothing. In this case, it began with wanting her to have her father's love and approval. There was nothing unusual about that. But in Mallory's twisted thinking, she'd found a way to justify harming Lexi and her sons and anyone else who might get in the way.

And there was more. On the same day, at about the same time the rest of them all converged on the clinic in Red Wing, a squad car was heading to the marina to check out a phone tip—a woman drinking in her car, with small children strapped in the backseat. Hopping into her own car and peeling out of there before everything hit the fan, Mallory had managed to sideswipe said squad car.

Waiving her rights, Mallory had insisted on making a full confession, which Courtney said was consistent with the mother she knew. Mallory's outbursts, she said, were always followed by deep remorse and self-loathing. She admitted putting vodka in Lexi's drink and setting her up for a DWI. She was fully aware it could have been more serious. No one had to point out what could have happened to Lexi and her small passengers and other drivers if she'd drunk the spiked fruit punch.

Mallory also confessed to attacking Robin and Cate, whom she alternately referred to as the Snoop Sisters and the Bloodhounds. She described hitting them with a single diagonal swipe of the wooden oar. The way she told it, the providential appearance of that oar had pretty much decided what she did next.

Telling this to Louise and Cate and Robin, Courtney broke down. She shook uncontrollably when she told the gathering how her mother had stood by, letting fate take its course when BJ and Brian ventured onto the dock, running and tussling and falling in, then walked away as they thrashed in the water and called for help.

Mallory was in a residential treatment facility, awaiting sentencing. Courtney said she would be incarcerated for months, maybe even years for child endangerment, attempted murder, and multiple counts of assault and battery.

She was pale and shaken by the retelling, but Courtney wasn't done. "Lexi wants me to stay here. I'm going to split my time between school and nannying the kids.

"Zan and her parents and I are all going to help so I have time to work toward my Masters in social work. I think my emphasis will be on family violence prevention. And you know the best part? Besides all this," she said, sweeping her hand to indicate her new home, "Lexi's not only paying me a salary, but she's paying for my schooling, too." Tears glistened on her cheeks.

Lexi gave a wry smile. "I prefer to think your father's paying for it. He always fought for social justice. We think he'd be very happy with our arrangement." The fondness between them was undeniable.

Looking to Lexi, Courtney asked, "Can I tell them?"

Lexi nodded.

"She's going to have twins in January."

For the first time, Louise noticed the baby bump on this otherwise slender woman. Louise looked from Courtney to Lexi to the small bulge where the babies were growing, and she was overwhelmed. "There's new life everywhere I look," she said.

Although she was still smiling, Courtney's eyes glistened with tears.

Louise thought she understood. "I grew up with a difficult parent, too. My father was a huge presence." She reached out for her hand. "No, that's sugarcoating it. He was downright destructive, but for all his faults, he raised me to take care of myself, and that's not a bad thing. I discovered I'm made of tougher stuff than my father, military rank and all. I need to remind myself I may be his daughter, but I'm not like him, and I'm not responsible for his behavior."

Courtney blinked rapidly and sniffled.

Robin's smile had a hint of sadness when she said, "Every woman in this room has dealt with some really hard things."

Cate agreed.

Surprise showed on Courtney's face. "I had no idea. You all hide it well."

Louise laughed. "The trick is not to hide it. It's to rise above it."

"Exactly," Lexi chimed in.

In a few minutes Louise, Robin and Cate, her arm in a sling, were at the door saying their good-byes, with promises of staying in touch.

Lexi bit her lip. "You'll have to come back when the babies are born."

On impulse, Louise said, "I remember my father talking about soldiers. He said the experiences they share in combat makes them closer than brothers."

"You're right about that," Cate said, "but don't expect any purple hearts."

Courtney said she was embarrassed that everyone was being so nice. "I still can't believe Lexi forgives me." She shook her head in wonderment.

Lexi placed a hand on her back. The gesture was so loving, so natural. "And why wouldn't I trust the young lady who saved my children? You don't need to give me any more proof than that."

58

Cate dreamed about the women again, only this time she was one of them. She looked at the smiling faces of Robin, Louise, Grace, and Foxy as they took each other's hands and formed a circle. Slowly they began to move, around and around, almost weightless, their hair streaming in the breeze as they danced and laughed.

When she woke, she clung to the image as long as possible.

She was on her first cup of coffee when the phone rang. She saw the name on caller ID and wondered why Simon was calling her.

"I'm making arrangements to investigate a state hospital north of the Cities. In its day, they performed barbaric experiments. With all sorts of allegations of abuse and neglect, it's no surprise people say the maze of tunnels underneath the hospital are haunted. People hear laughter and footsteps and feel the temperature drop, all the typical reports of ghosts. I'd sure like to get in those tunnels with the proper tools."

She stifled a giggle.

"I could use another volunteer if you're interested."

Her fingers automatically curled around her amulet. She ran her thumbnail along the fresh crack. "You know, Simon, I think I've had enough fun for a while."

Spirits of Pepin

* * *

"COFFEE'S COLD." HE JERKED his cup away. Pointing to the brown splatters on his white shirt, he said, "See?"

"Okay, Dad." Louise wet a washcloth to blot the stains.

"That's no good." He pushed her hand away. "It'll have to go in the wash now."

"We'll take care of it after breakfast," Dean said, winking at her.

"Do you want some jelly for your toast?" She handed him the jar.

"Goddamn it, I don't need you fussing over me. I'm not an invalid."

Louise rolled her eyes and waited for his rant to end. His hands had developed a tremor. He fixed her with a stare as he brought a spoonful of scrambled egg to his mouth. She thought the light in his eyes had dimmed ever so slightly in the short time since he'd come to Minnesota. More than once, she'd told Dean how she wished they could have worked out their difficulties while he still had his full faculties.

Back in his room, he sat ramrod straight in his leather chair and folded his hands in his lap like he was waiting for something. She wondered, as she had so many times, what he'd be like today if Bobby hadn't died, but she knew it wasn't their son's death that had made her parents bitter. It was the blame-a-thon that they would keep going until they were both dead and gone.

His eyes closed. The muscles of his face relaxed. He looked almost serene.

She and Dean were about to leave when her eyes fell on the unopened gift she'd brought her father. Tearing the tissue away, she looked at the calligraphy in the frame. They were the ancient words of Confucius: "To be wronged is nothing, unless you continue to remember it." She was about to set the frame on his nightstand when Dean took it out of her hands. "You know, Lou," he said, "I think he's already on his way to forgetting, don't you?"

She stared at the words a long time before rewrapping the gift and stuffing it in her purse. "You're right. I think the words were meant for me, anyway."

THE END